# Visible and Invisible

E. F. Benson

**Visible and Invisible**

The present edition is a reproduction of previous publication of this classic work. Minor typographical errors may have been corrected without note; however, for an authentic reading experience the spelling, punctuation, and capitalization have been retained from the original text.

ISBN: 978-1-63637-368-3

# Contents

# "And the Dead Spake— —"

There is not in all London a quieter spot, or one, apparently, more withdrawn from the heat and bustle of life than Newsome Terrace. It is a cul-de-sac, for at the upper end the roadway between its two lines of square, compact little residences is brought to an end by a high brick wall, while at the lower end, the only access to it is through Newsome Square, that small discreet oblong of Georgian houses, a relic of the time when Kensington was a suburban village sundered from the metropolis by a stretch of pastures stretching to the river. Both square and terrace are most inconveniently situated for those whose ideal environment includes a rank of taxicabs immediately opposite their door, a spate of 'buses roaring down the street, and a procession of underground trains, accessible by a station a few yards away, shaking and rattling the cutlery and silver on their dining tables. In consequence Newsome Terrace had come, two years ago, to be inhabited by leisurely and retired folk or by those who wished to pursue their work in quiet and tranquillity. Children with hoops and scooters are phenomena rarely encountered in the Terrace and dogs are equally uncommon.

In front of each of the couple of dozen houses of which the Terrace is composed lies a little square of railinged garden, in which you may often see the middle-aged or elderly mistress of the residence horticulturally employed. By five o'clock of a winter's evening the pavements will generally be empty of all passengers except the policeman, who with felted step, at intervals throughout the night, peers with his bull's-eye into these small front gardens, and never finds anything more suspicious there than an early crocus or an aconite. For by the time it is dark the inhabitants of the Terrace have got themselves home, where behind drawn curtains and bolted shutters they will pass a domestic and uninterrupted evening. No funeral (up to the time I speak of) had I ever seen leave the Terrace, no marriage party had strewed its pavements with confetti, and perambulators were unknown. It and its inhabitants seemed to be quietly mellowing like bottles of sound wine. No doubt there was stored within them the sunshine and summer of youth long past, and now, dozing in a cool place, they waited for the turn of the key in the cellar door, and the entry of one who would draw them forth and see what they were worth.

Yet, after the time of which I shall now speak, I have never passed down its pavement without wondering whether each house,

1

so seemingly-tranquil, is not, like some dynamo, softly and smoothly bringing into being vast and terrible forces, such as those I once saw at work in the last house at the upper end of the Terrace, the quietest, you would have said, of all the row. Had you observed it with continuous scrutiny, for all the length of a summer day, it is quite possible that you might have only seen issue from it in the morning an elderly woman whom you would have rightly conjectured to be the housekeeper, with her basket for marketing on her arm, who returned an hour later. Except for her the entire day might often pass without there being either ingress or egress from the door. Occasionally a middle-aged man, lean and wiry, came swiftly down the pavement, but his exit was by no means a daily occurrence, and indeed when he did emerge, he broke the almost universal usage of the Terrace, for his appearances took place, when such there were, between nine and ten in the evening. At that hour sometimes he would come round to my house in Newsome Square to see if I was at home and inclined for a talk a little later on. For the sake of air and exercise he would then have an hour's tramp through the lit and noisy streets, and return about ten, still pale and unflushed, for one of those talks which grew to have an absorbing fascination for me. More rarely through the telephone I proposed that I should drop in on him: this I did not often do, since I found that if he did not come out himself, it implied that he was busy with some investigation, and though he made me welcome, I could easily see that he burned for my departure, so that he might get busy with his batteries and pieces of tissue, hot on the track of discoveries that never yet had presented themselves to the mind of man as coming within the horizon of possibility.

My last sentence may have led the reader to guess that I am indeed speaking of none other than that recluse and mysterious physicist Sir James Horton, with whose death a hundred half-hewn avenues into the dark forest from which life comes must wait completion till another pioneer as bold as he takes up the axe which hitherto none but himself has been able to wield. Probably there was never a man to whom humanity owed more, and of whom humanity knew less. He seemed utterly independent of the race to whom (though indeed with no service of love) he devoted himself: for years he lived aloof and apart in his house at the end of the Terrace. Men and women were to him like fossils to the geologist, things to be tapped and hammered and dissected and studied with a view not only to the reconstruction of past ages, but to construction in the future. It is known, for instance, that he made an artificial being formed of the tissue, still living, of animals lately killed, with

2

the brain of an ape and the heart of a bullock, and a sheep's thyroid, and so forth. Of that I can give no first-hand account; Horton, it is true, told me something about it, and in his will directed that certain memoranda on the subject should on his death be sent to me. But on the bulky envelope there is the direction, "Not to be opened till January, 1925." He spoke with some reserve and, so I think, with slight horror at the strange things which had happened on the completion of this creature. It evidently made him uncomfortable to talk about it, and for that reason I fancy he put what was then a rather remote date to the day when his record should reach my eye. Finally, in these preliminaries, for the last five years before the war, he had scarcely entered, for the sake of companionship, any house other than his own and mine. Ours was a friendship dating from school-days, which he had never suffered to drop entirely, but I doubt if in those years he spoke except on matters of business to half a dozen other people. He had already retired from surgical practice in which his skill was unapproached, and most completely now did he avoid the slightest intercourse with his colleagues, whom he regarded as ignorant pedants without courage or the rudiments of knowledge. Now and then he would write an epoch-making little monograph, which he flung to them like a bone to a starving dog, but for the most part, utterly absorbed in his own investigations, he left them to grope along unaided. He frankly told me that he enjoyed talking to me about such subjects, since I was utterly unacquainted with them. It clarified his mind to be obliged to put his theories and guesses and confirmations with such simplicity that anyone could understand them.

I well remember his coming in to see me on the evening of the 4th of August, 1914.

"So the war has broken out," he said, "and the streets are impassable with excited crowds. Odd, isn't it? Just as if each of us already was not a far more murderous battlefield than any which can be conceived between warring nations."

"How's that?" said I.

"Let me try to put it plainly, though it isn't that I want to talk about. Your blood is one eternal battlefield. It is full of armies eternally marching and counter-marching. As long as the armies friendly to you are in a superior position, you remain in good health; if a detachment of microbes that, if suffered to establish themselves, would give you a cold in the head, entrench themselves in your mucous membrane, the commander-in-chief sends a regiment down and drives them out. He doesn't give his orders from your brain, mind you—those aren't his headquarters, for your brain

3

knows nothing about the landing of the enemy till they have made good their position and given you a cold."

He paused a moment.

"There isn't one headquarters inside you," he said, "there are many. For instance, I killed a frog this morning; at least most people would say I killed it. But had I killed it, though its head lay in one place and its severed body in another? Not a bit: I had only killed a piece of it. For I opened the body afterwards and took out the heart, which I put in a sterilised chamber of suitable temperature, so that it wouldn't get cold or be infected by any microbe. That was about twelve o'clock to-day. And when I came out just now, the heart was beating still. It was alive, in fact. That's full of suggestions, you know. Come and see it."

The Terrace had been stirred into volcanic activity by the news of war: the vendor of some late edition had penetrated into its quietude, and there were half a dozen parlour-maids fluttering about like black and white moths. But once inside Horton's door isolation as of an Arctic night seemed to close round me. He had forgotten his latch-key, but his housekeeper, then newly come to him, who became so regular and familiar a figure in the Terrace, must have heard his step, for before he rang the bell she had opened the door, and stood with his forgotten latch-key in her hand.

"Thanks, Mrs. Gabriel," said he, and without a sound the door shut behind us. Both her name and face, as reproduced in some illustrated daily paper, seemed familiar, rather terribly familiar, but before I had time to grope for the association, Horton supplied it.

"Tried for the murder of her husband six months ago," he said. "Odd case. The point is that she is the one and perfect housekeeper. I once had four servants, and everything was all mucky, as we used to say at school. Now I live in amazing comfort and propriety with one. She does everything. She is cook, valet, housemaid, butler, and won't have anyone to help her. No doubt she killed her husband, but she planned it so well that she could not be convicted. She told me quite frankly who she was when I engaged her."

Of course I remembered the whole trial vividly now. Her husband, a morose, quarrelsome fellow, tipsy as often as sober, had, according to the defence cut his own throat while shaving; according to the prosecution, she had done that for him. There was the usual discrepancy of evidence as to whether the wound could have been self-inflicted, and the prosecution tried to prove that the face had been lathered after his throat had been cut. So singular an exhibition of forethought and nerve had hurt rather than helped their case, and after prolonged deliberation on the part of the jury, she had been acquitted. Yet not less singular was Horton's selection of a probable murderess, however efficient, as housekeeper.

He anticipated this reflection.

"Apart from the wonderful comfort of having a perfectly appointed and absolutely silent house," he said, "I regard Mrs. Gabriel as a sort of insurance against my being murdered. If you had been tried for your life, you would take very especial care not to find yourself in suspicious proximity to a murdered body again: no more deaths in your house, if you could help it. Come through to my laboratory, and look at my little instance of life after death."

Certainly it was amazing to see that little piece of tissue still pulsating with what must be called life; it contracted and expanded faintly indeed but perceptibly, though for nine hours now it had been severed from the rest of the organisation. All by itself it went on living, and if the heart could go on living with nothing, you would say, to feed and stimulate its energy, there must also, so reasoned Horton, reside in all the other vital organs of the body other independent focuses of life.

"Of course a severed organ like that," he said, "will run down quicker than if it had the co-operation of the others, and presently I shall apply a gentle electric stimulus to it. If I can keep that glass bowl under which it beats at the temperature of a frog's body, in sterilised air, I don't see why it should not go on living. Food—of course there's the question of feeding it. Do you see what that opens up in the way of surgery? Imagine a shop with glass cases containing healthy organs taken from the dead. Say a man dies of pneumonia. He should, as soon as ever the breath is out of his body, be dissected, and though they would, of course, destroy his lungs, as they will be full of pneumococci, his liver and digestive organs are probably healthy. Take them out, keep them in a sterilised atmosphere with the temperature at 98·4, and sell the liver, let us say, to another poor devil who has cancer there. Fit him with a new healthy liver, eh?"

"And insert the brain of someone who has died of heart disease into the skull of a congenital idiot?" I asked.

"Yes, perhaps; but the brain's tiresomely complicated in its connections and the joining up of the nerves, you know. Surgery will have to learn a lot before it fits new brains in. And the brain has got such a lot of functions. All thinking, all inventing seem to belong to it, though, as you have seen, the heart can get on quite well without it. But there are other functions of the brain I want to study first. I've been trying some experiments already."

5

He made some little readjustment to the flame of the spirit lamp which kept at the right temperature the water that surrounded the sterilised receptacle in which the frog's heart was beating.

"Start with the more simple and mechanical uses of the brain," he said. "Primarily it is a sort of record office, a diary. Say that I rap your knuckles with that ruler. What happens? The nerves there send a message to the brain, of course, saying—how can I put it most simply—saying, 'Somebody is hurting me.' And the eye sends another, saying 'I perceive a ruler hitting my knuckles,' and the ear sends another, saying 'I hear the rap of it.' But leaving all that alone, what else happens? Why, the brain records it. It makes a note of your knuckles having been hit."

He had been moving about the room as he spoke, taking off his coat and waistcoat and putting on in their place a thin black dressing-gown, and by now he was seated in his favourite attitude cross-legged on the hearthrug, looking like some magician or perhaps the afrit which a magician of black arts had caused to appear. He was thinking intently now, passing through his fingers his string of amber beads, and talking more to himself than to me.

"And how does it make that note?" he went on. "Why, in the manner in which phonograph records are made. There are millions of minute dots, depressions, pockmarks on your brain which certainly record what you remember, what you have enjoyed or disliked, or done or said. The surface of the brain anyhow is large enough to furnish writing-paper for the record of all these things, of all your memories. If the impression of an experience has not been acute, the dot is not sharply impressed, and the record fades: in other words, you come to forget it. But if it has been vividly impressed, the record is never obliterated. Mrs. Gabriel, for instance, won't lose the impression of how she lathered her husband's face after she had cut his throat. That's to say, if she did it."

"Now do you see what I'm driving at? Of course you do. There is stored within a man's head the complete record of all the memorable things he has done and said: there are all his thoughts there, and all his speeches, and, most well-marked of all, his habitual thoughts and the things he has often said; for habit, there is reason to believe, wears a sort of rut in the brain, so that the life-principle, whatever it is, as it gropes and steals about the brain, is continually stumbling into it. There's your record, your gramophone plate all ready. What we want, and what I'm trying to arrive at, is a needle which, as it traces its minute way over these dots, will come across words or sentences which the dead have uttered, and will

6

reproduce them. My word, what Judgment Books! What a resurrection!"

Here in this withdrawn situation no remotest echo of the excitement which was seething through the streets penetrated; through the open window there came in only the tide of the midnight silence. But from somewhere closer at hand, through the wall surely of the laboratory, there came a low, somewhat persistent murmur.

"Perhaps our needle—unhappily not yet invented—as it passed over the record of speech in the brain, might induce even facial expression," he said. "Enjoyment or horror might even pass over dead features. There might be gestures and movements even, as the words were reproduced in our gramophone of the dead. Some people when they want to think intensely walk about: some, there's an instance of it audible now, talk to themselves aloud."

He held up his finger for silence.

"Yes, that's Mrs. Gabriel," he said. "She talks to herself by the hour together. She's always done that, she tells me. I shouldn't wonder if she has plenty to talk about."

It was that night when, first of all, the notion of intense activity going on below the placid house-fronts of the Terrace occurred to me. None looked more quiet than this, and yet there was seething here a volcanic activity and intensity of living, both in the man who sat cross-legged on the floor and behind that voice just audible through the partition wall. But I thought of that no more, for Horton began speaking of the brain-gramophone again.... Were it possible to trace those infinitesimal dots and pockmarks in the brain by some needle exquisitely fine, it might follow that by the aid of some such contrivance as translated the pockmarks on a gramophone record into sound, some audible rendering of speech might be recovered from the brain of a dead man. It was necessary, so he pointed out to me, that this strange gramophone record should be new; it must be that of one lately dead, for corruption and decay would soon obliterate these infinitesimal markings. He was not of opinion that unspoken thought could be thus recovered: the utmost he hoped for from his pioneering work was to be able to recapture actual speech, especially when such speech had habitually dwelt on one subject, and thus had worn a rut on that part of the brain known as the speech-centre.

"Let me get, for instance," he said, "the brain of a railway porter, newly dead, who has been accustomed for years to call out the name of a station, and I do not despair of hearing his voice through my gramophone trumpet. Or again, given that Mrs.

7

Gabriel, in all her interminable conversations with herself, talks about one subject, I might, in similar circumstances, recapture what she had been constantly saying. Of course my instrument must be of a power and delicacy still unknown, one of which the needle can trace the minutest irregularities of surface, and of which the trumpet must be of immense magnifying power, able to translate the smallest whisper into a shout. But just as a microscope will show you the details of an object invisible to the eye, so there are instruments which act in the same way on sound. Here, for instance, is one of remarkable magnifying power. Try it if you like."

He took me over to a table on which was standing an electric battery connected with a round steel globe, out of the side of which sprang a gramophone trumpet of curious construction. He adjusted the battery, and directed me to click my fingers quite gently opposite an aperture in the globe, and the noise, ordinarily scarcely audible, resounded through the room like a thunderclap.

"Something of that sort might permit us to hear the record on a brain," he said.

After this night my visits to Horton became far more common than they had hitherto been. Having once admitted me into the region of his strange explorations, he seemed to welcome me there. Partly, as he had said, it clarified his own thought to put it into simple language, partly, as he subsequently admitted, he was beginning to penetrate into such lonely fields of knowledge by paths so utterly untrodden, that even he, the most aloof and independent of mankind, wanted some human presence near him. Despite his utter indifference to the issues of the war—for, in his regard, issues far more crucial demanded his energies—he offered himself as surgeon to a London hospital for operations on the brain, and his services, naturally, were welcomed, for none brought knowledge or skill like his to such work. Occupied all day, he performed miracles of healing, with bold and dexterous excisions which none but he would have dared to attempt. He would operate, often successfully, for lesions that seemed certainly fatal, and all the time he was learning. He refused to accept any salary; he only asked, in cases where he had removed pieces of brain matter, to take these away, in order by further examination and dissection, to add to the knowledge and manipulative skill which he devoted to the wounded. He wrapped these morsels in sterilised lint, and took them back to the Terrace in a box, electrically heated to maintain the normal temperature of a man's blood. His fragment might then, so he reasoned, keep some sort of independent life of its own, even as the severed heart of a frog had continued to beat for hours without

8

connection with the rest of the body. Then for half the night he would continue to work on these sundered pieces of tissue scarcely dead, which his operations during the day had given him. Simultaneously, he was busy over the needle that must be of such infinite delicacy.

One evening, fatigued with a long day's work, I had just heard with a certain tremor of uneasy anticipation the whistles of warning which heralded an air-raid, when my telephone bell rang. My servants, according to custom, had already betaken themselves to the cellar, and I went to see what the summons was, determined in any case not to go out into the streets. I recognised Horton's voice. "I want you at once," he said.

"But the warning whistles have gone," said I, "And I don't like showers of shrapnel."

"Oh, never mind that," said he. "You must come. I'm so excited that I distrust the evidence of my own ears. I want a witness. Just come."

He did not pause for my reply, for I heard the click of his receiver going back into its place. Clearly he assumed that I was coming, and that I suppose had the effect of suggestion on my mind. I told myself that I would not go, but in a couple of minutes his certainty that I was coming, coupled with the prospect of being interested in something else than air-raids, made me fidget in my chair and eventually go to the street door and look out. The moon was brilliantly bright, the square quite empty, and far away the coughings of very distant guns. Next moment, almost against my will, I was running down the deserted pavements of Newsome Terrace. My ring at his bell was answered by Horton, before Mrs. Gabriel could come to the door, and he positively dragged me in.

"I shan't tell you a word of what I am doing," he said. "I want you to tell me what you hear. Come into the laboratory."

The remote guns were silent again as I sat myself, as directed, in a chair close to the gramophone trumpet, but suddenly through the wall I heard the familiar mutter of Mrs. Gabriel's voice. Horton, already busy with his battery, sprang to his feet.

"That won't do," he said. "I want absolute silence."

He went out of the room, and I heard him calling to her. While he was gone I observed more closely what was on the table. Battery, round steel globe, and gramophone trumpet were there, and some sort of a needle on a spiral steel spring linked up with the battery and the glass vessel, in which I had seen the frog's heart beat. In it now there lay a fragment of grey matter.

Horton came back in a minute or two, and stood in the middle of the room listening.

9

"That's better," he said. "Now I want you to listen at the mouth of the trumpet. I'll answer any questions afterwards."

With my ear turned to the trumpet, I could see nothing of what he was doing, and I listened till the silence became a rustling in my ears. Then suddenly that rustling ceased, for it was overscored by a whisper which undoubtedly came from the aperture on which my aural attention was fixed. It was no more than the faintest murmur, and though no words were audible, it had the timbre of a human voice.

"Well, do you hear anything?" asked Horton.

"Yes, something very faint, scarcely audible."

"Describe it," said he.

"Somebody whispering."

"I'll try a fresh place," said he.

The silence descended again; the mutter of the distant guns was still mute, and some slight creaking from my shirt front, as I breathed, alone broke it. And then the whispering from the gramophone trumpet began again, this time much louder than it had been before—it was as if the speaker (still whispering) had advanced a dozen yards—but still blurred and indistinct. More unmistakable, too, was it that the whisper was that of a human voice, and every now and then, whether fancifully or not, I thought I caught a word or two. For a moment it was silent altogether, and then with a sudden inkling of what I was listening to I heard something begin to sing. Though the words were still inaudible there was melody, and the tune was "Tipperary." From that convolvulus-shaped trumpet there came two bars of it.

"And what do you hear now?" cried Horton with a crack of exultation in his voice. "Singing, singing! That's the tune they all sang. Fine music that from a dead man. Encore! you say? Yes, wait a second, and he'll sing it again for you. Confound it, I can't get on to the place. Ah! I've got it: listen again."

Surely that was the strangest manner of song ever yet heard on the earth, this melody from the brain of the dead. Horror and fascination strove within me, and I suppose the first for the moment prevailed, for with a shudder I jumped up.

"Stop it!" I said. "It's terrible."

His face, thin and eager, gleamed in the strong ray of the lamp which he had placed close to him. His hand was on the metal rod from which depended the spiral spring and the needle, which just rested on that fragment of grey stuff which I had seen in the glass vessel.

"Yes, I'm going to stop it now," he said, "or the germs will be getting at my gramophone record, or the record will get cold. See, I spray it with carbolic vapour, I put it back into its nice warm bed. It will sing to us again. But terrible? What do you mean by terrible?"

Indeed, when he asked that I scarcely knew myself what I meant. I had been witness to a new marvel of science as wonderful perhaps as any that had ever astounded the beholder, and my nerves—these childish whimperers—had cried out at the darkness and the profundity. But the horror diminished, the fascination increased as he quite shortly told me the history of this phenomenon. He had attended that day and operated upon a young soldier in whose brain was embedded a piece of shrapnel. The boy was in extremis, but Horton had hoped for the possibility of saving him. To extract the shrapnel was the only chance, and this involved the cutting away of a piece of brain known as the speech-centre, and taking from it what was embedded there. But the hope was not realised, and two hours later the boy died. It was to this fragment of brain that, when Horton returned home, he had applied the needle of his gramophone, and had obtained the faint whisperings which had caused him to ring me up, so that he might have a witness of this wonder. Witness I had been, not to these whisperings alone, but to the fragment of singing.

"And this is but the first step on the new road," said he. "Who knows where it may lead, or to what new temple of knowledge it may not be the avenue? Well, it is late: I shall do no more to-night. What about the raid, by the way?"

To my amazement I saw that the time was verging on midnight. Two hours had elapsed since he let me in at his door; they had passed like a couple of minutes. Next morning some neighbours spoke of the prolonged firing that had gone on, of which I had been wholly unconscious.

Week after week Horton worked on this new road of research, perfecting the sensitiveness and subtlety of the needle, and, by vastly increasing the power of his batteries, enlarging the magnifying power of his trumpet. Many and many an evening during the next year did I listen to voices that were dumb in death, and the sounds which had been blurred and unintelligible mutterings in the earlier experiments, developed, as the delicacy of his mechanical devices increased, into coherence and clear articulation. It was no longer necessary to impose silence on Mrs. Gabriel when the gramophone was at work, for now the voice we listened to had risen to the pitch of ordinary human utterance, while as for the faithfulness and individuality of these records, striking testimony was given more than once by some living friend of the dead, who, without knowing what he was about to hear, recognised the tones of the speaker. More than once also, Mrs. Gabriel, bringing in syphons and whisky, provided us with three glasses, for she had heard, so she told us, three different voices in talk. But for the present no fresh phenomenon occurred: Horton was but perfecting the mechanism of his previous discovery and, rather grudging the time, was scribbling at a monograph, which presently he would toss to his colleagues, concerning the results he had already obtained. And then, even while Horton was on the threshold of new wonders, which he had already foreseen and spoken of as theoretically possible, there came an evening of marvel and of swift catastrophe.

I had dined with him that day, Mrs. Gabriel deftly serving the meal that she had so daintily prepared, and towards the end, as she was clearing the table for our dessert, she stumbled, I supposed, on a loose edge of carpet, quickly recovering herself. But instantly Horton checked some half-finished sentence, and turned to her.

"You're all right, Mrs. Gabriel?" he asked quickly.

"Yes, sir, thank you," said she, and went on with her serving.

"As I was saying," began Horton again, but his attention clearly wandered, and without concluding his narrative, he relapsed into silence, till Mrs. Gabriel had given us our coffee and left the room.

"I'm sadly afraid my domestic felicity may be disturbed," he said. "Mrs. Gabriel had an epileptic fit yesterday, and she confessed when she recovered that she had been subject to them when a child, and since then had occasionally experienced them."

"Dangerous, then?" I asked.

"In themselves not in the least," said he. "If she was sitting in her chair or lying in bed when one occurred, there would be nothing to trouble about. But if one occurred while she was cooking my dinner or beginning to come downstairs, she might fall into the fire or tumble down the whole flight. We'll hope no such deplorable calamity will happen. Now, if you've finished your coffee, let us go into the laboratory. Not that I've got anything very interesting in the way of new records. But I've introduced a second battery with a very strong induction coil into my apparatus. I find that if I link it up with my record, given that the record is a—a fresh one, it stimulates certain nerve centres. It's odd, isn't it, that the same forces which so encourage the dead to live would certainly encourage the living to die, if a man received the full current. One has to be careful in handling it. Yes, and what then? you ask."

The night was very hot, and he threw the windows wide before he settled himself cross-legged on the floor.

"I'll answer your question for you," he said, "though I believe we've talked of it before. Supposing I had not a fragment of brain-tissue only, but a whole head, let us say, or best of all, a complete corpse, I think I could expect to produce more than mere speech through the gramophone. The dead lips themselves perhaps might utter—God! what's that?"

From close outside, at the bottom of the stairs leading from the dining room which we had just quitted to the laboratory where we now sat, there came a crash of glass followed by the fall as of something heavy which bumped from step to step, and was finally flung on the threshold against the door with the sound as of knuckles rapping at it, and demanding admittance. Horton sprang up and threw the door open, and there lay, half inside the room and half on the landing outside, the body of Mrs. Gabriel. Round her were splinters of broken bottles and glasses, and from a cut in her forehead, as she lay ghastly with face upturned, the blood trickled into her thick grey hair.

Horton was on his knees beside her, dabbing his handkerchief on her forehead.

"Ah! that's not serious," he said; "there's neither vein nor artery cut. I'll just bind that up first."

He tore his handkerchief into strips which he tied together, and made a dexterous bandage covering the lower part of her forehead, but leaving her eyes unobscured. They stared with a fixed meaningless steadiness, and he scrutinised them closely.

"But there's worse yet," he said. "There's been some severe blow on the head. Help me to carry her into the laboratory. Get round to her feet and lift underneath the knees when I am ready. There! Now put your arm right under her and carry her."

Her head swung limply back as he lifted her shoulders, and he propped it up against his knee, where it mutely nodded and bowed, as his leg moved, as if in silent assent to what we were doing, and the mouth, at the extremity of which there had gathered a little lather, lolled open. He still supported her shoulders as I fetched a cushion on which to place her head, and presently she was lying close to the low table on which stood the gramophone of the dead. Then with light deft fingers he passed his hands over her skull, pausing as he came to the spot just above and behind her right ear. Twice and again his fingers groped and lightly pressed, while with shut eyes and concentrated attention he interpreted what his trained touch revealed.

"Her skull is broken to fragments just here," he said. "In the

13

middle there is a piece completely severed from the rest, and the edges of the cracked pieces must be pressing on her brain."

Her right arm was lying palm upwards on the floor, and with one hand he felt her wrist with finger-tips.

"Not a sign of pulse," he said. "She's dead in the ordinary sense of the word. But life persists in an extraordinary manner, you may remember. She can't be wholly dead: no one is wholly dead in a moment, unless every organ is blown to bits. But she soon will be dead, if we don't relieve the pressure on the brain. That's the first thing to be done. While I'm busy at that, shut the window, will you, and make up the fire. In this sort of case the vital heat, whatever that is, leaves the body very quickly. Make the room as hot as you can—fetch an oil-stove, and turn on the electric radiator, and stoke up a roaring fire. The hotter the room is the more slowly will the heat of life leave her."

Already he had opened his cabinet of surgical instruments, and taken out of it two drawers full of bright steel which he laid on the floor beside her. I heard the grating chink of scissors severing her long grey hair, and as I busied myself with laying and lighting the fire in the hearth, and kindling the oil-stove, which I found, by Horton's directions, in the pantry, I saw that his lancet was busy on the exposed skin. He had placed some vaporising spray, heated by a spirit lamp close to her head, and as he worked its fizzing nozzle filled the air with some clean and aromatic odour. Now and then he threw out an order.

"Bring me that electric lamp on the long cord," he said. "I haven't got enough light. Don't look at what I'm doing if you're squeamish, for if it makes you feel faint, I shan't be able to attend to you."

I suppose that violent interest in what he was doing overcame any qualm that I might have had, for I looked quite unflinching over his shoulder as I moved the lamp about till it was in such a place that it threw its beam directly into a dark hole at the edge of which depended a flap of skin. Into this he put his forceps, and as he withdrew them they grasped a piece of blood-stained bone.

"That's better," he said, "and the room's warming up well. But there's no sign of pulse yet. Go on stoking, will you, till the thermometer on the wall there registers a hundred degrees."

When next, on my journey from the coal-cellar, I looked, two more pieces of bone lay beside the one I had seen extracted, and presently referring to the thermometer, I saw that between the oil-stove and the roaring fire and the electric radiator, I had raised the room to the temperature he wanted. Soon, peering fixedly at the seat of his operation, he felt for her pulse again.

14

"Not a sign of returning vitality," he said, "and I've done all I can. There's nothing more possible that can be devised to restore her."

As he spoke the zeal of the unrivalled surgeon relaxed, and with a sigh and a shrug he rose to his feet and mopped his face. Then suddenly the fire and eagerness blazed there again. "The gramophone!" he said. "The speech centre is close to where I've been working, and it is quite uninjured. Good heavens, what a wonderful opportunity. She served me well living, and she shall serve me dead. And I can stimulate the motor nerve-centre, too, with the second battery. We may see a new wonder to-night."

Some qualm of horror shook me.

"No, don't!" I said. "It's terrible: she's just dead. I shall go if you do."

"But I've got exactly all the conditions I have long been wanting," said he. "And I simply can't spare you. You must be witness: I must have a witness. Why, man, there's not a surgeon or a physiologist in the kingdom who would not give an eye or an ear to be in your place now. She's dead. I pledge you my honour on that, and it's grand to be dead if you can help the living."

Once again, in a far fiercer struggle, horror and the intensest curiosity strove together in me.

"Be quick, then," said I.

"Ha! That's right," exclaimed Horton. "Help me to lift her on to the table by the gramophone. The cushion too; I can get at the place more easily with her head a little raised."

He turned on the battery and with the movable light close beside him, brilliantly illuminating what he sought, he inserted the needle of the gramophone into the jagged aperture in her skull. For a few minutes, as he groped and explored there, there was silence, and then quite suddenly Mrs. Gabriel's voice, clear and unmistakable and of the normal loudness of human speech, issued from the trumpet.

"Yes, I always said that I'd be even with him," came the articulated syllables. "He used to knock me about, he did, when he came home drunk, and often I was black and blue with bruises. But I'll give him a redness for the black and blue."

The record grew blurred; instead of articulate words there came from it a gobbling noise. By degrees that cleared, and we were listening to some dreadful suppressed sort of laughter, hideous to hear. On and on it went.

"I've got into some sort of rut," said Horton. "She must have laughed a lot to herself."

15

For a long time we got nothing more except the repetition of the words we had already heard and the sound of that suppressed laughter. Then Horton drew towards him the second battery.

"I'll try a stimulation of the motor nerve-centres," he said. "Watch her face."

He propped the gramophone needle in position, and inserted into the fractured skull the two poles of the second battery, moving them about there very carefully. And as I watched her face, I saw with a freezing horror that her lips were beginning to move.

"Her mouth's moving," I cried. "She can't be dead."

He peered into her face.

"Nonsense," he said. "That's only the stimulus from the current. She's been dead half an hour. Ah! what's coming now?"

The lips lengthened into a smile, the lower jaw dropped, and from her mouth came the laughter we had heard just now through the gramophone. And then the dead mouth spoke, with a mumble of unintelligible words, a bubbling torrent of incoherent syllables.

"I'll turn the full current on," he said.

The head jerked and raised itself, the lips struggled for utterance, and suddenly she spoke swiftly and distinctly.

"Just when he'd got his razor out," she said, "I came up behind him, and put my hand over his face, and bent his neck back over his chair with all my strength. And I picked up his razor and with one slit—ha, ha, that was the way to pay him out. And I didn't lose my head, but I lathered his chin well, and put the razor in his hand, and left him there, and went downstairs and cooked his dinner for him, and then an hour afterwards, as he didn't come down, up I went to see what kept him. It was a nasty cut in his neck that had kept him——"

Horton suddenly withdrew the two poles of the battery from her head, and even in the middle of her word the mouth ceased working, and lay rigid and open.

"By God!" he said. "There's a tale for dead lips to tell. But we'll get more yet."

Exactly what happened then I never knew. It appeared to me that as he still leaned over the table with the two poles of the battery in his hand, his foot slipped, and he fell forward across it. There came a sharp crack, and a flash of blue dazzling light, and there he lay face downwards, with arms that just stirred and quivered. With his fall the two poles that must momentarily have come into contact with his hand were jerked away again, and I lifted him and laid him on the floor. But his lips as well as those of the dead woman had spoken for the last time.

16

# The Outcast

When Mrs. Acres bought the Gate-house at Tarleton, which had stood so long without a tenant, and appeared in that very agreeable and lively little town as a resident, sufficient was already known about her past history to entitle her to friendliness and sympathy. Hers had been a tragic story, and the account of the inquest held on her husband's body, when, within a month of their marriage, he had shot himself before her eyes, was recent enough, and of as full a report in the papers as to enable our little community of Tarleton to remember and run over the salient grimness of the case without the need of inventing any further details—which, otherwise, it would have been quite capable of doing.

Briefly, then, the facts had been as follows. Horace Acres appeared to have been a heartless fortune-hunter—a handsome, plausible wretch, ten years younger than his wife. He had made no secret to his friends of not being in love with her but of having a considerable regard for her more than considerable fortune. But hardly had he married her than his indifference developed into violent dislike, accompanied by some mysterious, inexplicable dread of her. He hated and feared her, and on the morning of the very day when he had put an end to himself he had begged her to divorce him; the case he promised would be undefended, and he would make it indefensible. She, poor soul, had refused to grant this; for, as corroborated by the evidence of friends and servants, she was utterly devoted to him, and stated with that quiet dignity which distinguished her throughout this ordeal, that she hoped that he was the victim of some miserable but temporary derangement, and would come to his right mind again. He had dined that night at his club, leaving his month-old bride to pass the evening alone, and had returned between eleven and twelve that night in a state of vile intoxication. He had gone up to her bedroom, pistol in hand, had locked the door, and his voice was heard screaming and yelling at her. Then followed the sound of one shot. On the table in his dressing-room was found a half-sheet of paper, dated that day, and this was read out in court. "The horror of my position," he had written, "is beyond description and endurance. I can bear it no longer: my soul sickens...." The jury, without leaving the court, returned the verdict that he had committed suicide while temporarily insane, and the coroner, at their request, expressed their sympathy and his own with the poor lady, who, as testified on all hands, had treated her husband with the utmost tenderness and affection.

For six months Bertha Acres had travelled abroad, and then in the autumn she had bought Gate-house at Tarleton, and settled down to the absorbing trifles which make life in a small country town so busy and strenuous.

Our modest little dwelling is within a stone's throw of the Gate-house; and when, on the return of my wife and myself from two months in Scotland, we found that Mrs. Acres was installed as a neighbour, Madge lost no time in going to call on her. She returned with a series of pleasant impressions. Mrs. Acres, still on the sunny slope that leads up to the table-land of life which begins at forty years, was extremely handsome, cordial, and charming in manner, witty and agreeable, and wonderfully well dressed. Before the conclusion of her call Madge, in country fashion, had begged her to dispose with formalities, and, instead of a frigid return of the call, to dine with us quietly next day. Did she play bridge? That being so, we would just be a party of four; for her brother, Charles Alington, had proposed himself for a visit....

I listened to this with sufficient attention to grasp what Madge was saying, but what I was really thinking about was a chess-problem which I was attempting to solve. But at this point I became acutely aware that her stream of pleasant impressions dried up suddenly, and she became stonily silent. She shut speech off as by the turn of a tap, and glowered at the fire, rubbing the back of one hand with the fingers of another, as is her habit in perplexity.

"Go on," I said.

She got up, suddenly restless.

"All I have been telling you is literally and soberly true," she said. "I thought Mrs. Acres charming and witty and good-looking and friendly. What more could you ask from a new acquaintance? And then, after I had asked her to dinner, I suddenly found for no earthly reason that I very much disliked her; I couldn't bear her."

"You said she was wonderfully well dressed," I permitted myself to remark.... If the Queen took the Knight——

"Don't be silly!" said Madge. "I am wonderfully well dressed too. But behind all her agreeableness and charm and good looks I suddenly felt there was something else which I detested and dreaded. It's no use asking me what it was, because I haven't the slightest idea. If I knew what it was, the thing would explain itself. But I felt a horror—nothing vivid, nothing close, you understand, but somewhere in the background. Can the mind have a 'turn,' do

18

you think, just as the body can, when for a second or two you suddenly feel giddy? I think it must have been that—oh! I'm sure it was that. But I'm glad I asked her to dine. I mean to like her. I shan't have a 'turn' again, shall I?"

"No, certainly not," I said.... If the Queen refrained from taking the tempting Knight——

"Oh, do stop your silly chess-problem!" said Madge. "Bite him, Fungus!"

Fungus, so called because he is the son of Humour and Gustavus Adolphus, rose from his place on the hearthrug, and with a horse laugh nuzzled against my leg, which is his way of biting those he loves. Then the most amiable of bull-dogs, who has a passion for the human race, lay down on my foot and sighed heavily. But Madge evidently wanted to talk, and I pushed the chessboard away.

"Tell me more about the horror," I said.

"It was just horror," she said—"a sort of sickness of the soul."...

I found my brain puzzling over some vague reminiscence, surely connected with Mrs. Acres, which those words mistily evoked. But next moment that train of thought was cut short, for the old and sinister legend about the Gate-house came into my mind as accounting for the horror of which Madge spoke. In the days of Elizabethan religious persecutions it had, then newly built, been inhabited by two brothers, of whom the elder, to whom it belonged, had Mass said there every Sunday. Betrayed by the younger, he was arrested and racked to death. Subsequently the younger, in a fit of remorse, hanged himself in the panelled parlour. Certainly there was a story that the house was haunted by his strangled apparition dangling from the beams, and the late tenants of the house (which now had stood vacant for over three years) had quitted it after a month's occupation, in consequence, so it was commonly said, of unaccountable and horrible sights. What was more likely, then, than that Madge, who from childhood has been intensely sensitive to occult and psychic phenomena, should have caught, on that strange wireless receiver which is characteristic of "sensitives," some whispered message?

"But you know the story of the house," I said. "Isn't it quite possible that something of that may have reached you? Where did you sit, for instance? In the panelled parlour?"

She brightened at that.

"Ah, you wise man!" she said. "I never thought of that. That may account for it all. I hope it does. You shall be left in peace with your chess for being so brilliant."

19

I had occasion half an hour later to go to the post-office, a hundred yards up the High Street, on the matter of a registered letter which I wanted to despatch that evening. Dusk was gathering, but the red glow of sunset still smouldered in the west, sufficient to enable me to recognise familiar forms and features of passers-by. Just as I came opposite the post-office there approached from the other direction a tall, finely built woman, whom, I felt sure, I had never seen before. Her destination was the same as mine, and I hung on my step a moment to let her pass in first. Simultaneously I felt that I knew, in some vague, faint manner, what Madge had meant when she talked about a "sickness of the soul." It was no nearer realisation to me than is the running of a tune in the head to the audible external hearing of it, and I attributed my sudden recognition of her feeling to the fact that in all probability my mind had subconsciously been dwelling on what she had said, and not for a moment did I connect it with any external cause. And then it occurred to me who, possibly, this woman was....

She finished the transaction of her errand a few seconds before me, and when I got out into the street again she was a dozen yards down the pavement, walking in the direction of my house and of the Gate-house. Opposite my own door I deliberately lingered, and saw her pass down the steps that led from the road to the entrance of the Gate-house. Even as I turned into my own door the unbidden reminiscence which had eluded me before came out into the open, and I cast my net over it. It was her husband, who, in the inexplicable communication he had left on his dressing-room table, just before he shot himself, had written "my soul sickens." It was odd, though scarcely more than that, for Madge to have used those identical words.

Charles Alington, my wife's brother, who arrived next afternoon, is quite the happiest man whom I have ever come across. The material world, that perennial spring of thwarted ambition, physical desire, and perpetual disappointment, is practically unknown to him. Envy, malice, and all uncharitableness are equally alien, because he does not want to obtain what anybody else has got, and has no sense of possession, which is queer, since he is enormously rich. He fears nothing, he hopes for nothing, he has no abhorrences or affections, for all physical and nervous functions are in him in the service of an intense inquisitiveness. He never passed a moral judgment in his life, he only wants to explore and to know. Knowledge, in fact, is his entire preoccupation, and since chemists and medical scientists probe and mine in the world of tinctures and microbes far more efficiently than he could do, as he has so little

20

care for anything that can be weighed or propagated, he devotes himself, absorbedly and ecstatically, to that world that lies about the confines of conscious existence. Anything not yet certainly determined appeals to him with the call of a trumpet: he ceases to take an interest in a subject as soon as it shows signs of assuming a practical and definite status. He was intensely concerned, for instance, in wireless transmission, until Signor Marconi proved that it came within the scope of practical science, and then Charles abandoned it as dull. I had seen him last two months before, when he was in a great perturbation, since he was speaking at a meeting of Anglo-Israelites in the morning, to show that the Scone Stone, which is now in the Coronation Chair at Westminster, was for certain the pillow on which Jacob's head had rested when he saw the vision at Bethel; was addressing the Psychical Research Society in the afternoon on the subject of messages received from the dead through automatic script, and in the evening was, by way of a holiday, only listening to a lecture on reincarnation. None of these things could, as yet, be definitely proved, and that was why he loved them. During the intervals when the occult and the fantastic do not occupy him, he is, in spite of his fifty years and wizened mien, exactly like a schoolboy of eighteen back on his holidays and brimming with superfluous energy.

I found Charles already arrived when I got home next afternoon, after a round of golf. He was betwixt and between the serious and the holiday mood, for he had evidently been reading to Madge from a journal concerning reincarnation, and was rather severe to me....

"Golf!" he said, with insulting scorn. "What is there to know about golf? You hit a ball into the air——"

I was a little sore over the events of the afternoon.

"That's just what I don't do," I said. "I hit it along the ground!"

"Well, it doesn't matter where you hit it," said he. "It's all subject to known laws. But the guess, the conjecture: there's the thrill and the excitement of life. The charlatan with his new cure for cancer, the automatic writer with his messages from the dead, the reincarnationist with his positive assertions that he was Napoleon or a Christian slave—they are the people who advance knowledge. You have to guess before you know. Even Darwin saw that when he said you could not investigate without a hypothesis!"

"So what's your hypothesis this minute?" I asked.

"Why, that we've all lived before, and that we're going to live again here on this same old earth. Any other conception of a future life is impossible. Are all the people who have been born and have

21

died since the world emerged from chaos going to become inhabitants of some future world? What a squash, you know, my dear Madge! Now, I know what you're going to ask me. If we've all lived before, why can't we remember it? But that's so simple! If you remembered being Cleopatra, you would go on behaving like Cleopatra; and what would Tarleton say? Judas Iscariot, too! Fancy knowing you had been Judas Iscariot! You couldn't get over it! you would commit suicide, or cause everybody who was connected with you to commit suicide from their horror of you. Or imagine being a grocer's boy who knew he had been Julius Cæsar.... Of course, sex doesn't matter: souls, as far as I understand, are sexless—just sparks of life, which are put into physical envelopes, some male, some female. You might have been King David, Madge and poor Tony here one of his wives."

"That would be wonderfully neat," said I.

Charles broke out into a shout of laughter.

"It would indeed," he said. "But I won't talk sense any more to you scoffers. I'm absolutely tired out, I will confess, with thinking. I want to have a pretty lady to come to dinner, and talk to her as if she was just herself and I myself, and nobody else. I want to win two-and-sixpence at bridge with the expenditure of enormous thought. I want to have a large breakfast to-morrow and read The Times afterwards, and go to Tony's club and talk about crops and golf and Irish affairs and Peace Conferences, and all the things that don't matter one straw!"

"You're going to begin your programme to-night, dear," said Madge. "A very pretty lady is coming to dinner, and we're going to play bridge afterwards."

Madge and I were ready for Mrs. Acres when she arrived, but Charles was not yet down. Fungus, who has a wild adoration for Charles, quite unaccountable, since Charles has no feelings for dogs, was helping him to dress, and Madge, Mrs. Acres, and I waited for his appearance. It was certainly Mrs. Acres whom I had met last night at the door of the post-office, but the dim light of sunset had not enabled me to see how wonderfully handsome she was. There was something slightly Jewish about her profile: the high forehead, the very full-lipped mouth, the bridged nose, the prominent chin, all suggested rather than exemplified an Eastern origin. And when she spoke she had that rich softness of utterance, not quite hoarseness, but not quite of the clear-cut distinctness of tone which characterises northern nations. Something southern, something Eastern....

"I am bound to ask one thing," she said, when, after the usual

22

greetings, we stood round the fireplace, waiting for Charles—"but have you got a dog?"

Madge moved towards the bell.

"Yes, but he shan't come down if you dislike dogs," she said. "He's wonderfully kind, but I know——"

"Ah, it's not that," said Mrs. Acres. "I adore dogs. But I only wished to spare your dog's feelings. Though I adore them, they hate me, and they're terribly frightened of me. There's something anti-canine about me."

It was too late to say more. Charles's steps clattered in the little hall outside, and Fungus was hoarse and amused. Next moment the door opened, and the two came in.

Fungus came in first. He lolloped in a festive manner into the middle of the room, sniffed and snored in greeting, and then turned tail. He slipped and skidded on the parquet outside, and we heard him bundling down the kitchen stairs.

"Rude dog," said Madge. "Charles, let me introduce you to Mrs. Acres. My brother, Mrs. Acres: Sir Charles Alington."

Our little dinner-table of four would not permit of separate conversations, and general topics, springing up like mushrooms, wilted and died at their very inception. What mood possessed the others I did not at that time know, but for myself I was only conscious of some fundamental distaste of the handsome, clever woman who sat on my right, and seemed quite unaffected by the withering atmosphere. She was charming to the eye, she was witty to the ear, she had grace and gracefulness, and all the time she was something terrible. But by degrees, as I found my own distaste increasing, I saw that my brother-in-law's interest was growing correspondingly keen. The "pretty lady" whose presence at dinner he had desired and obtained was enchaining him—not, so I began to guess, for her charm and her prettiness, but for some purpose of study, and I wondered whether it was her beautiful Jewish profile that was confirming to his mind some Anglo-Israelitish theory, whether he saw in her fine brown eyes the glance of the seer and the clairvoyante, or whether he divined in her some reincarnation of one of the famous or the infamous dead. Certainly she had for him some fascination beyond that of the legitimate charm of a very handsome woman; he was studying her with intense curiosity.

"And you are comfortable in the Gate-house?" he suddenly rapped out at her, as if asking some question of which the answer was crucial.

"Ah! but so comfortable," she said—"such a delightful atmosphere. I have never known a house that 'felt' so peaceful and

23

homelike. Or is it merely fanciful to imagine that some houses have a sense of tranquillity about them and others are uneasy and even terrible?"

Charles stared at her a moment in silence before he recollected his manners.

"No, there may easily be something in it, I should say," he answered. "One can imagine long centuries of tranquillity actually investing a home with some sort of psychical aura perceptible to those who are sensitive."

She turned to Madge.

"And yet I have heard a ridiculous story that the house is supposed to be haunted," she said. "If it is, it is surely haunted by delightful, contented spirits."

Dinner was over. Madge rose.

"Come in very soon, Tony," she said to me, "and let's get to our bridge."

But her eyes said, "Don't leave me long alone with her."

Charles turned briskly round when the door had shut.

"An extremely interesting woman," he said.

"Very handsome," said I.

"Is she? I didn't notice. Her mind, her spirit—that's what intrigued me. What is she? What's behind? Why did Fungus turn tail like that? Queer, too, about her finding the atmosphere of the Gate-house so tranquil. The late tenants, I remember, didn't find that soothing touch about it!"

"How do you account for that?" I asked.

"There might be several explanations. You might say that the late tenants were fanciful, imaginative people, and that the present tenant is a sensible, matter-of-fact woman. Certainly she seemed to be."

"Or——" I suggested.

He laughed.

"Well, you might say—mind, I don't say so—but you might say that the—the spiritual tenants of the house find Mrs. Acres a congenial companion, and want to retain her. So they keep quiet, and don't upset the cook's nerves!"

Somehow this answer exasperated and jarred on me.

"What do you mean?" I said. "The spiritual tenant of the house, I suppose, is the man who betrayed his brother and hanged himself. Why should he find a charming woman like Mrs. Acres a congenial companion?"

Charles got up briskly. Usually he is more than ready to discuss such topics, but to-night it seemed that he had no such inclination.

24

"Didn't Madge tell us not to be long?" he asked. "You know how I run on if I once get on that subject, Tony, so don't give me the opportunity."

"But why did you say that?" I persisted.

"Because I was talking nonsense. You know me well enough to be aware that I am an habitual criminal in that respect."

It was indeed strange to find how completely both the first impression that Madge had formed of Mrs. Acres and the feeling that followed so quickly on its heels were endorsed by those who, during the next week or two, did a neighbour's duty to the newcomer. All were loud in praise of her charm, her pleasant, kindly wit, her good looks, her beautiful clothes, but even while this Lob-gesang was in full chorus it would suddenly die away, and an uneasy silence descended, which somehow was more eloquent than all the appreciative speech. Odd, unaccountable little incidents had occurred, which were whispered from mouth to mouth till they became common property. The same fear that Fungus had shown of her was exhibited by another dog. A parallel case occurred when she returned the call of our parson's wife. Mrs. Dowlett had a cage of canaries in the window of her drawing-room. These birds had manifested symptoms of extreme terror when Mrs. Acres entered the room, beating themselves against the wires of their cage, and uttering the alarm-note.... She inspired some sort of inexplicable fear, over which we, as trained and civilised human beings, had control, so that we behaved ourselves. But animals, without that check, gave way altogether to it, even as Fungus had done.

Mrs. Acres entertained; she gave charming little dinner-parties of eight, with a couple of tables at bridge to follow, but over these evenings there hung a blight and a blackness. No doubt the sinister story of the panelled parlour contributed to this.

This curious secret dread of her, of which as on that first evening at my house, she appeared to be completely unconscious differed very widely in degree. Most people, like myself, were conscious of it, but only very remotely so, and we found ourselves at the Gate-house behaving quite as usual, though with this unease in the background. But with a few, and most of all with Madge, it grew into a sort of obsession. She made every effort to combat it; her will was entirely set against it, but her struggle seemed only to establish its power over her. The pathetic and pitiful part was that Mrs. Acres from the first had taken a tremendous liking to her, and used to drop in continually, calling first to Madge at the window, in that pleasant, serene voice of hers, to tell Fungus that the hated one was imminent.

25

Then came a day when Madge and I were bidden to a party at the Gate-house on Christmas evening. This was to be the last of Mrs. Acres's hospitalities for the present, since she was leaving immediately afterwards for a couple of months in Egypt. So, with this remission ahead, Madge almost gleefully accepted the bidding. But when the evening came she was seized with so violent an attack of sickness and shivering that she was utterly unable to fulfil her engagement. Her doctor could find no physical trouble to account for this: it seemed that the anticipation of her evening alone caused it, and here was the culmination of her shrinking from our kindly and pleasant neighbour. She could only tell me that her sensations, as she began to dress for the party, were like those of that moment in sleep when somewhere in the drowsy brain nightmare is ripening. Something independent of her will revolted at what lay before her....

Spring had begun to stretch herself in the lap of winter when next the curtain rose on this veiled drama of forces but dimly comprehended and shudderingly conjectured; but then, indeed, nightmare ripened swiftly in broad noon. And this was the way of it.

Charles Alington had again come to stay with us five days before Easter, and expressed himself as humorously disappointed to find that the subject of his curiosity was still absent from the Gate-house. On the Saturday morning before Easter he appeared very late for breakfast, and Madge had already gone her ways. I rang for a fresh teapot, and while this was on its way he took up The Times.

"I only read the outside page of it," he said. "The rest is too full of mere materialistic dullnesses—politics, sports, money-market—"

He stopped, and passed the paper over to me.

"There, where I'm pointing," he said—"among the deaths. The first one."

What I read was this:

"Acres, Bertha. Died at sea, Thursday night, 30th March, and by her own request buried at sea. (Received by wireless from P. & O. steamer Peshawar.)"

He held out his hand for the paper again, and turned over the leaves.

"Lloyd's," he said. "The Peshawar arrived at Tilbury yesterday afternoon. The burial must have taken place somewhere in the English Channel."

On the afternoon of Easter Sunday Madge and I motored out to the golf links three miles away. She proposed to walk along the

26

beach just outside the dunes while I had my round, and return to the club-house for tea in two hours' time. The day was one of most lucid spring: a warm south-west wind bowled white clouds along the sky, and their shadows jovially scudded over the sandhills. We had told her of Mrs. Acres's death, and from that moment something dark and vague which had been lying over her mind since the autumn seemed to join this fleet of the shadows of clouds and leave her in sunlight. We parted at the door of the club-house, and she set out on her walk.

Half an hour later, as my opponent and I were waiting on the fifth tee, where the road crosses the links, for the couple in front of us to move on, a servant from the club-house, scudding along the road, caught sight of us, and, jumping from his bicycle, came to where we stood.

"You're wanted at the club-house, sir," he said to me. "Mrs. Carford was walking along the shore, and she found something left by the tide. A body, sir. 'Twas in a sack, but the sack was torn, and she saw—— It's upset her very much, sir. We thought it best to come for you."

I took the boy's bicycle and went back to the club-house as fast as I could turn the wheel. I felt sure I knew what Madge had found, and, knowing that, realised the shock.... Five minutes later she was telling me her story in gasps and whispers.

"The tide was going down," she said, "and I walked along the high-water mark.... There were pretty shells; I was picking them up.... And then I saw it in front of me—just shapeless, just a sack ... and then, as I came nearer, it took shape; there were knees and elbows. It moved, it rolled over, and where the head was the sack was torn, and I saw her face. Her eyes were open, Tony, and I fled.... All the time I felt it was rolling along after me. Oh, Tony! she's dead, isn't she? She won't come back to the Gate-house? Do you promise me?... There's something awful! I wonder if I guess. The sea gives her up. The sea won't suffer her to rest in it."...

The news of the finding had already been telephoned to Tarleton, and soon a party of four men with a stretcher arrived. There was no doubt as to the identity of the body, for though it had been in the water for three days no corruption had come to it. The weights with which at burial it had been laden must by some strange chance have been detached from it, and by a chance stranger yet it had drifted to the shore closest to her home. That night it lay in the mortuary, and the inquest was held on it next day, though that was a bank-holiday. From there it was taken to the Gate-house and coffined, and it lay in the panelled parlour for the funeral on the morrow.

Madge, after that one hysterical outburst, had completely recovered herself, and on the Monday evening she made a little wreath of the spring-flowers which the early warmth had called into blossom in the garden, and I went across with it to the Gate-house. Though the news of Mrs. Acres's death and the subsequent finding of the body had been widely advertised, there had been no response from relations or friends, and as I laid the solitary wreath on the coffin a sense of the utter loneliness of what lay within seized and encompassed me. And then a portent, no less, took place before my eyes. Hardly had the freshly gathered flowers been laid on the coffin than they drooped and wilted. The stalks of the daffodils bent, and their bright chalices closed; the odour of the wallflowers died, and they withered as I watched.... What did it mean, that even the petals of spring shrank and were moribund?

I told Madge nothing of this; and she, as if through some pang of remorse, was determined to be present next day at the funeral. No arrival of friends or relations had taken place, and from the Gate-house there came none of the servants. They stood in the porch as the coffin was brought out of the house, and even before it was put into the hearse had gone back again and closed the door. So, at the cemetery on the hill above Tarleton, Madge and her brother and I were the only mourners.

The afternoon was densely overcast, though we got no rainfall, and it was with thick clouds above and a sea-mist drifting between the grave-stones that we came, after the service in the cemetery-chapel, to the place of interment. And then—I can hardly write of it now—when it came for the coffin to be lowered into the grave, it was found that by some faulty measurement it could not descend, for the excavation was not long enough to hold it.

Madge was standing close to us, and at this moment I heard her sob.

"And the kindly earth will not receive her," she whispered.

There was awful delay: the diggers must be sent for again, and meantime the rain had begun to fall thick and tepid. For some reason—perhaps some outlying feeler of Madge's obsession had wound a tentacle round me—I felt that I must know that earth had gone to earth, but I could not suffer Madge to wait. So, in this miserable pause, I got Charles to take her home, and then returned.

Pick and shovel were busy, and soon the resting-place was ready. The interrupted service continued, the handful of wet earth splashed on the coffin-lid, and when all was over I left the cemetery, still feeling, I knew not why, that all was not over. Some restlessness and want of certainty possessed me, and instead of going home I fared forth into the rolling wooded country inland, with the intention of walking off these bat-like terrors that flapped around me. The rain had ceased, and a blurred sunlight penetrated the sea-mist which still blanketed the fields and woods, and for half an hour, moving briskly, I endeavoured to fight down some fantastic conviction that had gripped my mind in its claws. I refused to look straight at that conviction, telling myself how fantastic, how unreasonable it was; but as often as I put out a hand to throttle it there came the echo of Madge's words: "The sea will not suffer her; the kindly earth will not receive her." And if I could shut my eyes to that there came some remembrance of the day she died, and of half-forgotten fragments of Charles's superstitious belief in reincarnation. The whole thing, incredible though its component parts were, hung together with a terrible tenacity.

Before long the rain began again, and I turned, meaning to go by the main-road into Tarleton, which passes in a wide-flung curve some half-mile outside the cemetery. But as I approached the path through the fields, which, leaving the less direct route, passes close to the cemetery and brings you by a steeper and shorter descent into the town, I felt myself irresistibly impelled to take it. I told myself, of course, that I wished to make my wet walk as short as possible; but at the back of my mind was the half-conscious, but none the less imperative need to know by ocular evidence that the grave by which I had stood that afternoon had been filled in, and that the body of Mrs. Acres now lay tranquil beneath the soil. My path would be even shorter if I passed through the graveyard, and so presently I was fumbling in the gloom for the latch of the gate, and closed it again behind me. Rain was falling now thick and sullenly, and in the bleared twilight I picked my way among the mounds and slipped on the dripping grass, and there in front of me was the newly turned earth. All was finished: the grave-diggers had done their work and departed, and earth had gone back again into the keeping of the earth.

It brought me some great lightening of the spirit to know that, and I was on the point of turning away when a sound of stir from the heaped soil caught my ear, and I saw a little stream of pebbles mixed with clay trickle down the side of the mound above the grave: the heavy rain, no doubt, had loosened the earth. And then came another and yet another, and with terror gripping at my heart I perceived that this was no loosening from without, but from within, for to right and left the piled soil was falling away with the press of something from below. Faster and faster it poured off the grave, and ever higher at the head of it rose a mound of earth pushed upwards from beneath. Somewhere out of sight there came the sound as of creaking and breaking wood, and then through that mound of earth there protruded the end of the coffin. The lid was shattered: loose pieces of the boards fell off it, and from within the cavity there faced me white features and wide eyes. All this I saw, while sheer terror held me motionless; then, I suppose, came the breaking-point, and with such panic as surely man never felt before I was stumbling away among the graves and racing towards the kindly human lights of the town below.

I went to the parson who had conducted the service that afternoon with my incredible tale, and an hour later he, Charles Alington, and two or three men from the undertaker's were on the spot. They found the coffin, completely disinterred, lying on the ground by the grave, which was now three-quarters full of the earth which had fallen back into it. After what had happened it was decided to make no further attempt to bury it; and next day the body was cremated.

Now, it is open to anyone who may read this tale to reject the incident of this emergence of the coffin altogether, and account for the other strange happenings by the comfortable theory of coincidence. He can certainly satisfy himself that one Bertha Acres did die at sea on this particular Thursday before Easter, and was buried at sea: there is nothing extraordinary about that. Nor is it the least impossible that the weights should have slipped from the canvas shroud, and that the body should have been washed ashore on the coast by Tarleton (why not Tarleton, as well as any other little town near the coast?); nor is there anything inherently significant in the fact that the grave, as originally dug, was not of sufficient dimensions to receive the coffin. That all these incidents should have happened to the body of a single individual is odd, but then the nature of coincidence is to be odd. They form a startling series, but unless coincidences are startling they escape observation altogether. So, if you reject the last incident here recorded, or account for it by some local disturbance, an earthquake, or the breaking of a spring just below the grave, you can comfortably recline on the cushion of coincidence....

For myself, I give no explanation of these events, though my brother-in-law brought forward one with which he himself is perfectly satisfied. Only the other day he sent me, with considerable jubilation, a copy of some extracts from a mediæval treatise on the subject of reincarnation which sufficiently indicates his theory. The original work was in Latin, which, mistrusting my scholarship, he kindly translated for me. I transcribe his quotations exactly as he sent them to me.

"We have these certain instances of his reincarnation. In one his spirit was incarnated in the body of a man; in the other, in that of a woman, fair of outward aspect, and of a pleasant conversation, but held in dread and in horror by those who came into more than casual intercourse with her.... She, it is said, died on the anniversary of the day on which he hanged himself, after the betrayal, but of this I have no certain information. What is sure is that, when the time came for her burial, the kindly earth would receive her not, but though the grave was dug deep and well it spewed her forth again.... Of the man in whom his cursed spirit was reincarnated it is said that, being on a voyage when he died, he was cast overboard with weights to sink him; but the sea would not suffer him to rest in her bosom, but slipped the weights from him, and cast him forth again on to the coast.... Howbeit, when the full time of his expiation shall have come and his deadly sin forgiven, the corporal body which is the cursed receptacle of his spirit shall at length be purged with fire, and so he shall, in the infinite mercy of the Almighty, have rest, and shall wander no more."

# The Horror-Horn

For the past ten days Alhubel had basked in the radiant midwinter weather proper to its eminence of over 6,000 feet. From rising to setting the sun (so surprising to those who have hitherto associated it with a pale, tepid plate indistinctly shining through the murky air of England) had blazed its way across the sparkling blue, and every night the serene and windless frost had made the stars sparkle like illuminated diamond dust. Sufficient snow had fallen before Christmas to content the skiers, and the big rink, sprinkled every evening, had given the skaters each morning a fresh surface on which to perform their slippery antics. Bridge and dancing served to while away the greater part of the night, and to me, now for the first time tasting the joys of a winter in the Engadine, it seemed that a new heaven and a new earth had been lighted, warmed, and refrigerated for the special benefit of those who like myself had been wise enough to save up their days of holiday for the winter.

But a break came in these ideal conditions: one afternoon the sun grew vapour-veiled and up the valley from the north-west a wind frozen with miles of travel over ice-bound hill-sides began scouting through the calm halls of the heavens. Soon it grew dusted with snow, first in small flakes driven almost horizontally before its congealing breath and then in larger tufts as of swansdown. And though all day for a fortnight before the fate of nations and life and death had seemed to me of far less importance than to get certain tracings of the skate-blades on the ice of proper shape and size, it now seemed that the one paramount consideration was to hurry back to the hotel for shelter: it was wiser to leave rocking-turns alone than to be frozen in their quest.

I had come out here with my cousin, Professor Ingram, the celebrated physiologist and Alpine climber. During the serenity of the last fortnight he had made a couple of notable winter ascents, but this morning his weather-wisdom had mistrusted the signs of the heavens, and instead of attempting the ascent of the Piz Passug he had waited to see whether his misgivings justified themselves. So there he sat now in the hall of the admirable hotel with his feet on the hot-water pipes and the latest delivery of the English post in his hands. This contained a pamphlet concerning the result of the Mount Everest expedition, of which he had just finished the perusal when I entered.

"A very interesting report," he said, passing it to me, "and they certainly deserve to succeed next year. But who can tell, what that final six thousand feet may entail? Six thousand feet more when you have already accomplished twenty-three thousand does not seem much, but at present no one knows whether the human frame can stand exertion at such a height. It may affect not the lungs and heart only, but possibly the brain. Delirious hallucinations may occur. In fact, if I did not know better, I should have said that one such hallucination had occurred to the climbers already."

"And what was that?" I asked.

"You will find that they thought they came across the tracks of some naked human foot at a great altitude. That looks at first sight like an hallucination. What more natural than that a brain excited and exhilarated by the extreme height should have interpreted certain marks in the snow as the footprints of a human being? Every bodily organ at these altitudes is exerting itself to the utmost to do its work, and the brain seizes on those marks in the snow and says 'Yes, I'm all right, I'm doing my job, and I perceive marks in the snow which I affirm are human footprints.' You know, even at this altitude, how restless and eager the brain is, how vividly, as you told me, you dream at night. Multiply that stimulus and that consequent eagerness and restlessness by three, and how natural that the brain should harbour illusions! What after all is the delirium which often accompanies high fever but the effort of the brain to do its work under the pressure of feverish conditions? It is so eager to continue perceiving that it perceives things which have no existence!"

"And yet you don't think that these naked human footprints were illusions," said I. "You told me you would have thought so, if you had not known better."

He shifted in his chair and looked out of the window a moment. The air was thick now with the density of the big snow-flakes that were driven along by the squealing north-west gale.

"Quite so," he said. "In all probability the human footprints were real human footprints. I expect that they were the footprints, anyhow, of a being more nearly a man than anything else. My reason for saying so is that I know such beings exist. I have even seen quite near at hand—and I assure you I did not wish to be nearer in spite of my intense curiosity—the creature, shall we say, which would make such footprints. And if the snow was not so dense, I could show you the place where I saw him."

He pointed straight out of the window, where across the valley lies the huge tower of the Ungeheuerhorn with the carved pinnacle of rock at the top like some gigantic rhinoceros-horn. On one side

33

only, as I knew, was the mountain practicable, and that for none but the finest climbers; on the other three a succession of ledges and precipices rendered it unscalable. Two thousand feet of sheer rock form the tower; below are five hundred feet of fallen boulders, up to the edge of which grow dense woods of larch and pine.

"Upon the Ungeheuerhorn?" I asked.

"Yes. Up till twenty years ago it had never been ascended, and I, like several others, spent a lot of time in trying to find a route up it. My guide and I sometimes spent three nights together at the hut beside the Blumen glacier, prowling round it, and it was by luck really that we found the route, for the mountain looks even more impracticable from the far side than it does from this. But one day we found a long, transverse fissure in the side which led to a negotiable ledge; then there came a slanting ice couloir which you could not see till you got to the foot of it. However, I need not go into that."

The big room where we sat was filling up with cheerful groups driven indoors by this sudden gale and snowfall, and the cackle of merry tongues grew loud. The band, too, that invariable appanage of tea-time at Swiss resorts, had begun to tune up for the usual potpourri from the works of Puccini. Next moment the sugary, sentimental melodies began.

"Strange contrast!" said Ingram. "Here are we sitting warm and cosy, our ears pleasantly tickled with these little baby tunes and outside is the great storm growing more violent every moment, and swirling round the austere cliffs of the Ungeheuerhorn: the Horror-Horn, as indeed it was to me."

"I want to hear all about it," I said. "Every detail: make a short story long, if it's short. I want to know why it's your Horror-horn?"

"Well, Chanton and I (he was my guide) used to spend days prowling about the cliffs, making a little progress on one side and then being stopped, and gaining perhaps five hundred feet on another side and then being confronted by some insuperable obstacle, till the day when by luck we found the route. Chanton never liked the job, for some reason that I could not fathom. It was not because of the difficulty or danger of the climbing, for he was the most fearless man I have ever met when dealing with rocks and ice, but he was always insistent that we should get off the mountain and back to the Blumen hut before sunset. He was scarcely easy even when we had got back to shelter and locked and barred the door, and I well remember one night when, as we ate our supper, we heard some animal, a wolf probably, howling somewhere out in the night. A positive panic seized him, and I don't think he closed his eyes till morning. It struck me then that there might be some grisly legend about the mountain, connected possibly with its name, and next day I asked him why the peak was called the Horror-horn. He put the question off at first, and said that, like the Schreckhorn, its name was due to its precipices and falling stones; but when I pressed him further he acknowledged that there was a legend about it, which his father had told him. There were creatures, so it was supposed, that lived in its caves, things human in shape, and covered, except for the face and hands, with long black hair. They were dwarfs in size, four feet high or thereabouts, but of prodigious strength and agility, remnants of some wild primeval race. It seemed that they were still in an upward stage of evolution, or so I guessed, for the story ran that sometimes girls had been carried off by them, not as prey, and not for any such fate as for those captured by cannibals, but to be bred from. Young men also had been raped by them, to be mated with the females of their tribe. All this looked as if the creatures, as I said, were tending towards humanity. But naturally I did not believe a word of it, as applied to the conditions of the present day. Centuries ago, conceivably, there may have been such beings, and, with the extraordinary tenacity of tradition, the news of this had been handed down and was still current round the hearths of the peasants. As for their numbers, Chanton told me that three had been once seen together by a man who owing to his swiftness on skis had escaped to tell the tale. This man, he averred, was no other than his grandfather, who had been benighted one winter evening as he passed through the dense woods below the Ungeheuerhorn, and Chanton supposed that they had been driven down to these lower altitudes in search of food during severe winter weather, for otherwise the recorded sights of them had always taken place among the rocks of the peak itself. They had pursued his grandfather, then a young man, at an extraordinarily swift canter, running sometimes upright as men run, sometimes on all-fours in the manner of beasts, and their howls were just such as that we had heard that night in the Blumen hut. Such at any rate was the story Chanton told me, and, like you, I regarded it as the very moonshine of superstition. But the very next day I had reason to reconsider my judgment about it.

"It was on that day that after a week of exploration we hit on the only route at present known to the top of our peak. We started as soon as there was light enough to climb by, for, as you may guess, on very difficult rocks it is impossible to climb by lantern or moonlight. We hit on the long fissure I have spoken of, we explored the ledge which from below seemed to end in nothingness, and with an hour's step-cutting ascended the couloir which led upwards from it. From there onwards it was a rock-climb, certainly of considerable difficulty, but with no heart-breaking discoveries ahead, and it was about nine in the morning that we stood on the top. We did not wait there long, for that side of the mountain is raked by falling stones loosened, when the sun grows hot, from the ice that holds them, and we made haste to pass the ledge where the falls are most frequent. After that there was the long fissure to descend, a matter of no great difficulty, and we were at the end of our work by midday, both of us, as you may imagine, in the state of the highest elation.

"A long and tiresome scramble among the huge boulders at the foot of the cliff then lay before us. Here the hill-side is very porous and great caves extend far into the mountain. We had unroped at the base of the fissure, and were picking our way as seemed good to either of us among these fallen rocks, many of them bigger than an ordinary house, when, on coming round the corner of one of these, I saw that which made it clear that the stories Chanton had told me were no figment of traditional superstition.

"Not twenty yards in front of me lay one of the beings of which he had spoken. There it sprawled naked and basking on its back with face turned up to the sun, which its narrow eyes regarded unwinking. In form it was completely human, but the growth of hair that covered limbs and trunk alike almost completely hid the sun-tanned skin beneath. But its face, save for the down on its cheeks and chin, was hairless, and I looked on a countenance the sensual and malevolent bestiality of which froze me with horror. Had the creature been an animal, one would have felt scarcely a shudder at the gross animalism of it; the horror lay in the fact that it was a man. There lay by it a couple of gnawed bones, and, its meal finished, it was lazily licking its protuberant lips, from which came a purring murmur of content. With one hand it scratched the thick hair on its belly, in the other it held one of these bones, which presently split in half beneath the pressure of its finger and thumb. But my horror was not based on the information of what happened to those men whom these creatures caught, it was due only to my proximity to a thing so human and so infernal. The peak, of which the ascent had a moment ago filled us with such elated satisfaction, became to me an Ungeheuerhorn indeed, for it was the home of beings more awful than the delirium of nightmare could ever have conceived.

"Chanton was a dozen paces behind me, and with a backward wave of my hand I caused him to halt. Then withdrawing myself with infinite precaution, so as not to attract the gaze of that basking creature, I slipped back round the rock, whispered to him what I had seen, and with blanched faces we made a long detour, peering round every corner, and crouching low, not knowing that at any step we might not come upon another of these beings, or that from the mouth of one of these caves in the mountain-side there might not appear another of those hairless and dreadful faces, with perhaps this time the breasts and insignia of womanhood. That would have been the worst of all.

"Luck favoured us, for we made our way among the boulders and shifting stones, the rattle of which might at any moment have betrayed us, without a repetition of my experience, and once among the trees we ran as if the Furies themselves were in pursuit. Well now did I understand, though I dare say I cannot convey, the qualms of Chanton's mind when he spoke to me of these creatures. Their very humanity was what made them so terrible, the fact that they were of the same race as ourselves, but of a type so abysmally degraded that the most brutal and inhuman of men would have seemed angelic in comparison."

The music of the small band was over before he had finished the narrative, and the chattering groups round the tea-table had dispersed. He paused a moment.

"There was a horror of the spirit," he said, "which I experienced then, from which, I verily believe, I have never entirely recovered. I saw then how terrible a living thing could be, and how terrible, in consequence, was life itself. In us all I suppose lurks some inherited germ of that ineffable bestiality, and who knows whether, sterile as it has apparently become in the course of centuries, it might not fructify again. When I saw that creature sun itself, I looked into the abyss out of which we have crawled. And these creatures are trying to crawl out of it now, if they exist any longer. Certainly for the last twenty years there has been no record of their being seen, until we come to this story of the footprint seen by the climbers on Everest. If that is authentic, if the party did not mistake the footprint of some bear, or what not, for a human tread, it seems as if still this bestranded remnant of mankind is in existence."

Now, Ingram, had told his story well; but sitting in this warm and civilised room, the horror which he had clearly felt had not communicated itself to me in any very vivid manner. Intellectually, I agreed, I could appreciate his horror, but certainly my spirit felt no shudder of interior comprehension.

"But it is odd," I said, "that your keen interest in physiology did not disperse your qualms. You were looking, so I take it, at some form of man more remote probably than the earliest human remains. Did not something inside you say 'This is of absorbing significance'?"

He shook his head.

"No: I only wanted to get away," said he. "It was not, as I have told you, the terror of what according to Chanton's story, might await us if we were captured; it was sheer horror at the creature itself. I quaked at it."

The snowstorm and the gale increased in violence that night, and I slept uneasily, plucked again and again from slumber by the fierce battling of the wind that shook my windows as if with an imperious demand for admittance. It came in billowy gusts, with strange noises intermingled with it as for a moment it abated, with flutings and moanings that rose to shrieks as the fury of it returned. These noises, no doubt, mingled themselves with my drowsed and sleepy consciousness, and once I tore myself out of nightmare, imagining that the creatures of the Horror-horn had gained footing on my balcony and were rattling at the window-bolts. But before morning the gale had died away, and I awoke to see the snow falling dense and fast in a windless air. For three days it continued, without intermission, and with its cessation there came a frost such as I have never felt before. Fifty degrees were registered one night, and more the next, and what the cold must have been on the cliffs of the Ungeheuerhorn I cannot imagine. Sufficient, so I thought, to have made an end altogether of its secret inhabitants: my cousin, on that day twenty years ago, had missed an opportunity for study which would probably never fall again either to him or another.

I received one morning a letter from a friend saying that he had arrived at the neighbouring winter resort of St. Luigi, and proposing that I should come over for a morning's skating and lunch afterwards. The place was not more than a couple of miles off, if one took the path over the low, pine-clad foot-hills above which lay the steep woods below the first rocky slopes of the Ungeheuerhorn; and accordingly, with a knapsack containing skates on my back, I went on skis over the wooded slopes and down by an easy descent again on to St. Luigi. The day was overcast, clouds entirely obscured the higher peaks though the sun was visible, pale and unluminous, through the mists. But as the morning went on, it gained the upper hand, and I slid down into St. Luigi beneath a sparkling firmament. We skated and lunched, and then, since it looked as if thick weather was coming up again, I set out early about three o'clock for my return journey.

Hardly had I got into the woods when the clouds gathered

thick above, and streamers and skeins of them began to descend among the pines through which my path threaded its way. In ten minutes more their opacity had so increased that I could hardly see a couple of yards in front of me. Very soon I became aware that I must have got off the path, for snow-cowled shrubs lay directly in my way, and, casting back to find it again, I got altogether confused as to direction. But, though progress was difficult, I knew I had only to keep on the ascent, and presently I should come to the brow of these low foot-hills, and descend into the open valley where Alhubel stood. So on I went, stumbling and sliding over obstacles, and unable, owing to the thickness of the snow, to take off my skis, for I should have sunk over the knees at each step. Still the ascent continued, and looking at my watch I saw that I had already been near an hour on my way from St. Luigi, a period more than sufficient to complete my whole journey. But still I stuck to my idea that though I had certainly strayed far from my proper route a few minutes more must surely see me over the top of the upward way, and I should find the ground declining into the next valley. About now, too, I noticed that the mists were growing suffused with rose-colour, and, though the inference was that it must be close on sunset, there was consolation in the fact that they were there and might lift at any moment and disclose to me my whereabouts. But the fact that night would soon be on me made it needful to bar my mind against that despair of loneliness which so eats out the heart of a man who is lost in woods or on mountain-side, that, though still there is plenty of vigour in his limbs, his nervous force is sapped, and he can do no more than lie down and abandon himself to whatever fate may await him.... And then I heard that which made the thought of loneliness seem bliss indeed, for there was a worse fate than loneliness. What I heard resembled the howl of a wolf, and it came from not far in front of me where the ridge—was it a ridge?—still rose higher in vestment of pines.

From behind me came a sudden puff of wind, which shook the frozen snow from the drooping pine-branches, and swept away the mists as a broom sweeps the dust from the floor. Radiant above me were the unclouded skies, already charged with the red of the sunset, and in front I saw that I had come to the very edge of the wood through which I had wandered so long. But it was no valley into which I had penetrated, for there right ahead of me rose the steep slope of boulders and rocks soaring upwards to the foot of the Ungeheuerhorn. What, then, was that cry of a wolf which had made my heart stand still? I saw.

Not twenty yards from me was a fallen tree, and leaning

against the trunk of it was one of the denizens of the Horror-Horn, and it was a woman. She was enveloped in a thick growth of hair grey and tufted, and from her head it streamed down over her shoulders and her bosom, from which hung withered and pendulous breasts. And looking on her face I comprehended not with my mind alone, but with a shudder of my spirit, what Ingram had felt. Never had nightmare fashioned so terrible a countenance; the beauty of sun and stars and of the beasts of the field and the kindly race of men could not atone for so hellish an incarnation of the spirit of life. A fathomless bestiality modelled the slavering mouth and the narrow eyes; I looked into the abyss itself and knew that out of that abyss on the edge of which I leaned the generations of men had climbed. What if that ledge crumbled in front of me and pitched me headlong into its nethermost depths?...

In one hand she held by the horns a chamois that kicked and struggled. A blow from its hindleg caught her withered thigh, and with a grunt of anger she seized the leg in her other hand, and, as a man may pull from its sheath a stem of meadow-grass, she plucked it off the body, leaving the torn skin hanging round the gaping wound. Then putting the red, bleeding member to her mouth she sucked at it as a child sucks a stick of sweetmeat. Through flesh and gristle her short, brown teeth penetrated, and she licked her lips with a sound of purring. Then dropping the leg by her side, she looked again at the body of the prey now quivering in its death-convulsion, and with finger and thumb gouged out one of its eyes. She snapped her teeth on it, and it cracked like a soft-shelled nut.

It must have been but a few seconds that I stood watching her, in some indescribable catalepsy of terror, while through my brain there pealed the panic-command of my mind to my stricken limbs "Begone, begone, while there is time." Then, recovering the power of my joints and muscles, I tried to slip behind a tree and hide myself from this apparition. But the woman—shall I say?—must have caught my stir of movement, for she raised her eyes from her living feast and saw me. She craned forward her neck, she dropped her prey, and half rising began to move towards me. As she did this, she opened her mouth, and gave forth a howl such as I had heard a moment before. It was answered by another, but faintly and distantly.

Sliding and slipping, with the toes of my skis tripping in the obstacles below the snow, I plunged forward down the hill between the pine-trunks. The low sun already sinking behind some rampart of mountain in the west reddened the snow and the pines with its ultimate rays. My knapsack with the skates in it swung to and fro on my back, one ski-stick had already been twitched out of my hand by a fallen branch of pine, but not a second's pause could I allow myself to recover it. I gave no glance behind, and I knew not at what pace my pursuer was on my track, or indeed whether any pursued at all, for my whole mind and energy, now working at full power again under the stress of my panic, was devoted to getting away down the hill and out of the wood as swiftly as my limbs could bear me. For a little while I heard nothing but the hissing snow of my headlong passage, and the rustle of the covered undergrowth beneath my feet, and then, from close at hand behind me, once more the wolf-howl sounded and I heard the plunging of footsteps other than my own.

The strap of my knapsack had shifted, and as my skates swung to and fro on my back it chafed and pressed on my throat, hindering free passage of air, of which, God knew, my labouring lungs were in dire need, and without pausing I slipped it free from my neck, and held it in the hand from which my ski-stick had been jerked. I seemed to go a little more easily for this adjustment, and now, not so far distant, I could see below me the path from which I had strayed. If only I could reach that, the smoother going would surely enable me to out-distance my pursuer, who even on the rougher ground was but slowly overhauling me, and at the sight of that riband stretching unimpeded downhill, a ray of hope pierced the black panic of my soul. With that came the desire, keen and insistent, to see who or what it was that was on my tracks, and I spared a backward glance. It was she, the hag whom I had seen at her gruesome meal; her long grey hair flew out behind her, her mouth chattered and gibbered, her fingers made grabbing movements, as if already they closed on me.

But the path was now at hand, and the nearness of it I suppose made me incautious. A hump of snow-covered bush lay in my path, and, thinking I could jump over it, I tripped and fell, smothering myself in snow. I heard a maniac noise, half scream, half laugh, from close behind, and before I could recover myself the grabbing fingers were at my neck, as if a steel vice had closed there. But my right hand in which I held my knapsack of skates was free, and with a blind back-handed movement I whirled it behind me at the full length of its strap, and knew that my desperate blow had found its billet somewhere. Even before I could look round I felt the grip on my neck relax, and something subsided into the very bush which had entangled me. I recovered my feet and turned.

There she lay, twitching and quivering. The heel of one of my skates piercing the thin alpaca of the knapsack had hit her full on the temple, from which the blood was pouring, but a hundred yards

41

away I could see another such figure coming downwards on my tracks, leaping and bounding. At that panic rose again within me, and I sped off down the white smooth path that led to the lights of the village already beckoning. Never once did I pause in my headlong going: there was no safety until I was back among the haunts of men. I flung myself against the door of the hotel, and screamed for admittance, though I had but to turn the handle and enter; and once more as when Ingram had told his tale, there was the sound of the band, and the chatter of voices, and there, too, was he himself, who looked up and then rose swiftly to his feet as I made my clattering entrance.

"I have seen them too," I cried. "Look at my knapsack. Is there not blood on it? It is the blood of one of them, a woman, a hag, who tore off the leg of a chamois as I looked, and pursued me through the accursed wood. I——"

Whether it was I who spun round, or the room which seemed to spin round me, I knew not, but I heard myself falling, collapsed on the floor, and the next time that I was conscious at all I was in bed. There was Ingram there, who told me that I was quite safe, and another man, a stranger, who pricked my arm with the nozzle of a syringe, and reassured me....

A day or two later I gave a coherent account of my adventure, and three or four men, armed with guns, went over my traces. They found the bush in which I had stumbled, with a pool of blood which had soaked into the snow, and, still following my ski-tracks, they came on the body of a chamois, from which had been torn one of its hindlegs and one eye-socket was empty. That is all the corroboration of my story that I can give the reader, and for myself I imagine that the creature which pursued me was either not killed by my blow or that her fellows removed her body.... Anyhow, it is open to the incredulous to prowl about the caves of the Ungeheuerhorn, and see if anything occurs that may convince them.

# Machaon

I was returning at the close of the short winter day from my visit to St. James's Hospital, where my old servant Parkes, who had been in my service for twenty years, was lying. I had sent him there three days before, not for treatment, but for observation, and this afternoon I had gone up to London, to hear the doctor's report on the case. He told me that Parkes was suffering from an internal tumour, the nature of which could not be diagnosed for certain, but all the symptoms pointed directly to its being cancerous. That, however, must not be regarded as proved; it could only be proved by an exploratory operation to reveal the nature and the extent of the growth, which must then, if possible, be excised. It might involve, so my old friend Godfrey Symes told me, certain tissues and would be found to be inoperable, but he hoped this would not be the case, and that it would be possible to remove it: removal gave the only chance of recovery. It was fortunate that the patient had been sent for examination in an early stage, for thus the chances of success were much greater than if the growth had been one of long standing. Parkes was not, however, in a fit state to stand the operation at once; a recuperative week or ten days in bed was advisable. In these circumstances Symes recommended that he should not be told at once what lay in front of him.

"I can see that he is a nervous fellow," he said, "and to lie in bed thinking of what he has got to face will probably undo all the good that lying in bed will bring to him. You don't get used to the idea of being cut open; the more you think about it, the more intolerable it becomes. If that sort of adventure faced me, I should infinitely prefer not to be told about it until they came to give me the anæsthetic. Naturally, he will have to consent to the operation, but I shouldn't tell him anything about it till the day before. He's not married, I think, is he?"

"No: he's alone in the world," said I. "He's been with me twenty years."

"Yes, I remember Parkes almost as long as I remember you. But that's all I can recommend. Of course, if the pain became severe, it might be better to operate sooner, but at present he suffers hardly at all, and he sleeps well, so the nurse tells me."

"And there's nothing else that you can try for it?" I asked.

"I'll try anything you like, but it will be perfectly useless. I'll let him have any quack nostrum you and he wish, as long as it doesn't injure his health, or make you put off the operation. There are X-rays and ultra-violet rays, and violet leaves and radium; there are fresh cures for cancer discovered every day, and what's the result? They only make people put off the operation till it's no longer possible to operate. Naturally, I will welcome any further opinion you want."

Now Godfrey Symes is easily the first authority on this subject, and has a far higher percentage of cures to his credit than anyone else.

"No, I don't want any fresh opinion," said I.

"Very well, I'll have him carefully watched. By the way, can't you stop in town and dine with me? There are one or two people coming, and among them a perfectly mad spiritualist who has more messages from the other world than I ever get on my telephone. Trunk-calls, eh? I wonder where the exchange is. Do come! You like cranks, I know!"

"I can't, I'm afraid," said I. "I've a couple of guests coming to stay with me to-day down in the country. They are both cranks: one's a medium."

He laughed.

"Well, I can only offer you one crank, and you've got two," he said. "I must get back to the wards. I'll write to you in about a week's time or so, unless there's any urgency which I don't foresee, and I should suggest your coming up to tell Parkes. Good-bye."

I caught my train at Charing Cross with about three seconds to spare, and we slid clanking out over the bridge through the cold, dense air. Snow had been falling intermittently since morning, and when we got out of the grime and fog of London, it was lying thickly on field and hedgerow, retarding by its reflection of such light as lingered the oncoming of darkness, and giving to the landscape an aloof and lonely austerity. All day I had felt that drowsiness which accompanies snowfall, and sometimes, half losing myself in a doze, my mind crept, like a thing crawling about in the dark, over what Godfrey Symes had told me. For all these years Parkes, as much friend as servant, had given me his faithfulness and devotion, and now, in return for that, all that apparently I could do was to tell him of his plight. It was clear, from what the surgeon had said, that he expected a serious disclosure, and I knew from the experience of two friends of mine who had been in his condition what might be expected of this "exploratory operation." Exactly similar had been these cases; there was clear evidence of an internal growth possibly not malignant, and in each case the same dismal sequence had followed. The growth had been removed, and within a couple of months there had been a recrudescence of it. Indeed, surgery had proved no more than a pruning-knife, which had stimulated that which the surgeon had hoped to extirpate into swifter activity. And that apparently was the best chance that Symes held out: the rest of the treatments were but rubbish or quackery....

My mind crawled away towards another subject: probably the two visitors whom I expected, Charles Hope and the medium whom he was bringing with him, were in the same train as I, and I ran over in my mind all that he had told me of Mrs. Forrest. It was certainly an odd story he had brought me two days before. Mrs. Forrest was a medium of considerable reputation in psychical circles, and had produced some very extraordinary book-tests which, by all accounts, seemed inexplicable, except on a spiritualistic hypothesis, and no imputation of trickery had, at any rate as yet, come near her. When in trance, she spoke and wrote, as is invariably the case with mediums, under the direction of a certain "control"—that is to say, a spiritual and discarnate intelligence which for the time was in possession of her. But lately there had been signs that a fresh control had inspired her, the nature of whom, his name, and his identity was at present unknown. And then came the following queer incident.

Last week only when in trance, and apparently under the direction of this new control, she began describing in considerable detail a certain house where the control said that he had work to do. At first the description aroused no association in Charles Hope's mind, but as it went on, it suddenly struck him that Mrs. Forrest was speaking of my house in Tilling. She gave its general features, its position in a small town on a hill, its walled-in garden, and then went on to speak with great minuteness of a rather peculiar feature in the house. She described a big room built out in the garden a few yards away from the house itself at right-angles to its front, and approached by half a dozen stone steps. There was a railing, so she said, on each side of them, and into the railing were twisted, like snake coils, the stems of a tree which bore pale mauve flowers. This was all a correct description of my garden room and the wistaria which writhes in and out of the railings which line the steps. She then went on to speak of the interior of the room. At one end was a fireplace, at the other a big bow-window looking out on to the street and the front of the house, and there were two other windows opposite each other, in one of which was a table, while the other, looking out on to the garden, was shadowed by the tree that twisted itself about the railings. Book-cases lined the walls, and there was a big sofa at right-angles to the fire....

Now all this, though it was a perfectly accurate description of a place that, as far as could be ascertained, Mrs. Forrest had never seen, might conceivably have been derived from Charles Hope's mind, since he knew the room well, having often stayed with me. But the medium added a detail which could not conceivably have been thus derived, for Charles believed it to be incorrect. She said that there was a big piano near the bow-window, while he was sure that there was not. But oddly enough I had hired a piano only a week or so ago, and it stood in the place that she mentioned. The "control" then repeated that there was work for him to do in that house. There was some situation or complication there in which he could help, and he could "get through" better (that is, make a clearer communication) if the medium could hold a séance there. Charles Hope then told the control that he believed he knew the house that he had been speaking of, and promised to do his best. Shortly afterwards Mrs. Forrest came out of trance, and, as usual, had no recollection of what had passed.

So Charles came to me with the story exactly as I have given it here, and though I could not think of any situation or complication in which an unknown control of a medium I had never seen could be of assistance, the whole thing (and in especial that detail about the piano) was so odd that I asked him to bring the medium down for a sitting or a series of sittings. The day of their arrival was arranged, but when three days ago Parkes had to go into hospital, I was inclined to put them off. But a neighbour away for a week obligingly lent me a parlour-maid, and I let the engagement stand. With regard to the situation in which the control would be of assistance, I can but assure the reader that as far as I thought about it at all, I only wondered whether it was concerned with a book on which I was engaged, which dealt (if I could ever succeed in writing it) with psychical affairs. But at present I could not get on with it at all. I had made half a dozen beginnings which had all gone into the waste-paper basket.

My guests proved not to have come by the same train as I, but arrived shortly before dinner-time, and after Mrs. Forrest had gone to her room, I had a few words with Charles, who told me exactly how the situation now stood.

"I know your caution and your captiousness in these affairs," he said, "so I have told Mrs. Forrest nothing about the description she gave of this house, or of the reason why I asked her to come here. I said only, as we settled, that you were a great friend of mine and immensely interested in psychical affairs, but a country-mouse whom it was difficult to get up to town. But you would be delighted if she would come down for a few days and give some sittings here."

"And does she recognise the house, do you think?" I asked.

"No sign of it. As I told you, when she comes out of trance she never seems to have the faintest recollection of what she has said or written. We shall have a séance, I hope, to-night after dinner."

"Certainly, if she will," said I. "I thought we had better hold it in the garden-room, for that was the place that was so minutely described. It's quite warm there, central-heating and a fire, and it's only half a dozen yards from the house. I've had the snow swept from the steps."

Mrs. Forrest turned out to be a very intelligent woman, well spiced with humour, gifted with a sane appreciation of the comforts of life, and most agreeably furnished with the small change of talk. She was inclined to be stout, but carried herself with briskness, and neither in body nor mind did she suggest that she was one who held communication with the unseen: there was nothing wan or occult about her. Her general outlook on life appeared to be rather materialistic than otherwise, and she was very interesting on the topic when, about half-way through dinner, the subject of her mediumship came on the conversational board.

"My gifts, such as they are," she said, "have nothing to do with this person who sits eating and drinking and talking to you. She, as Mr. Hope may have told you, is quite expunged before the subconscious part of me—that is the latest notion, is it not?—gets into touch with discarnate intelligences. Until that happens, the door is shut, and when it is over, the door is shut again, and I have no recollection of what I have said or written. The control uses my hand and my voice, but that is all. I know no more about it than a piano on which a tune has been played."

"And there is a new control who has lately been using you?" I asked.

She laughed.

"You must ask Mr. Hope about that," she said. "I know nothing whatever of it. He tells me it is so, and he tells me—don't you, Mr. Hope?—that he hasn't any idea who or what the new control is. I look forward to its development; my idea is that the control has to get used to me, as in learning a new instrument. I assure you I am as eager as anyone that he should gain facility in communication through me. I hope, indeed, that we are to have a séance to-night."

The talk veered again, and I learned that Mrs. Forrest had never been in Tilling before, and was enchanted with the snowy

47

moonlit glance she had had of its narrow streets and ancient residences. She liked, too, the atmosphere of the house: it seemed tranquil and kindly; especially so was the little drawing-room where we had assembled before dinner.

I glanced at Charles.

"I had thought of proposing that we should sit in the garden-room," I said, "if you don't mind half a dozen steps in the open. It adjoins the house."

"Just as you wish," she said, "though I think we have excellent conditions in here without going there."

This confirmed her statement that she had no idea after she had come out of trance what she had said, for otherwise she must have recognised at the mention of the garden-room her own description of it, and when soon after dinner we adjourned there, it was clear that, unless she was acting an inexplicable part, the sight of it twanged no chord of memory. There we made the very simple arrangements to which she was accustomed.

As the procedure in such sittings is possibly unfamiliar to the reader, I will describe quite shortly what our arrangements were. We had no idea what form these manifestations—if there were any—might take, and therefore we, Charles and I, were prepared to record them on the spot. We three sat round a small table about a couple of yards from the fire, which was burning brightly; Mrs. Forrest seated herself in a big armchair. Exactly in front of her on the table were a pencil and a block of paper in case, as often happened, the manifestation took the form of automatic script—writing, that is, while in a state of trance. Charles and I sat on each side of her, also provided with pencil and paper in order to take down what she said if and when (as lawyers say) the control took possession of her. In case materialised spirits appeared, a phenomenon not as yet seen at her séances, our idea was to jot down as quickly as possible whatever we saw or thought we saw. Should there be rappings or movements of furniture, we were to make similar notes of our impressions. The lamp was then turned down, so that just a ring of flame encircled the wick, but the firelight was of sufficient brightness, as we tested before the séance began, to enable us to write and to see what we had written. The red glow of it illuminated the room, and it was settled that Charles should note by his watch the time at which anything occurred. Occasionally, throughout the séance a bubble of coal-gas caught fire, and then the whole room started into strong light. I had given orders that my servants should not interrupt the sitting at all, unless somebody rang the bell from the garden-room. In that case it was to be answered. Finally, before the séance began, we bolted all the windows on the inside and locked the door. We took no other precautions against trickery, though, as a matter of fact, Mrs. Forrest suggested that she should be tied into her chair. But in the firelight any movement of hers would be so visible that we did not adopt this precaution. Charles and I had settled to read to each other the notes we made during the sitting, and cut out anything that both of us had not recorded. The accounts, therefore, of this sitting and of that which followed next day are founded on our joint evidence. The sitting began.

Mrs. Forrest was leaning back at ease with her eyes open and her hands on the arms of her chair. Then her eyes closed and a violent trembling seized her. That passed, and shortly afterwards her head fell forward and her breathing became very rapid. Presently that quieted to normal pace again, and she began to speak at first in a scarcely audible whisper and then in a high shrill voice, quite unlike her usual tones.

I do not think that in all England there was a more disappointed man than I during the next half-hour. "Starlight," it appeared, was in control, and Starlight was a personage of platitudes. She had been a nun in the time of Henry VII, and her work was to help those who had lately passed over. She was very busy and very happy, and was in the third sphere where they had a great deal of beautiful music. We must all be good, said Starlight, and it didn't matter much whether we were clever or not. Love was the great thing; we had to love each other and help each other, and death was no more than the gate of life, and everything would be tremendously jolly.... Starlight, in fact, might be better described as clap-trap, and I began thinking about Parkes....

And then I ceased to think about Parkes, for the shrill moralities of Starlight ceased, and Mrs. Forrest's voice changed again. The stale facility of her utterance stopped and she began to speak, quite unintelligibly, in a voice of low baritone range. Charles leaned across the table and whispered to me.

"That's the new control," he said.

The voice that was speaking stumbled and hesitated: it was like that of a man trying to express himself in some language which he knew very imperfectly. Sometimes it stopped altogether, and in one of these pauses I asked:

"Can you tell us your name?"

There was no reply, but presently I saw Mrs. Forrest's hand reach out for the pencil. Charles put it into her fingers and placed the writing-pad more handily for her. I watched the letters, in capitals, being traced. They were made hesitatingly, but were perfectly legible. "Swallow," she wrote, and again "Swallow," and stopped.

"The bird?" I asked.

The voice spoke in answer; now I could hear the words, uttered in that low baritone voice.

"No, not a bird," it said. "Not a bird, but it flies."

I was utterly at sea; my mind could form no conjecture whatever as to what was meant. And then the pencil began writing again. "Swallow, swallow," and then with a sudden briskness of movement, as if the guiding intelligence had got over some difficulty, it wrote "Swallow-tail."

This seemed more abstrusely senseless than ever. The only connection with swallow-tail in my mind was a swallow-tailed coat, but whoever heard of a swallow-tailed coat flying?

"I've got it," said Charles. "Swallow-tail butterfly. Is it that?"

There came three sudden raps on the table, loud and startling. These raps, I may explain, in the usual code mean "Yes." As if to confirm it the pencil began to write again, and spelled out "Swallow-tail butterfly."

"Is that your name?" I asked.

There was one rap, which signifies "No," followed by three, which means "Yes." I had not the slightest idea of what it all signified (indeed it seemed to signify nothing at all), but the sitting had become extraordinarily interesting if only for its very unexpectedness. The control was trying to establish himself by three methods simultaneously—by the voice, by the automatic writing, and by rapping. But how a swallow-tail butterfly could assist in some situation which was now existing in my house was utterly beyond me.... Then an idea struck me: the swallow-tail butterfly no doubt had a scientific name, and that we could easily ascertain, for I knew that there was on my shelves a copy of Newman's Butterflies and Moths of Great Britain, a sumptuous volume bound in morocco, which I had won as an entomological prize at school. A moment's search gave me the book, and by the firelight I turned up the description of this butterfly in the index. Its scientific name was Papilio Machaon.

"Is Machaon your name?" I asked.

The voice came clear now.

"Yes, I am Machaon," it said.

With that came the end of the séance, which had lasted not more than an hour. Whatever the power was that had made Mrs. Forrest speak in that male voice and struggle, through that roundabout method of "swallow, swallow-tail, Machaon," to establish its identity, it now began to fail. Mrs. Forrest's pencil made a few illegible scribbles, she whispered a few inaudible words, and presently with a stretch and a sigh she came out of trance. We told her that the name of the control was established, but apparently Machaon meant nothing to her. She was much exhausted, and very soon I took her across to the house to go to bed, and presently rejoined Charles.

"Who was Machaon, anyhow?" he asked. "He sounds classical: more in your line than mine."

I remembered enough Greek mythology to supply elementary facts, while I hunted for a particular book about Athens.

"Machaon was the son of Asclepios," I said, "and Asclepios was the Greek god of healing. He had precincts, hydropathic establishments, where people went to be cured. The Romans called him Aesculapius."

"What can he do for you then?" asked Charles. "You're fairly fit, aren't you?"

Not till he spoke did a light dawn on me. Though I had been thinking so much of Parkes that day, I had not consciously made the connection.

"But Parkes isn't," said I. "Is that possible?"

"By Jove!" said he.

I found my book, and turned to the accounts of the precinct of Asclepios in Athens.

"Yes, Asclepios had two sons," I said—"Machaon and Podaleirios. In Homeric times he wasn't a god, but only a physician, and his sons were physicians too. The myth of his godhead is rather a late one——"

I shut the book.

"Best not to read any more," I said. "If we know all about Asclepios, we shall possibly be suggesting things to the medium's mind. Let's see what Machaon can tell us about himself, and we can verify it afterwards."

It was therefore with no further knowledge than this on the subject of Machaon that we proposed to hold another séance the next day. All morning the bitter air had been laden with snow, and now the street in front of my house, a by-way at the best in the slender traffic of the town, lay white and untrodden, save on the pavement where a few passengers had gone by. Mrs. Forrest had not appeared at breakfast, and from then till lunch-time I sat in the bow-window of the garden-room, for the warmth of the central heating, of which a stack of pipes was there installed, and for

51

securing the utmost benefit of light that penetrated this cowl of snow-laden sky, busy with belated letters. The drowsiness that accompanies snowfall weighed heavily on my faculties, but as far as I can assert anything, I can assert that I did not sleep. From one letter I went on to another, and then for the sixth or seventh time I tried to open my story. It promised better now than before, and searching for a word that would not come to my pen, I happened to look up along the street which lay in front of me. I expected nothing: I was thinking of nothing but my work; probably I had looked up like that a dozen times before, and had seen the empty street, with snow lying thickly on the roadway.

But now the roadway was not untenanted. Someone was walking down the middle of it, and his aspect, incredible though it seemed, was not startling. Why I was not startled I have no idea: I can only say that the vision appeared perfectly natural. The figure was that of a young man, whose hair, black and curly, lay crisply over his forehead. A large white cloak reaching down to his knees enveloped him, and he had thrown the end of it over his shoulder. Below his knees his legs and feet were bare, so too was the arm up to the elbow, with which he pressed his cloak to him, and there he was walking briskly down the snowy street. As he came directly below the window where I sat, he raised his head and looked at me directly, and smiled. And now I saw his face: there was the low brow, the straight nose, the curved and sunny mouth, the short chin, and I thought to myself that this was none other than the Hermes of Praxiteles, he whose statue at Olympia makes all those who look on it grow young again. There, anyhow, was a boyish Greek god, stepping blithely and with gay, incomparable grace along the street, and raising his face to smile at this stolid, middle-aged man who blankly regarded him. Then with the certainty of one returning home, he mounted the steps outside the front door, and seemed to pass into and through it. Certainly he was no longer in the street, and, so real and solid-seeming had he been to my vision, that I jumped up, ran across the few steps of garden, and went into the house, and I should not have been amazed if I had found him standing in the hall. But there was no one there, and I opened the front door: the snow lay smooth and untrodden down the centre of the road where he had walked and on my doorstep. And at that moment the memory of the séance the evening before, about which up till now I had somehow felt distrustful and suspicious, passed into the realm of sober fact, for had not Machaon just now entered my house, with a smile as of recognition on some friendly mission?

We sat again that afternoon by daylight, and now, I must

52

suppose, the control was more actively and powerfully present, for hardly had Mrs. Forrest passed into trance than the voice began, louder than it had been the night before, and far more distinct. He—Machaon I must call him—seemed to be anxious to establish his identity beyond all doubt, like some newcomer presenting his credentials, and he began to speak of the precinct of Asclepios in Athens. Often he hesitated for a word in English, often he put in a word in Greek, and as he spoke, fragments of things I had learned when an archæological student in Athens came back into my mind, and I knew that he was accurately describing the portico and the temple and the well. All this I toss to the sceptic to growl and worry over and tear to bits; for certainly it seems possible that my mind, holding these facts in its subconsciousness, was suggesting them to the medium's mind, who thereupon spoke of them and, conveying them back to me, made me aware that I had known them.... My forgotten knowledge of these things and of the Greek language came flooding back on me, as he told us, now half in Greek, and half in English, of the patients who came to consult the god, how they washed in the sacred well for purification, and lay down to sleep in the portico. They often dreamed, and in the interpretation of their dreams, which they told to the priest next day, lay the indication of the cure. Or sometimes the god healed more directly, and accompanied by the sacred snake walked among the sleepers and by his touch made them whole. His temple was hung with ex-votos, the gifts of those whom he had cured. And at Epidaurus, where was another shrine of his, there were great mural tablets recording the same....

Then the voice stopped, and as if to prove identity by another means, the medium drew the pencil and paper to her, and in Greek characters, unknown apparently to her, she traced the words "Machaon, son of Asclepios...."

There was a pause, and I asked a direct question, which now had been long simmering in my mind.

"Have you come to help me about Parkes?" I asked. "Can you tell me what will cure him?"

The pencil began to move again, tracing out characters in Greek. It wrote φέγγος ξ, and repeated it. I did not at once guess what it meant, and asked for an explanation. There was no answer, and presently the medium stirred, stretched herself and sighed, and came out of trance. She took up the paper on which she had written.

"Did that come through?" she asked. "And what does it mean? I don't even know the characters...."

Then suddenly the possible significance of φέγγος ξ flashed on me, and I marvelled at my slowness. φέγγος, a beam of light, a ray, and the letter ξ, the equivalent of the English x. That had come in direct answer to my question as to what would cure Parkes, and it was without hesitation or delay that I wrote to Symes. I reminded him that he had said that he had no objection to any possible remedy, provided it was not harmful, being tried on his patient, and I asked him to treat him with X-rays. The whole sequence of events had been so frankly amazing, that I believe the veriest sceptic would not have done otherwise than I did.

Our sittings continued, but after this day we had no further evidence of this second control. It looked as if the intelligence (even the most incredulous will allow me, for the sake of convenience, to call that intelligence Machaon) that had described this room, and told Mrs. Forrest that he had work to do here, had finished his task. Machaon had said, or so my interpretation was, that X-rays would cure Parkes. In justification of this view it is proper to quote from a letter which I got from Symes a week later.

"There is no need for you to come up to break to Parkes that an operation lies in front of him. In answer to your request, and without a grain of faith in its success, I treated him with X-rays, which I assured you were useless. To-day, to speak quite frankly, I don't know what to think, for the growth has been steadily diminishing in size and hardness, and it is perfectly evident that it is being absorbed and is disappearing.

"The treatment through which I put Parkes is that of ——. Here in this hospital we have had patients to whom it brought no shadow of benefit. Often it had been continued on these deluded wretches till any operation which might possibly have been successful was out of the question owing to the encroachment of the growth. But from the first dose of the X-rays, Parkes began to get better, the growth was first arrested, and then diminished.

"I am trying to put the whole thing before you with as much impartiality as I can command. So, on the other side, you must remember that Parkes's was never a proved case of cancer. I told you that it could not be proved till the exploratory operation took place. All the symptoms pointed to cancer—you see, I am trying to save my own face—but my diagnosis, though confirmed by ——, may have been wrong. If he only had what we call a benign tumour, the case is not so extraordinary; there have been plenty of cases when a benign tumour has disappeared by absorption or what not. It is unusual, but by no means unknown. For instance....

"But Parkes's case was quite different. I certainly believe he had a cancerous growth, and thought that an operation was inevitable if his life was to be saved. Even then, the most I hoped for was an alleviation of pain, as the disease progressed, and a year or two more, at the most, of life. Instead, I apply another remedy, at your suggestion, and if he goes on as he has been doing, the growth will be a nodule in another week or two, and I should expect it to disappear altogether. Taking everything into consideration, if you asked me the question whether this X-ray treatment was the cause of the cure, I should be obliged to say 'Yes.' I don't believe in such a treatment, but I believe it is curing him. I suppose that it was suggested to you by a fraudulent, spiritualistic medium in a feigned trance, who was inspired by Aesculapius or some exploded heathen deity, for I remember you said you were going down into the country for some spiritual business....

"Well, Parkes is getting better, and I am so old-fashioned a fellow that I would sooner a patient of mine got better by incredible methods, than died under my skilful knife.... Of course, we trained people know nothing, but we have to act according to the best chances of our ignorance. I entirely believed that the knife was the only means of saving the man, and now, when I stand confuted, the only thing that I can save is my honesty, which I hereby have done. Let me know, at your leisure, whether you just thought you would, on your own idea, like me to try X-rays, or whether some faked voice from the grave suggested it.

"Ever yours,
"Godfrey Symes.

"P.S.—If it was some beastly voice from the grave, you might tell me in confidence who the medium was. I want to be fair...."

That is the story; the reader will explain it according to his temperament. And as I have told Parkes, who is now back with me again, to look into the garden-room before post-time and take a registered packet to the office, it is time that I got it ready for him.

So here is the completed packet in manuscript, to be sent to the printer's. From my window I shall see him go briskly along the street down which Machaon walked on a snowy morning.

# Negotium Perambulans....

The casual tourist in West Cornwall may just possibly have noticed, as he bowled along over the bare high plateau between Penzance and the Land's End, a dilapidated signpost pointing down a steep lane and bearing on its battered finger the faded inscription "Polearn 2 miles," but probably very few have had the curiosity to traverse those two miles in order to see a place to which their guide-books award so cursory a notice. It is described there, in a couple of unattractive lines, as a small fishing village with a church of no particular interest except for certain carved and painted wooden panels (originally belonging to an earlier edifice) which form an altar-rail. But the church at St. Creed (the tourist is reminded) has a similar decoration far superior in point of preservation and interest, and thus even the ecclesiastically disposed are not lured to Polearn. So meagre a bait is scarce worth swallowing, and a glance at the very steep lane which in dry weather presents a carpet of sharp-pointed stones, and after rain a muddy watercourse, will almost certainly decide him not to expose his motor or his bicycle to risks like these in so sparsely populated a district. Hardly a house has met his eye since he left Penzance, and the possible trundling of a punctured bicycle for half a dozen weary miles seems a high price to pay for the sight of a few painted panels.

Polearn, therefore, even in the high noon of the tourist season, is little liable to invasion, and for the rest of the year I do not suppose that a couple of folk a day traverse those two miles (long ones at that) of steep and stony gradient. I am not forgetting the postman in this exiguous estimate, for the days are few when, leaving his pony and cart at the top of the hill, he goes as far as the village, since but a few hundred yards down the lane there stands a large white box, like a sea-trunk, by the side of the road, with a slit for letters and a locked door. Should he have in his wallet a registered letter or be the bearer of a parcel too large for insertion in the square lips of the sea-trunk, he must needs trudge down the hill and deliver the troublesome missive, leaving it in person on the owner, and receiving some small reward of coin or refreshment for his kindness. But such occasions are rare, and his general routine is to take out of the box such letters as may have been deposited there, and insert in their place such letters as he has brought. These will be called for, perhaps that day or perhaps the next, by an emissary from the Polearn post-office. As for the fishermen of the place, who, in their export trade, constitute the chief link of movement between Polearn and the outside world, they would not dream of taking their catch up the steep lane and so, with six miles farther of travel, to the market at Penzance. The sea route is shorter and easier, and they deliver their wares to the pier-head. Thus, though the sole industry of Polearn is sea-fishing, you will get no fish there unless you have bespoken your requirements to one of the fishermen. Back come the trawlers as empty as a haunted house, while their spoils are in the fish-train that is speeding to London.

Such isolation of a little community, continued, as it has been, for centuries, produces isolation in the individual as well, and nowhere will you find greater independence of character than among the people of Polearn. But they are linked together, so it has always seemed to me, by some mysterious comprehension: it is as if they had all been initiated into some ancient rite, inspired and framed by forces visible and invisible. The winter storms that batter the coast, the vernal spell of the spring, the hot, still summers, the season of rains and autumnal decay, have made a spell which, line by line, has been communicated to them, concerning the powers, evil and good, that rule the world, and manifest themselves in ways benignant or terrible....

I came to Polearn first at the age of ten, a small boy, weak and sickly, and threatened with pulmonary trouble. My father's business kept him in London, while for me abundance of fresh air and a mild climate were considered essential conditions if I was to grow to manhood. His sister had married the vicar of Polearn, Richard Bolitho, himself native to the place, and so it came about that I spent three years, as a paying guest, with my relations. Richard Bolitho owned a fine house in the place, which he inhabited in preference to the vicarage, which he let to a young artist, John Evans, on whom the spell of Polearn had fallen, for from year's beginning to year's end he never left it. There was a solid roofed shelter, open on one side to the air, built for me in the garden, and here I lived and slept, passing scarcely one hour out of the twenty-four behind walls and windows. I was out on the bay with the fisher-folk, or wandering along the gorse-clad cliffs that climbed steeply to right and left of the deep combe where the village lay, or pottering about on the pier-head, or bird's-nesting in the bushes with the boys of the village. Except on Sunday and for the few daily hours of my lessons, I might do what I pleased so long as I remained in the open air. About the lessons there was nothing formidable; my uncle conducted me through flowering bypaths among the thickets of arithmetic, and made pleasant excursions into the elements of Latin grammar, and above all, he made me daily give him an account, in clear and grammatical sentences, of what had been occupying my mind or my movements. Should I select to tell him about a walk along the cliffs, my speech must be orderly, not vague, slip-shod notes of what I had observed. In this way, too, he trained my observation, for he would bid me tell him what flowers were in bloom, and what birds hovered fishing over the sea or were building in the bushes. For that I owe him a perennial gratitude, for to observe and to express my thoughts in the clear spoken word became my life's profession.

But far more formidable than my weekday tasks was the prescribed routine for Sunday. Some dark embers compounded of Calvinism and mysticism smouldered in my uncle's soul, and made it a day of terror. His sermon in the morning scorched us with a foretaste of the eternal fires reserved for unrepentant sinners, and he was hardly less terrifying at the children's service in the afternoon. Well do I remember his exposition of the doctrine of guardian angels. A child, he said, might think himself secure in such angelic care, but let him beware of committing any of those numerous offences which would cause his guardian to turn his face from him, for as sure as there were angels to protect us, there were also evil and awful presences which were ready to pounce; and on them he dwelt with peculiar gusto. Well, too, do I remember in the morning sermon his commentary on the carved panels of the altar-rails to which I have already alluded. There was the angel of the Annunciation there, and the angel of the Resurrection, but not less was there the witch of Endor, and, on the fourth panel, a scene that concerned me most of all. This fourth panel (he came down from his pulpit to trace its time-worn features) represented the lych-gate of the church-yard at Polearn itself, and indeed the resemblance when thus pointed out was remarkable. In the entry stood the figure of a robed priest holding up a Cross, with which he faced a terrible creature like a gigantic slug, that reared itself up in front of him. That, so ran my uncle's interpretation, was some evil agency, such as he had spoken about to us children, of almost infinite malignity and power, which could alone be combated by firm faith and a pure heart. Below ran the legend "Negotium perambulans in tenebris" from the ninety-first Psalm. We should find it translated there, "the pestilence that walketh in darkness," which but feebly rendered the Latin. It was more deadly to the soul than any pestilence that can only kill the body: it was the Thing, the Creature, the Business that trafficked in the outer Darkness, a minister of God's wrath on the unrighteous....

I could see, as he spoke, the looks which the congregation exchanged with each other, and knew that his words were evoking a surmise, a remembrance. Nods and whispers passed between them, they understood to what he alluded, and with the inquisitiveness of boyhood I could not rest till I had wormed the story out of my friends among the fisher-boys, as, next morning, we sat basking and naked in the sun after our bathe. One knew one bit of it, one another, but it pieced together into a truly alarming legend. In bald outline it was as follows:

A church far more ancient than that in which my uncle terrified us every Sunday had once stood not three hundred yards away, on the shelf of level ground below the quarry from which its stones were hewn. The owner of the land had pulled this down, and erected for himself a house on the same site out of these materials, keeping, in a very ecstasy of wickedness, the altar, and on this he dined and played dice afterwards. But as he grew old some black melancholy seized him, and he would have lights burning there all night, for he had deadly fear of the darkness. On one winter evening there sprang up such a gale as was never before known, which broke in the windows of the room where he had supped, and extinguished the lamps. Yells of terror brought in his servants, who found him lying on the floor with the blood streaming from his throat. As they entered some huge black shadow seemed to move away from him, crawled across the floor and up the wall and out of the broken window.

"There he lay a-dying," said the last of my informants, "and him that had been a great burly man was withered to a bag o' skin, for the critter had drained all the blood from him. His last breath was a scream, and he hollered out the same words as parson read off the screen."

"Negotium perambulans in tenebris," I suggested eagerly.

"Thereabouts. Latin anyhow."

"And after that?" I asked.

"Nobody would go near the place, and the old house rotted and fell in ruins till three years ago, when along comes Mr. Dooliss from Penzance, and built the half of it up again. But he don't care much about such critters, nor about Latin neither. He takes his bottle of whisky a day and gets drunk's a lord in the evening. Eh, I'm gwine home to my dinner."

Whatever the authenticity of the legend, I had certainly heard the truth about Mr. Dooliss from Penzance, who from that day became an object of keen curiosity on my part, the more so because the quarry-house adjoined my uncle's garden. The Thing that walked in the dark failed to stir my imagination, and already I was so used to sleeping alone in my shelter that the night had no terrors for me. But it would be intensely exciting to wake at some timeless hour and hear Mr. Dooliss yelling, and conjecture that the Thing had got him.

But by degrees the whole story faded from my mind, overscored by the more vivid interests of the day, and, for the last two years of my out-door life in the vicarage garden, I seldom thought about Mr. Dooliss and the possible fate that might await him for his temerity in living in the place where that Thing of darkness had done business. Occasionally I saw him over the garden fence, a great yellow lump of a man, with slow and staggering gait, but never did I set eyes on him outside his gate, either in the village street or down on the beach. He interfered with none, and no one interfered with him. If he wanted to run the risk of being the prey of the legendary nocturnal monster, or quietly drink himself to death, it was his affair. My uncle, so I gathered, had made several attempts to see him when first he came to live at Polearn, but Mr. Dooliss appeared to have no use for parsons, but said he was not at home and never returned the call.

After three years of sun, wind, and rain, I had completely outgrown my early symptoms and had become a tough, strapping youngster of thirteen. I was sent to Eton and Cambridge, and in due course ate my dinners and became a barrister. In twenty years from that time I was earning a yearly income of five figures, and had already laid by in sound securities a sum that brought me dividends which would, for one of my simple tastes and frugal habits, supply me with all the material comforts I needed on this side of the grave. The great prizes of my profession were already within my reach, but I had no ambition beckoning me on, nor did I want a wife and children, being, I must suppose, a natural celibate. In fact there was only one ambition which through these busy years had held the lure of blue and far-off hills to me, and that was to get back to Polearn, and live once more isolated from the world with the sea and the gorse-clad hills for play-fellows, and the secrets that lurked there for exploration. The spell of it had been woven about my heart, and I can truly say that there had hardly passed a day in all those years in which the thought of it and the desire for it had been wholly absent from my mind. Though I had been in frequent communication with my uncle there during his lifetime, and, after his death, with his widow who still lived there, I had never been back to it since I embarked on my profession, for I knew that if I went there, it would be a wrench beyond my power to tear myself away again. But I had made up my mind that when once I had provided for my own independence, I would go back there not to leave it again. And yet I did leave it again, and now nothing in the world would induce me to turn down the lane from the road that leads from Penzance to the Land's End, and see the sides of the combe rise steep above the roofs of the village and hear the gulls chiding as they fish in the bay. One of the things invisible, of the dark powers, leaped into light, and I saw it with my eyes.

The house where I had spent those three years of boyhood had been left for life to my aunt, and when I made known to her my intention of coming back to Polearn, she suggested that, till I found a suitable house or found her proposal unsuitable, I should come to live with her.

"The house is too big for a lone old woman," she wrote, "and I have often thought of quitting and taking a little cottage sufficient for me and my requirements. But come and share it, my dear, and if you find me troublesome, you or I can go. You may want solitude— most people in Polearn do—and will leave me. Or else I will leave you: one of the main reasons of my stopping here all these years was a feeling that I must not let the old house starve. Houses starve, you know, if they are not lived in. They die a lingering death; the spirit in them grows weaker and weaker, and at last fades out of them. Isn't this nonsense to your London notions?..."

Naturally I accepted with warmth this tentative arrangement, and on an evening in June found myself at the head of the lane leading down to Polearn, and once more I descended into the steep valley between the hills. Time had stood still apparently for the combe, the dilapidated signpost (or its successor) pointed a rickety finger down the lane, and a few hundred yards farther on was the white box for the exchange of letters. Point after remembered point met my eye, and what I saw was not shrunk, as is often the case with the revisited scenes of childhood, into a smaller scale. There stood the post-office, and there the church and close beside it the vicarage, and beyond, the tall shrubberies which separated the house for which I was bound from the road, and beyond that again the grey roofs of the quarry-house damp and shining with the moist evening wind from the sea. All was exactly as I remembered it, and, above all, that sense of seclusion and isolation. Somewhere above the tree-tops climbed the lane which joined the main road to Penzance, but all that had become immeasurably distant. The years that had passed since last I turned in at the well-known gate faded like a frosty breath, and vanished in this warm, soft air. There were law-courts somewhere in memory's dull book which, if I cared to turn the pages, would tell me that I had made a name and a great income there. But the dull book was closed now, for I was back in Polearn, and the spell was woven around me again.

And if Polearn was unchanged, so too was Aunt Hester, who met me at the door. Dainty and china-white she had always been, and the years had not aged but only refined her. As we sat and talked after dinner she spoke of all that had happened in Polearn in that score of years, and yet somehow the changes of which she spoke seemed but to confirm the immutability of it all. As the recollection of names came back to me, I asked her about the quarry-house and Mr. Dooliss, and her face gloomed a little as with the shadow of a cloud on a spring day.

"Yes, Mr. Dooliss," she said, "poor Mr. Dooliss, how well I remember him, though it must be ten years and more since he died. I never wrote to you about it, for it was all very dreadful, my dear, and I did not want to darken your memories of Polearn. Your uncle always thought that something of the sort might happen if he went on in his wicked, drunken ways, and worse than that, and though nobody knew exactly what took place, it was the sort of thing that might have been anticipated."

"But what more or less happened, Aunt Hester?" I asked.

"Well, of course I can't tell you everything, for no one knew it. But he was a very sinful man, and the scandal about him at Newlyn was shocking. And then he lived, too, in the quarry-house.... I wonder if by any chance you remember a sermon of your uncle's when he got out of the pulpit and explained that panel in the altar-rails, the one, I mean, with the horrible creature rearing itself up outside the lych-gate?"

"Yes, I remember perfectly," said I.

"Ah. It made an impression on you, I suppose, and so it did on all who heard him, and that impression got stamped and branded on us all when the catastrophe occurred. Somehow Mr. Dooliss got to hear about your uncle's sermon, and in some drunken fit he broke into the church and smashed the panel to atoms. He seems to have thought that there was some magic in it, and that if he destroyed that he would get rid of the terrible fate that was threatening him. For I must tell you that before he committed that dreadful sacrilege he had been a haunted man: he hated and feared darkness, for he thought that the creature on the panel was on his track, but that as long as he kept lights burning it could not touch him. But the panel, to his disordered mind, was the root of his terror, and so, as I said, he broke into the church and attempted— you will see why I said 'attempted'—to destroy it. It certainly was

63

found in splinters next morning, when your uncle went into church for matins, and knowing Mr. Dooliss's fear of the panel, he went across to the quarry-house afterwards and taxed him with its destruction. The man never denied it; he boasted of what he had done. There he sat, though it was early morning, drinking his whisky.

"'I've settled your Thing for you,' he said, 'and your sermon too. A fig for such superstitions.'

"Your uncle left him without answering his blasphemy, meaning to go straight into Penzance and give information to the police about this outrage to the church, but on his way back from the quarry-house he went into the church again, in order to be able to give details about the damage, and there in the screen was the panel, untouched and uninjured. And yet he had himself seen it smashed, and Mr. Dooliss had confessed that the destruction of it was his work. But there it was, and whether the power of God had mended it or some other power, who knows?"

This was Polearn indeed, and it was the spirit of Polearn that made me accept all Aunt Hester was telling me as attested fact. It had happened like that. She went on in her quiet voice.

"Your uncle recognised that some power beyond police was at work, and he did not go to Penzance or give information about the outrage, for the evidence of it had vanished."

A sudden spate of scepticism swept over me.

"There must have been some mistake," I said. "It hadn't been broken...."

She smiled.

"Yes, my dear, but you have been in London so long," she said. "Let me, anyhow, tell you the rest of my story. That night, for some reason, I could not sleep. It was very hot and airless; I dare say you will think that the sultry conditions accounted for my wakefulness. Once and again, as I went to the window to see if I could not admit more air, I could see from it the quarry-house, and I noticed the first time that I left my bed that it was blazing with lights. But the second time I saw that it was all in darkness, and as I wondered at that, I heard a terrible scream, and the moment afterwards the steps of someone coming at full speed down the road outside the gate. He yelled as he ran; 'Light, light!' he called out. 'Give me light, or it will catch me!' It was very terrible to hear that, and I went to rouse my husband, who was sleeping in the dressing-room across the passage. He wasted no time, but by now the whole village was aroused by the screams, and when he got down to the pier he found that all was over. The tide was low, and on the rocks at its foot was lying the body of Mr. Dooliss. He must have cut some artery when he fell on those sharp edges of stone, for he had bled to death, they thought, and though he was a big burly man, his corpse was but skin and bones. Yet there was no pool of blood round him, such as you would have expected. Just skin and bones as if every drop of blood in his body had been sucked out of him!"

She leaned forward.

"You and I, my dear, know what happened," she said, "or at least can guess. God has His instruments of vengeance on those who bring wickedness into places that have been holy. Dark and mysterious are His ways."

Now what I should have thought of such a story if it had been told me in London I can easily imagine. There was such an obvious explanation: the man in question had been a drunkard, what wonder if the demons of delirium pursued him? But here in Polearn it was different.

"And who is in the quarry-house now?" I asked. "Years ago the fisher-boys told me the story of the man who first built it and of his horrible end. And now again it has happened. Surely no one has ventured to inhabit it once more?"

I saw in her face, even before I asked that question, that somebody had done so.

"Yes, it is lived in again," said she, "for there is no end to the blindness.... I don't know if you remember him. He was tenant of the vicarage many years ago."

"John Evans," said I.

"Yes. Such a nice fellow he was too. Your uncle was pleased to get so good a tenant. And now——"

She rose.

"Aunt Hester, you shouldn't leave your sentences unfinished," I said.

She shook her head.

"My dear, that sentence will finish itself," she said. "But what a time of night! I must go to bed, and you too, or they will think we have to keep lights burning here through the dark hours."

Before getting into bed I drew my curtains wide and opened all the windows to the warm tide of the sea air that flowed softly in. Looking out into the garden I could see in the moonlight the roof of the shelter, in which for three years I had lived, gleaming with dew. That, as much as anything, brought back the old days to which I had now returned, and they seemed of one piece with the present, as if no gap of more than twenty years sundered them. The two flowed into one like globules of mercury uniting into a softly shining globe, of mysterious lights and reflections. Then, raising my eyes a little, I saw against the black hill-side the windows of the quarry-house still alight.

Morning, as is so often the case, brought no shattering of my illusion. As I began to regain consciousness, I fancied that I was a boy again waking up in the shelter in the garden, and though, as I grew more widely awake, I smiled at the impression, that on which it was based I found to be indeed true. It was sufficient now as then to be here, to wander again on the cliffs, and hear the popping of the ripened seed-pods on the gorse-bushes; to stray along the shore to the bathing-cove, to float and drift and swim in the warm tide, and bask on the sand, and watch the gulls fishing, to lounge on the pier-head with the fisher-folk, to see in their eyes and hear in their quiet speech the evidence of secret things not so much known to them as part of their instincts and their very being. There were powers and presences about me; the white poplars that stood by the stream that babbled down the valley knew of them, and showed a glimpse of their knowledge sometimes, like the gleam of their white underleaves; the very cobbles that paved the street were soaked in it.... All that I wanted was to lie there and grow soaked in it too; unconsciously, as a boy, I had done that, but now the process must be conscious. I must know what stir of forces, fruitful and mysterious, seethed along the hill-side at noon, and sparkled at night on the sea. They could be known, they could even be controlled by those who were masters of the spell, but never could they be spoken of, for they were dwellers in the innermost, grafted into the eternal life of the world. There were dark secrets as well as these clear, kindly powers, and to these no doubt belonged the negotium perambulans in tenebris which, though of deadly malignity, might be regarded not only as evil, but as the avenger of sacrilegious and impious deeds.... All this was part of the spell of Polearn, of which the seeds had long lain dormant in me. But now they were sprouting, and who knew what strange flower would unfold on their stems?

It was not long before I came across John Evans. One morning, as I lay on the beach, there came shambling across the sand a man stout and middle-aged with the face of Silenus. He paused as he drew near and regarded me from narrow eyes.

"Why, you're the little chap that used to live in the parson's garden," he said. "Don't you recognise me?"

I saw who it was when he spoke: his voice, I think, instructed me, and recognising it, I could see the features of the strong, alert young man in this gross caricature.

"Yes, you're John Evans," I said. "You used to be very kind to me: you used to draw pictures for me."

"So I did, and I'll draw you some more. Been bathing? That's a risky performance. You never know what lives in the sea, nor what lives on the land for that matter. Not that I heed them. I stick to work and whisky. God! I've learned to paint since I saw you, and drink too for that matter. I live in the quarry-house, you know, and it's a powerful thirsty place. Come and have a look at my things if you're passing. Staying with your aunt, are you? I could do a wonderful portrait of her. Interesting face; she knows a lot. People who live at Polearn get to know a lot, though I don't take much stock in that sort of knowledge myself."

I do not know when I have been at once so repelled and interested. Behind the mere grossness of his face there lurked something which, while it appalled, yet fascinated me. His thick lisping speech had the same quality. And his paintings, what would they be like?...

"I was just going home," I said. "I'll gladly come in, if you'll allow me."

He took me through the untended and overgrown garden into the house which I had never yet entered. A great grey cat was sunning itself in the window, and an old woman was laying lunch in a corner of the cool hall into which the door opened. It was built of stone, and the carved mouldings let into the walls, the fragments of gargoyles and sculptured images, bore testimony to the truth of its having been built out of the demolished church. In one corner was an oblong and carved wooden table littered with a painter's apparatus and stacks of canvases leaned against the walls.

He jerked his thumb towards a head of an angel that was built into the mantelpiece and giggled.

"Quite a sanctified air," he said, "so we tone it down for the purposes of ordinary life by a different sort of art. Have a drink? No? Well, turn over some of my pictures while I put myself to rights."

He was justified in his own estimate of his skill: he could paint (and apparently he could paint anything), but never have I seen pictures so inexplicably hellish. There were exquisite studies of trees, and you knew that something lurked in the flickering shadows. There was a drawing of his cat sunning itself in the window, even as I had just now seen it, and yet it was no cat but some beast of awful malignity. There was a boy stretched naked on the sands, not human, but some evil thing which had come out of the sea. Above all there were pictures of his garden overgrown and

67

jungle-like, and you knew that in the bushes were presences ready to spring out on you....

"Well, do you like my style?" he said as he came up, glass in hand. (The tumbler of spirits that he held had not been diluted.) "I try to paint the essence of what I see, not the mere husk and skin of it, but its nature, where it comes from and what gave it birth. There's much in common between a cat and a fuchsia-bush if you look at them closely enough. Everything came out of the slime of the pit, and it's all going back there. I should like to do a picture of you some day. I'd hold the mirror up to Nature, as that old lunatic said."

After this first meeting I saw him occasionally throughout the months of that wonderful summer. Often he kept to his house and to his painting for days together, and then perhaps some evening I would find him lounging on the pier, always alone, and every time we met thus the repulsion and interest grew, for every time he seemed to have gone farther along a path of secret knowledge towards some evil shrine where complete initiation awaited him.... And then suddenly the end came.

I had met him thus one evening on the cliffs while the October sunset still burned in the sky, but over it with amazing rapidity there spread from the west a great blackness of cloud such as I have never seen for denseness. The light was sucked from the sky, the dusk fell in ever thicker layers. He suddenly became conscious of this.

"I must get back as quick as I can," he said. "It will be dark in a few minutes, and my servant is out. The lamps will not be lit."

He stepped out with extraordinary briskness for one who shambled and could scarcely lift his feet, and soon broke out into a stumbling run. In the gathering darkness I could see that his face was moist with the dew of some unspoken terror.

"You must come with me," he panted, "for so we shall get the lights burning the sooner. I cannot do without light."

I had to exert myself to the full to keep up with him, for terror winged him, and even so I fell behind, so that when I came to the garden gate, he was already half-way up the path to the house. I saw him enter, leaving the door wide, and found him fumbling with matches. But his hand so trembled that he could not transfer the light to the wick of the lamp.

"But what's the hurry about?" I asked.

Suddenly his eyes focused themselves on the open door behind me, and he jumped from his seat beside the table which had once been the altar of God, with a gasp and a scream.

"No, no!" he cried. "Keep it off!..."

I turned and saw what he had seen. The Thing had entered and now was swiftly sliding across the floor towards him, like some gigantic caterpillar. A stale phosphorescent light came from it, for though the dusk had grown to blackness outside, I could see it quite distinctly in the awful light of its own presence. From it too there came an odour of corruption and decay, as from slime that has long lain below water. It seemed to have no head, but on the front of it was an orifice of puckered skin which opened and shut and slavered at the edges. It was hairless, and slug-like in shape and in texture. As it advanced its fore-part reared itself from the ground, like a snake about to strike, and it fastened on him....

At that sight, and with the yells of his agony in my ears, the panic which had struck me relaxed into a hopeless courage, and with palsied, impotent hands I tried to lay hold of the Thing. But I could not: though something material was there, it was impossible to grasp it; my hands sunk in it as in thick mud. It was like wrestling with a nightmare.

I think that but a few seconds elapsed before all was over. The screams of the wretched man sank to moans and mutterings as the Thing fell on him: he panted once or twice and was still. For a moment longer there came gurglings and sucking noises, and then it slid out even as it had entered. I lit the lamp which he had fumbled with, and there on the floor he lay, no more than a rind of skin in loose folds over projecting bones.

# At the Farmhouse

The dusk of a November day was falling fast when John Aylsford came out of his lodging in the cobbled street and started to walk briskly along the road which led eastwards by the shore of the bay. He had been at work while the daylight served him, and now, when the gathering darkness weaned him from his easel, he was accustomed to go out for air and exercise and cover half a dozen miles before he returned to his solitary supper.

To-night there were but few folk abroad, and those scudded along before the strong south-westerly gale which had roared and raged all day, or, leaning forward, beat their way against it. No fishing-boats had put forth on that maddened sea, but had lain moored behind the quay-wall, tossing uneasily with the backwash of the great breakers that swept by the pier-head. The tide was low now, and they rested on the sandy beach, black blots against the smooth wet surface which sombrely reflected the last flames in the west. The sun had gone down in a wrack of broken and flying clouds, angry and menacing with promise of a wild night to come.

For many days past, at this hour John Aylsford had started eastwards for his tramp along the rough coast road by the bay. The last high tide had swept shingle and sand over sections of it, and fragments of seaweed, driven by the wind, bowled along the ruts. The heavy boom of the breakers sounded sullenly in the dusk, and white towers of foam appearing and disappearing showed how high they leaped over the reefs of rock beyond the headland. For half a mile or so, slanting himself against the gale he pursued this road, then turned up a narrow muddy lane sunk deep between the banks on either side of it. It ran steeply uphill, dipped down again, and joined the main road inland. Having arrived at the junction, John Aylsford went eastwards no more, but turned his steps to the west, arriving, half an hour after he had set out, on the top of the hill above the village he had quitted, though five minutes' ascent would have taken him from his lodgings to the spot where he now stood looking down on the scattered lights below him. The wind had blown all wayfarers indoors, and now in front of him the road that crossed this high and desolate table-land, sprinkled here and there with lonely cottages and solitary farms, lay empty and greyly glimmering in the wind-swept darkness, not more than faintly visible.

Many times during this past month had John Aylsford made

this long detour, starting eastwards from the village and coming back by a wide circuit, and now, as on these other occasions, he paused in the black shelter of the hedge through which the wind hissed and whistled, crouching there in the shadow as if to make sure that none had followed him, and that the road in front lay void of passengers, for he had no mind to be observed by any on these journeyings. And as he paused he let his hate blaze up, warming him for the work the accomplishment of which alone could enable him to recapture any peace or profit from life. To-night he was determined to release himself from the millstone which for so many years had hung round his neck, drowning him in bitter waters. From long brooding over the idea of the deed, he had quite ceased to feel any horror of it. The death of that drunken slut was not a matter for qualms or uneasiness; the world would be well rid of her, and he more than well.

No spark of tenderness for the handsome fisher-girl who once had been his model and for twenty years had been his wife pierced the blackness of his purpose. Just here it was that he had seen her first when on a summer holiday he had lodged with a couple of friends in the farmhouse towards which his way now lay. She was coming up the hill with the late sunset gilding her face, and, breathing quickly from the ascent, had leaned on the wall close by with a smile and a glance for the young man. She had sat to him, and the autumn brought the sequel to the summer in his marriage. He had bought from her uncle the little farmhouse where he had lodged, adding to its modest accommodation a studio and a bedroom above it, and there he had seen the flicker of what had never been love, die out, and over the cold ashes of its embers the poisonous lichen of hatred spread fast. Early in their married life she had taken to drink, and had sunk into a degradation of soul and body that seemed bottomless, dragging him with her, down and down, in the grip of a force that was hardly human in its malignity.

Often during the wretched years that followed he had tried to leave her; he had offered to settle the farm on her and make adequate provision for her, but she had clung to the possession of him, not, it would seem, from any affection for him, but for a reason exactly opposite, namely, that her hatred of him fed and glutted itself on the sight of his ruin. It was as if, in obedience to some hellish power, she set herself to spoil his life, his powers, his possibilities, by tying him to herself. And by the aid of that power, so sometimes he had thought, she enforced her will on him, for, plan as he might to cut the whole dreadful business and leave the wreck behind him, he had never been able to consolidate his resolve into action. There, but a few miles away, was the station from which ran the train that would bear him out of this ancient western kingdom, where the beliefs in spells and superstitions grew rank as the herbage in that soft enervating air, and set him in the dry hard light of cities. The way lay open, but he could not take it; something unseen and potent, of grim inflexibility, held him back....

He had passed no one on his way here, and satisfied now that in the darkness he could proceed without fear of being recognised if a chance wayfarer came from the direction in which he was going, he left the shelter of the hedge, and struck out into the stormy sea of that stupendous gale. Even as a man in the grip of imminent death sees his past life spread itself out in front of him for his final survey before the book is closed, so now, on the brink of the new life from which the deed on which he was determined alone separated him, John Aylsford, as he battled his advance through this great tempest, turned over page after page of his own wretched chronicles, feeling already strangely detached from them; it was as if he read the sordid and enslaved annals of another, wondering at them, half-pitying, half-despising him who had allowed himself to be bound so long in this ruinous noose.

Yes; it had been just that, a noose drawn ever tighter round his neck, while he choked and struggled all unavailingly. But there was another noose which should very soon now be drawn rapidly and finally tight, and the drawing of that in his own strong hands would free him. As he dwelt on that for a moment, his fingers stroked and patted the hank of whipcord that lay white and tough in his pocket. A noose, a knot drawn quickly taut, and he would have paid her back with justice and swifter mercy for the long strangling which he had suffered.

Voluntarily and eagerly at the beginning had he allowed her to slip the noose about him, for Ellen Trenair's beauty in those days, so long past and so everlastingly regretted, had been enough to ensnare a man. He had been warned at the time, by hint and half-spoken suggestion, that it was ill for a man to mate with a girl of that dark and ill-famed family, or for a woman to wed a boy in whose veins ran the blood of Jonas Trenair, once Methodist preacher, who learned on one All-Hallows' Eve a darker gospel than he had ever preached before. What had happened to the girls who had married into that dwindling family, now all but extinct? One, before her marriage was a year old, had gone off her head, and now, a withered and ancient crone, mowed and gibbered about the streets of the village, picking garbage from the gutter and munching it in her toothless jaws. Another, Ellen's own mother, had been found hanging from the banister of her stairs, stark and grim. Then there was young Frank Pencarris, who had wed Ellen's sister. He had sunk into an awful melancholy, and sat tracing on sheets of paper the visions that beset his eyes, headless shapes, and foaming mouths, and the images of the spawn of hell.... John Aylsford, in those early days, had laughed to scorn these old-wife tales of spells and sorceries: they belonged to ages long past, whereas fair Ellen Trenair was of the lovely present, and had lit desire in his heart which she alone could assuage. He had no use, in the brightness of her eye, for such shadows and superstitions; her beams dispelled them.

Bitter and black as midnight had his enlightenment been, darkening through dubious dusks till the mirk of the pit itself enveloped him. His laughter at the notion that in this twentieth century spells and sorceries could survive, grew silent on his lips. He had seen the cattle of a neighbour who had offended one whom it was wiser not to cross, dwindle and pine, though there were rich pastures for their grazing, till the rib-bones stuck out like the timbers of stranded wrecks. He had seen the spring on another farm run dry at lambing-time because the owner, sceptic like himself, had refused that bounty, which all prudent folk paid to the wizard of Mareuth, who, like Ellen, was of the blood of Jonas Trenair. From scorn and laughter he had wavered to an uneasy wonder, and from wonder his mind had passed to the conviction that there were powers occult and terrible which strove in darkness and prevailed, secrets and spells that could send disease on man and beast, dark incantations, known to few, which could maim and cripple, and of these few his wife was one. His reason revolted, but some conviction, deeper than reason, held its own. To such a view it seemed that the deed he contemplated was no crime, but rather an act of obedience to the ordinance "Thou shalt not suffer a witch to live." And the sense of detachment was over that, even as over the memories that oozed up in his mind. Somebody—not he—who had planned everything very carefully was in the next hour going to put an end to his bondage.

So the years had passed, he floundering ever deeper in the slough into which he was plunged, out of which while she lived he could never emerge. For the last year, she, wearying of his perpetual presence at the farm, had allowed him to take a lodging in the village. She did not loose her hold over him, for the days were few on which she did not come with demands for a handful of shillings to procure her the raw spirits which alone could slake her thirst. Sometimes as he sat at work there in the north room looking on to the small garden-yard, she would come lurching up the path, with her bloated crimson face set on the withered neck, and tap at his window with fingers shrivelled like bird's claws. Body and limbs were no more than bones over which the wrinkled skin was stretched, but her face bulged monstrously with layers of fat. He would give her whatever he had about him, and if it was not enough, she would plant herself there, grinning at him and wheedling him, or with screams and curses threatening him with such fate as he had known to overtake those who crossed her will. But usually he gave her enough to satisfy her for that day and perhaps the next, for thus she would the more quickly drink herself to death. Yet death seemed long in coming....

He remembered well how first the notion of killing her came into his head, just a little seed, small as that of mustard, which lay long in barrenness. Only the bare idea of it was there, like an abstract proposition. Then imperceptibly in the fruitful darkness of his mind, it must have begun to sprout, for presently a tendril, still soft and white, prodded out into the daylight. He almost pushed it back again, for fear that she, by some divining art, should probe his purpose. But when next she came for supplies, he saw no gleam of surmise in her red-rimmed eyes, and she took her money and went her way, and his purpose put forth another leaf, and the stem of it grew sappy. All autumn through it had flourished, and grown tree-like, and fresh ideas, fresh details, fresh precautions, flocked there like building birds and made it gay with singing. He sat under the shadow of it and listened with brightening hopes to their song; never had there been such peerless melody. They knew their tunes now, there was no need for any further rehearsal.

He began to wonder how soon he would be back on the road again, with face turned from this buffeting wind, and on his way home. His business would not take him long; the central deed of it would be over in a couple of minutes, and he did not anticipate delay about the setting to work on it, for by seven o'clock of the evening, as well he knew, she was usually snoring in the oblivion of complete drunkenness, and even if she was not as far gone as that, she would certainly be incapable of any serious resistance. After that, a quarter of an hour more would finish the job, and he would leave the house secure already from any chance of detection. Night after night during these last ten days he had been up here, peering from the darkness into the lighted room where she sat, then listening for her step on the stairs as she stumbled up to bed, or hearing her snorings as she slept in her chair below. The out-house, he knew, was well stocked with paraffin; he needed no further apparatus than the whipcord and the matches he carried with him. Then back he would go along the exact route by which he had come, re-entering the village again from the eastwards, in which direction he had set out.

This walk of his was now a known and established habit; half the village during the last week or two had seen him every evening set forth along the coast road, for a tramp in the dusk when the light failed for his painting, and had seen him come back again as they hung about and smoked in the warm dusk, a couple of hours later. None knew of his detour to the main road which took him westwards again above the village and so to the stretch of bleak upland along which now he fought his way against the gale. Always round about the hour of eight he had entered the village again from the other side, and had stopped and chatted with the loiterers. To-night, no later than was usual, he would come up the cobbled road again, and give "good night" to any who lingered there outside the public-house. In this wild wind it was not likely that there would be such, and if so, no matter; he had been seen already setting forth on his usual walk by the coast of the bay, and if none outside saw him return, none could see the true chart of his walk. By eight he should be back to his supper, there would be a soused herring for him, and a cut of cheese, and the kettle would be singing on the hob for his hot whisky-toddy. He would have a keen edge for the enjoyment of them to-night; he would drink long healths to the damned and the dead. Not till to-morrow, probably, would the news of what had happened reach him, for the farmhouse lay lonely and sheltered by the wood of firs. However high might mount the beacon of its blazing, it would scarcely, screened by the tall trees, light up the western sky, and be seen from the village nestling below the steep hill-crest.

By now John Aylsford had come to the fir wood which bordered the road on the left, and, as he passed into its shelter, cut off from him the violence of the gale. All its branches were astir with the sound of some vexed, overhead sea, and the trunks that upheld them creaked and groaned in the fury of the tempest. Somewhere behind the thick scud of flying cloud the moon must have risen, for the road glimmered more visibly, and the tossing blackness of the branches was clear enough against the grey tumult overhead. Behind the tempest she rode in serene skies, and in the murderous clarity of his mind he likened himself to her. Just for half an hour more he would still grope and scheme and achieve in this hurly-burly, and then, like a balloon released, soar through the clouds and find serenity. A couple of hundred yards now would take him round

75

the corner of the wood; from there the miry lane led from the high-road to the farm.

He hastened rather than retarded his going as he drew near, for the wood, though it roared with the gale, began to whisper to him of memories. Often in that summer before his marriage had he strayed out at dusk into it, certain that before he had gone many paces he would see a shadow flitting towards him through the firs, or hear the crack of dry twigs in the stillness. Here was their tryst; she would come up from the village with the excuse of bringing fish to the farmhouse, after the boats had come in, and deserting the high-road make a short cut through the wood. Like some distant blink of lightning the memory of those evenings quivered distantly on his mind, and he quickened his step. The years that followed had killed and buried those recollections, but who knew what stirring of corpses and dry bones might not yet come to them if he lingered there? He fingered the whipcord in his pocket, and launched out, beyond the trees, into the full fury of the gale.

The farmhouse was near now and in full view, a black blot against the clouds. A beam of light shone from an uncurtained window on the ground-floor, and the rest was dark. Even thus had he seen it for many nights past, and well knew what sight would greet him as he stole up nearer. And even so it was to-night, for there she sat in the studio he had built, betwixt table and fireplace with the bottle near her, and her withered hands stretched out to the blaze, and the huge bloated face swaying on her shoulders. Beside her to-night were the wrecked remains of a chair, and the first sight that he caught of her was to show her feeding the fire with the broken pieces of it. It had been too troublesome to bring fresh logs from the store of wood; to break up a chair was the easier task.

She stirred and sat more upright, then reached out for the bottle that stood beside her, and drank from the mouth of it. She drank and licked her lips and drank again, and staggered to her feet, tripping on the edge of the hearthrug. For the moment that seemed to anger her, and with clenched teeth and pointing finger she mumbled at it; then once more she drank, and lurching forward, took the lamp from the table. With it in her hand she shuffled to the door, and the room was left to the flickering firelight. A moment afterwards, the bedroom window above sprang into light, an oblong of bright illumination.

As soon as that appeared he crept round the house to the door. He gently turned the handle of it, and found it unlocked. Inside was a small passage entrance, on the left of which ascended the stairs to the bedroom above the studio. All was silent there, but from where he stood he could see that the door into the bedroom was open, for a shaft of light from the lamp she had carried up with her was shed on to the landing there.... Everything was smoothing itself out to render his course most easy. Even the gale was his friend, for it would be bellows for the fire. He slipped off his shoes, leaving them on the mat, and drew the whipcord from his pocket. He made a noose in it, and began to ascend the stairs. They were well-built of seasoned oak, and no creak betrayed his advancing footfall.

At the top he paused, listening for any stir of movement within, but there was nothing to be heard but the sound of heavy breathing from the bed that lay to the left of the door and out of sight. She had thrown herself down there, he guessed, without undressing, leaving the lamp to burn itself out. He could see it through the open door already beginning to flicker; on the wall behind it were a couple of water-colours, pictures of his own, one of the little walled garden by the farm, the other of the pinewood of their tryst. Well he remembered painting them: she would sit by him as he worked with prattle and singing. He looked at them now quite detachedly; they seemed to him wonderfully good, and he envied the artist that fresh, clean skill. Perhaps he would take them down presently and carry them away with him.

Very softly now he advanced into the room, and looking round the corner of the door, he saw her, sprawling and fully dressed on the broad bed. She lay on her back, eyes closed and mouth open, her dull grey hair spread over the pillow. Evidently she had not made the bed that day, for she lay stretched on the crumpled back-turned blankets. A hair-brush was on the floor beside her; it seemed to have fallen from her hand. He moved quickly towards her.

He put on his shoes again when he came to the foot of the stairs, carrying the lamp with him and the two pictures which he had taken down from the wall, and went into the studio. He set the lamp on the table and drew down the blinds, and his eye fell on the half-empty whisky bottle from which he had seen her drinking. Though his hand was quite steady and his mind composed and tranquil, there was yet at the back of it some impression that was slowly developing, and a good dose of spirits would no doubt expunge that. He drank half a tumbler of it raw and undiluted, and though it seemed no more than water in his mouth, he soon felt that it was doing its work and sponging away from his mind the picture that had been outlining itself there. In a couple of minutes he was quite himself again, and could afford to wonder and laugh at the illusion, for it was no less than that, which had been gaining on him.

For though he could distinctly remember drawing the noose tight, and seeing the face grow black, and struggling with the convulsive movements of those withered limbs that soon lay quiet again, there had sprung up in his mind some unaccountable impression that what he had left there huddled on the bed was not just the bundle of withered limbs and strangled neck, but the body of a young girl, smooth of skin and golden of hair, with mouth that smiled drowsily. She had been asleep when he came in, and now was half-awake, and was stirring and stretching herself. In what dim region of his mind that image had formed itself, he had no idea; all he cared about now was that his drink had shattered it again, and he could proceed with order and method to make all secure. Just one drop more first: how lucky it was that this morning he had been liberal with his money when she came to the village, for he would have been sorry to have gone without that fillip to his nerves.

He looked at his watch, and saw to his satisfaction that it was still only a little after seven o'clock. Half an hour's walking, with this gale to speed his steps, would easily carry him from door to door, round the detour which approached the village from the east, and a quarter of an hour, so he reckoned, would be sufficient to accomplish thoroughly what remained to be done here. He must not hurry and thus overlook some precaution needful for his safety, though, on the other hand, he would be glad to be gone from the house as soon as might be, and he proceeded to set about his work without delay. There was brushwood and fire-kindling to be brought in from the wood-shed in the yard, and he made three journeys, returning each time with his arms full, before he had brought in what he judged to be sufficient. Most of this he piled in a loose heap in the studio; with the rest he ascended once more to the bedroom above and made a heap of it there in the middle of the floor. He took the curtains down from the windows, for they would make a fine wick for the paraffin, and stuffed them into the pile. Before he left, he looked once more at what lay on the bed, and marvelled at the illusion which the whisky had dispelled, and as he looked, the sense that he was free mounted and bubbled in his head. The thing seemed scarcely human at all; it was a monster from which he had delivered himself, and now, with the thought of that to warm him, he was no longer eager to get through with his work and be gone, for it was all part of that act of riddance which he had accomplished, and he gloried in it. Soon, when all was ready, he would come back once more and soak the fuel and set light to it, and purge with fire the corruption that lay humped on the bed.

The fury of the gale had increased with nightfall, and as he went downstairs again he heard the rattle of loosened tiles on the roof, and the crash as they shattered themselves on the cobbles of the yard. At that a sudden misgiving made his breath to catch in his throat, as he pictured to himself some maniac blast falling on the house and crashing in the walls that now trembled and shuddered. Supposing the whole house fell, even if he escaped with his life from the toppling ruin, what would his life be worth? There would be search made in the fallen débris to find the body of her who lay strangled with the whipcord round her neck, and he pictured to himself the slow, relentless march of justice. He had bought whipcord only yesterday at a shop in the village, insisting on its strength and toughness ... would it be wiser now, this moment, to untie the noose and take it back with him or add it to his brushwood?... He paused on the staircase, pondering that; but his flesh quaked at the thought, and master of himself though he had been during those few struggling minutes, he distrusted his power of making himself handle once more that which could struggle no longer. But even as he tried to screw his courage to the point, the violence of the squall passed, and the shuddering house braced itself again. He need not fear that; the gale was his friend that would blow on the flames, not his enemy. The blasts that trumpeted overhead were the voices of the allies who had come to aid him.

All was arranged then upstairs for the pouring of the paraffin and the lighting of the pyre; it remained but to make similar dispositions in the studio. He would stay to feed the flames till they raged beyond all power of extinction; and now he began to plan the line of his retreat. There were two doors in the studio: one by the fireplace which opened on to the little garden; the other gave into the passage entrance from which mounted the stairs and so to the door through which he had come into the house. He decided to use the garden-door for his exit; but when he came to open it, he found that the key was stiff in the rusty lock, and did not yield to his efforts. There was no use in wasting time over that; it made no difference through which door he finally emerged, and he began piling up his heap of wood at that end of the room. The lamp was burning low; but the fire, which only so few minutes ago she had fed with a broken chair, shone brightly, and a flaming ember from it would serve to set light to his conflagration. There was a straw mat in front of it, which would make fine kindling, and with these two fires, one in the bedroom upstairs and the other here, there would be no mistake about the incineration of the house and all that it contained. His own crime, if crime it was, would perish, too, and all evidence thereof, victim and whipcord, and the very walls of the house of sin and hate. It was a great deed and a fine adventure, and as the liquor he had drunk began to circulate more buoyantly through his veins, he gloried at the thought of the approaching consummation. He would slip out of the sordid tragedy of his past life, as from a discarded garment that he threw into the bonfire he would soon kindle.

All was ready now for the soaking of the fuel he had piled with the paraffin, and he went out to the shed in the yard where the barrel stood. A big tin ewer stood beside it, which he filled and carried indoors. That would be sufficient for the soaking of the pile upstairs, and fetching the smoky and flickering lamp from the studio, he went up again, and like a careful gardener watering some bed of choice blossoms, he sprinkled and poured till his ewer was empty. He gave but one glance to the bed behind him, where the huddled thing lay so quietly, and as he turned, lamp in hand, to go down again, the draught that came in through the window against which the gale blew, extinguished it. A little blue flame of burning vapour rose in the chimney and went out; so, having no further use for it, he pitched it on to the pile of soaked material. As he left the room he thought he heard some small stir of movement behind him, but he told himself that it was but something slipping in the heap he had built there.

Again he went out into the storm. The clouds that scudded overhead were thinner now, though the gale blew not less fiercely, and the blurred, watery moonlight was brighter. Once for a moment, as he approached the shed, he caught sight of the full orb plunging madly among the streaming vapours; then she was hidden again behind the wrack. Close in front of him were the fir trees of the wood where those sweet trysts had been held, and once again the vision of her as she had been broke into his mind and the queer conviction that it was no withered and bloated hag, who lay on the bed upstairs but the fair, comely limbs and the golden head. It was even more vivid now, and he made haste to get back to the studio, where he would find the trusty medicine that had dispelled that vision before. He would have to make two journeys at least with his tin ewer before he transported enough oil to feed the larger pyre below, and so, to save time, he took the barrel off its stand, and rolled it along the path and into the house. He paused at the foot of the stairs, listening to hear if anything stirred, but all was silent. Whatever had slipped up there was steady again; from outside only came the squeal and bellow of the wind.

The studio was brightly but fitfully lit by the flames on the hearth; at one moment a noonday blazed there, the next but the last smoulder of some red sunset. It was easier to decant from the barrel into his ewer than carry the heavy keg and sprinkle from it, and once and once again he filled and emptied it. One more application would be sufficient, and after that he could let what remained trickle out on to the floor. But by some awkward movement he managed to spill a splash of it down the front of his trousers: he must be sure, therefore (how quickly his brain responded with counsels of precautions), to have some accident with his lamp when he came in to his supper, which should account for this little misadventure. Or, probably, the wind through which he would presently be walking would dry it before he reached the village.

So, for the last time with matches ready in his hand, he mounted the stairs to set light to the fuel piled in the room above. His second dose of whisky sang in his head, and he said to himself, smiling at the humour of the notion, "She always liked a fire in her bedroom; she shall have it now." That seemed a very comical idea, and it dwelt in his head as he struck the match which should light it for her. Then, still grinning, he gave one glance to the bed, and the smile died on his face, and the wild cymbals of panic crashed in his brain. The bed was empty; no huddled shape lay there.

Distraught with terror, he thrust the match into the soaked pile and the flame flared up. Perhaps the body had rolled off the bed. It must, in any case, be here somewhere, and when once the room was alight there would be nothing more to fear. High rose the smoky flame, and banging the door, he leaped down the stairs to set light to the pile below and be gone from the house. Yet, whatever monstrous miracle his eye had assured him of, it could not be that she still lived and had left the place where she lay, for she had ceased to breathe when the noose was tight round her neck, and her fight for life and air had long been stilled. But, if by some hideous witchcraft, she was not dead, it would soon be over now with her in the stupefaction of the smoke and the scorching flames. Let be; the door was shut and she within, for him it remained to be finished with the business, and flee from the house of terror, lest he leave the sanity of his soul behind him.

The red glare from the hearth in the studio lit his steps down the passage from the stairway, and already he could hear from above the dry crack and snap from the fire that prospered there. As he shuffled in, he held his hands to his head, as if pressing the brain back into its cool case, from which it seemed eager to fly out into the welter of storm and fire and hideous imagination. If he could only control himself for a few moments more, all would be done and he would escape from this disordered haunted place into the night and the gale, leaving behind him the blaze that would burn away all perilous stuff. Again the flames broke out in the embers on the hearth, bravely burning, and he took from the heart of the glare a fragment on which the fire was bursting into yellow flowers. He heeded not the scorching of his hand, for it was but for a moment that he held it, and then plunged it into the pile that dripped with the oil he had poured on it. A tower of flame mounted, licking the rafters of the low ceiling, then died away as if suffocated by its own smoke, but crept onwards, nosing its way along till it reached the straw mat, which blazed fiercely. That blaze kindled the courage in him; whatever trick his imagination had played on him just now, he had nothing to fear except his own terror, which now he mastered again, for nothing real could ever escape from the conflagration, and it was only the real that he feared. Spells and witchcrafts and superstitions, such as for the last twenty years had battened on him, were all enclosed in that tight-drawn noose.

It was time to be gone, for all was safe now, and the room was growing to oven-heat. But as he picked his way across the floor over which runnels of flames from the split barrel were beginning to spread this way and that, he heard from above the sound of a door unlatched, and footsteps light and firm tapped on the stairs. For one second the sheer catalepsy of panic seized him, but he recovered his control, and with hands that groped through the thick smoke he found the door. At that moment the fire shot up in a blaze of blinding flame, and there in the doorway stood Ellen. It was no withered body and bloated face that confronted him, but she with whom he had trysted in the wood, with the bloom of eternal youth upon her, and the smooth soft hand, on which was her wedding-ring, pointed at him.

It was in vain that he called on himself to rush forward out of that torrid and suffocating air. The front door was open, he had but to pass her and speed forth safe into the night. But no power from his will reached his limbs; his will screamed to him, "Go, go! Push by her: it is but a phantom which you fear!" but muscle and sinew were in mutiny, and step by step he retreated before that pointing finger and the radiant shape that advanced on him. The flames that flickered over the floor had discovered the paraffin he had spilt, and leaped up his leg.

Just one spot in his brain retained lucidity from the encompassing terror. Somewhere behind that barrier of fire there was the second door into the garden. He had but cursorily attempted to unlock its rusty wards; now, surely, the knowledge that there alone was escape would give strength to his hand. He leaped backwards through the flames, still with eyes fixed on her who ever advanced in time with his retreat, and turning, wrestled and strove with the key. Something snapped in his hand, and there still in the keyhole was the bare shaft.

Holding his breath, for the heat scorched his throat, he groped towards where he knew was the window through which he had first seen her that night. The flames licked fiercely round it, but there, beneath his hand, was the hasp, and he threw it open. At that the wind poured in as through the nozzle of a plied bellows, and Death rose high and bright around him. Through the flames, as he sank to the floor, a face radiant with revenge smiled on him.

# Inscrutable Decrees

I had found nothing momentous in the more august pages of The Times that morning, and so, just because I was lazy and unwilling to embark on a host of businesses that were waiting for me, I turned to the first page and, beginning with the seventh column, pondered profoundly over "Situations Vacant," and hoped that the "Gentlewoman fond of games," who desired the position of governess, would find the very thing to suit her. I glanced at the notices of lectures to be delivered under the auspices of various learned societies, and was thankful that I had not got to give or to listen to any of them. I debated over "Business Opportunities"; I vainly tried to conjecture clues to mysterious "Personal" paragraphs, and, still pursuing my sideways, crab-fashion course, came to "Deaths Continued."

There, with a shock of arrest, I saw that Sybil Rorke, widow of the late Sir Ernest Rorke, had died at Torquay, suddenly, at the age of thirty-two. It seemed strange that there should be only this bare announcement concerning a woman who at one time had been so well-known and dazzling a figure; and turning to the obituary notices, I found that my inattentive skimming had overlooked a paragraph there of appreciation and regret. She had died during her sleep, and it was announced that an inquest would be held. My laziness then had been of some use, for Archie Rorke, distant cousin but successor to Sir Ernest's estates and title, was arriving that evening to spend a few country days with me, and I was glad to have known this before he came. How it would affect him, or whether, indeed, it would affect him at all, I had no idea.

What a mysterious affair it had been! No one, I supposed, knew the history of it except he, now that Lady Rorke was dead. If anyone knew, it should have been myself, and yet Archie, my oldest friend, whose best man I was to have been, had never opened his lips to a syllable of explanation. I knew, in fact, no whit more than the whole world knew, namely, that a year after Sir Ernest Rorke's death the engagement of his widow to the new baronet, Sir Archibald Rorke, was made public, and that within a fortnight of the date fixed for the wedding it was laconically announced that the marriage would not take place. When, on seeing that, I rang Archie up on the telephone, I was told that he had already left London, and he wrote to me a few days later from Lincote—the place in Hampshire, which he had inherited from his cousin—saying that he had nothing to tell me about the breaking off of his engagement beyond the fact that it was true. The whole—he had written a word and carefully erased it—episode was now an excised leaf from his life. He was proposing to stay down at Lincote alone for a month or so, and would then turn on to the new page.

Lady Rorke, so I heard, had also left London immediately and passed the summer in Italy. Then she took a furnished house in Torquay, where she lived for the remainder of the year which intervened between the breaking off of her engagement and her death. She cut herself completely off from all her friends—and no woman, surely, ever commanded a larger host of them—saw nobody, seldom went outside her house and garden, and observed the same unbroken silence as did Archie about what had happened. And now, with all her youth and charm and beauty, she had gone down dumb into the Great Silence.

With the prospect of seeing Archie that evening it was no wonder that the thought of Lady Rorke ran all day in my head like a tune heard long ago which now recalled itself to my mind in scattered staves of melody. Meetings and talks with her, phrase by phrase, reconstructed themselves, and as these memories grew definite and complete I found that, even as before, when I was actually experiencing them, there lurked underneath the gay rhythms and joyousness something macabre and mysterious. To-day that was accentuated, whereas before when I listened for it, trying to isolate it from the rest and so perhaps dispel it, it was always overscored by some triumphant crescendo: her presence diverted eye and ear alike. Yet such a simile halts; perhaps, still in simile, I shall more accurately define this underlying "something" by saying that her presence was like some gorgeous rose-bush, full of flowers, and sun, and sweetness; then, even as one admired and applauded and inhaled, one saw that among its buds and blossoms there emerged the spikes of some other plant, bitter and poisonous, but growing from the same soil as the rose, and intertwined with it. But immediately a fresh glory met your eye, a fresh fragrance enchanted you.

As I rummaged among my memories of her, certain scenes which significantly illustrated this curiously vivid impression stirred and made themselves manifest to me, and now they were not broken in upon by her presence. One such occurred on the first evening that I ever met her, which was in the summer before the death of her husband. The moment that she entered the room where we were waiting before dinner for her arrival, the stale, sultry air of a June evening grew fresh and effervescent; never have I come

85

across so radiant and infectious a vitality. She was tall and big, with the splendour of the Juno-type, and though she was then close on thirty, the iridescence of girlhood was still hers. Without effort she Pied-pipered a rather stodgy party to dance to her flutings, she caused everyone to become silly and pleased and full of laughter. At her bidding we indulged in ridiculous games, dumb-crambo, and what not, and after that the carpet was rolled up and we capered to the strains of a gramophone. And then the incident occurred.

I was standing with her, for a breath of air, on the balcony outside the drawing-room windows which faced the park. She had just made a great curtsey to a slip of the moon that rose above the trees and had borrowed a shilling of me in order to turn it.

"No, I can't swear that I believe in moon-luck," she said, "but after all it does no harm, and, in case it's true, you can't afford to make an enemy of her. Ah, what's that?"

A thrush, attracted by the lights inside, had flown between us, dashed itself against the window, and now lay fluttering on the ground at our feet. Instantly she was all pity and tenderness. She picked up the bird, examined it, and found that its wing was broken.

"Ah, poor thing!" she said. "Look, its wing-bone is snapped; the end protrudes. And how terrified it is! What are we to do?"

It was clear that the kindest thing to do would be to put the bird out of its pain, but when I suggested that, she took a step back from me, and covered it with her other hand. Her eyes gleamed, her mouth smiled, and I saw the tip of her tongue swiftly pass over her lips as if licking them.

"No, that would be a terrible thing to do," she said. "I shall take it home with me ever so carefully, and watch over it. I am afraid it is badly hurt. But it may live."

Suddenly—perhaps it was that swift licking of her lips that suggested the thought to me—I felt instinctively that she was not so much pitiful as pleased. She stood there with eyes fixed on it, as it feebly struggled in her hands.

And then her face clouded; over its brightness there came a look of displeasure, of annoyance.

"I'm afraid it is dying," she said. "Its poor frightened eyes are closing."

The bird fluttered once more, then its legs stretched themselves stiffly out, and it lay still. She tossed it out of her hands on to the paved balcony, with a little shrug of her shoulders.

"What a fuss over a bird," she said. "It was silly of it to fly against the glass. But I have too soft a heart; I cannot bear that the poor creatures should die. Let us go in and have one more romp.

Oh, here is your shilling; I hope it will have brought me good luck. And then I must get home. My husband—do you know him?—always sits up till I get back, and he will scold me for being so late!"

There, then, was my first meeting with her, and there, too, were the spikes of the poisonous plant pushing up among the magnificence of her roses. And yet, so I thought to myself then, and so I think to myself now, I perhaps was utterly wrong about it all, in thus attributing to her a secret glee of which she was wholly incapable. So, with a certain effort I wiped the impression I had received off my mind, determining to consider myself quite mistaken. But, involuntarily, my mind as if to justify itself in having delineated such a picture, proceeded to delineate another.

Very shortly after that first meeting I received from her a charming note, asking me to dine with her on a date not far distant. I telephoned a delighted acceptance, for, indeed, I wanted then, even as I did this morning, to convince myself that I was wholly in error concerning my interpretation of that incident concerning the thrush. Though I hold that no man has the right to accept the hospitality offered by one he does not like, in all points except one I admired and liked Lady Rorke immensely and wished to get rid of that one. So I gratefully accepted, and then hurried out on a dismal and overdue visit to the dentist's. In the waiting-room was a girl of about twelve, with a hand nursing a rueful face, and from time to time she stifled a sob of pain or apprehension. I was just wondering whether it would be a breach of waiting-room etiquette to attempt to administer comfort or supply diversion, when the door opened and in came Lady Rorke. She laughed delightfully when she saw me.

"Hurrah! You're another occupant of the condemned cell," she said, "and very soon we shall both be sent for to the scaffold. I can't describe to you what a coward I am about it. Why haven't we got beaks like birds?——"

Her glance fell on the forlorn little figure by the window, with the rueful face and the wet eyes.

"Why, here's another of us," she said. "And have they sent you to the dentist's all alone, my dear?"

"Y—yes."

"How horrid of them!" said Lady Rorke. "They've sent me alone, too, and I think it's most unfeeling. But you shan't be alone, anyhow, I'll come in with you, and sit by you, if you like that, and box the man's ears for him if he hurts you. Or shall you and I set on him, as soon as we've got him by himself, and take out all his teeth one after the other? Just to teach him to be a dentist."

A faint smile began the break through the clouds.

"Oh, will you come in with me?" she asked. "I shan't mind nearly so much, then. It's—it's got to come out, you know, and I mayn't have gas."

Just the same gleam of a smile as I had seen on Lady Rorke's face once before quivered there now, a light not of pity, surely.

"Ah, but it won't ache any more after that," she said, "and after all, it is so soon over. You'll just open your mouth as if you were going to put the largest of all strawberries into it, and you'll hold tight on to my hand, and the dentist takes up something which you needn't look at——"

There was a want of tact in the vividness of this picture, and the child began to sob again.

"Oh, don't, don't!" she cried.

Again the door opened, and she clung to Lady Rorke.

"Oh, I know it's for me!" she wailed.

Lady Rorke bent over her, scanning her terrified face.

"Come along, my dear," she said, "and it will be over in no time. You'll be back here again before this gentleman can count a hundred, and he'll have all his troubles in front of him still."

Again this morning I tried to expunge from that picture, so trivial and yet so vivid to me, the sinister something which seemed to connect it with the incident about the thrush, and, leaving it, my mind strayed on over other reminiscences of Lady Rorke. Before the season was over I had got to know her well, and the better I knew her the more I marvelled at that many-petalled vitality, which never ceased unfolding itself. She entertained largely, and had that crowning gift of a good hostess, namely, that she enjoyed her own parties quite enormously. She was a very fine horsewoman, and after being up till dawn at some dance, she would be in the Row by half-past eight on a peculiarly vicious mare to whom she seemed to pay only the most cursory attention. She had a good knowledge of music, she dressed amazingly, she was charming to her meagre little husband, playing piquet with him by the hour (which was the only thing, apart from herself, that he cared about), and if in this modern democratic London there could be said to be a queen, there is no doubt who that season would have worn the crown. Less publicly, she was a great student of the psychical and occult, and I remembered hearing that she was herself possessed of very remarkable mediumistic gifts. But to me that was a matter of hearsay, for I never was present at any séance of hers.

Yet through the triumphant music of her pageant, there sounded, to my ears at least, fragments of a very ugly tune. It was not only in these two instances of its emergence that I heard it, it was chiefly and most persistently audible in her treatment of Archie Rorke, her husband's cousin. Everyone knew, for none could help knowing, that he was desperately in love with her, and it is impossible to imagine that she alone was ignorant of it. It is, no doubt, the instinct of many women to fan a passion which they do not share, and which they have no intention of indulging, just as the male instinct is to gratify a passion that he does not really feel, but there are limits to mercilessness. She was not "cruel to be kind"; she was kind to be demoniacally cruel. She had him always by her; she gave him those little touches and comrade-like licences which meant nothing to her, but crazed him with thirst; she held the glass close to his lips and then tilted it up and showed it him empty. The more charitable explanation was that she, perhaps, knew that her husband could not live long, and that she intended to marry Archie, and such, so it subsequently appeared, her intentions were. But when I saw her feeding him with husks and putting an empty glass to his lips, nothing, to my mind, could account for her treatment of him except a rapture of cruelty at the sight of his aching. And somehow, awfully and aptly, that seemed to fit in with the affair of the thrush, and the meeting with the forlorn child in the dentist's waiting-room. Yet ever, through that gruesome twilight, there blazed forth her charm and her beauty and the beam of her joyous vitality, and I would cudgel myself for my nasty interpretations.

It was early in the spring of next year that I was spending a week-end with her and her husband at Lincote. She had suggested my coming down on Saturday morning before the party assembled later in the day, and at lunch I was alone with her husband and her. Sir Ernest was very silent; he looked ill and haggard, and, in fact, hardly spoke a word except when suddenly he turned to the butler and said, "Has anything been heard of the child yet?" He was told that there was no news, and subsided into silence again. I thought that some queer shadow as of suspense or anxiety crossed Lady Rorke's face at the question; but on the answer, it cleared off again, and, as if to sweep the subject wholly away, she asked me if I could tolerate a saunter with her through the woods till her guests arrived.

Out she came like some splendid Diana of the Forests, and like the goddess's was the swift, swinging pace of her saunter. Spring all round was riotous in blossom and bird-song; it was just that ecstatic moment of the year when the hounds of spring have run winter to death, and as we gained the high ridge of down above the woods she stopped and threw her arms wide.

"Oh, the sense of spring!" she cried. "The daffodils, and the west wind, and the shadows of the clouds. How I wish I could take the whole lot into my arms and hug them. Miracles are flowering every moment now in the country, while the only miracle in London is the mud. What sunshine, what air! Drink them in, for they are the one divine medicine. One wants that medicine sometimes, for there are sad things and terrible things all round us, pain and anguish, and decay. Yet I suppose that even those call out the splendour of fortitude or endurance. Even when one looks on a struggle which one knows is hopeless, it warms the heart to see it."

The gleam that shone from her paled, her arms dropped, and she moved on. Then, soft of voice and soft of eye, she spoke again.

"Such a sad thing happened here two days ago," she said. "A small girl—now what was her name? Yes—Ellen Davenport—brought a note from the village up to the house. I was out, so she left it, and started, it is supposed, to go back home. She has not been seen since. Descriptions of her were circulated in all the villages for miles round; but, as you heard at lunch, there has been no news of her, and the copses and coverts in the park have been searched, but with no result. And yet out of that comes splendour. I went to see her mother yesterday, bowed down with grief, but she won't give up hope. 'If it is God's will,' she said to me, 'we shall find my Ellen alive; and if we find her dead, it will be God's will, too.'"

She paused.

"But I didn't ask you down here to moan over tragedies," she said. "I wanted you after all your weeks in town to come and have a spring-cleaning. Doesn't the wind take the dust out of you, like one of those sucking-machines which you put on to carpets? And the sun! Make a sponge of yourself and soak it up till you're dripping with it."

For a couple of miles, at the least, we kept along this high ridge of down, and the larks were springing from the grass, vocal with song uncongealed, as they aspired and sank again, dropping at last dumb and spent with rapture. Then we descended steeply, through the woods and glades of the park, past thickets of catkinned sallows, and of willows with soft moleskin buttons, and in the hollows the daffodils were dancing, and the herbs of the springtime were pushing up through the brittle withered stuff of the winter. Then, passing along the one street of the red-tiled village, in which my companion pointed me out the house where the poor vanished girl had lived, we turned homewards across the grass and joined the road again at the bottom of the great lake that lies below the terraced gardens of the house.

This lake was artificial, made a hundred years ago by the erection of a huge dam across the dip of the valley, so that the stream which flowed down it was thereby confined and must needs form this sheet of water before it found outlet again through the sluices. At the centre the dam is some twenty-five feet in height, and by the side of the road which crosses it clumps of rhododendrons lean out over the deep water. The margin on the side towards the lake is reinforced with concrete, now mossy and overgrown with herbage, and the face of it, burrows down to the level of the bottom of the dam through four fathoms of dusky water. The lake was high and the overflow poured sonorously through the sluices, and the sun in the west made broken rainbows in the foam of its outpouring.

As we paused there a moment, my companion seemed the incarnation of the sights and sounds that went to the spell of the spring; singing larks and dancing daffodils, west wind and rainbowed foam and, no less, the dark, deep water, were all distilled into her radiant vitality.

"And now for the house again," she said, going briskly up the steep slope. "Is it inhospitable of me to wish that no one was coming except, of course, our delightful Archie? A houseful brings London into the country, and we shall talk scandal and stir up mud instead of watching miracles."

Another faint memory of her lingered somewhere in the dusk, and I groped for it, as one gropes in slime for the roots of a water-plant, and pulled it out. A notorious murderer had been guillotined that morning in France, and in some Sunday paper next day there was a brutal, brilliant, inexcusable little sketch of his being led out between guards for the final scene at dawn outside the prison at Versailles. And, as I wrote my name in Lady Rorke's visitors' book on Monday morning, I spilt a blot of ink on the page and hastily had recourse to the blotting-pad on her writing-table in order to minimize the disfigurement. Inside it was this unpardonable picture, cut out and put away, and I thought of the thrush and the dentist's waiting-room——

A month afterwards her husband died, after three weeks of intolerable torment. The doctor insisted on his having two trained nurses, but Lady Rorke never left him. She was present at the painful dressings of the wound from the operation that only prolonged the misery of his existence, and even slept on the sofa of the room where he lay.

Archie Rorke arrived that evening. He let me know at once that he had seen the announcement of Lady Rorke's death, and said no more about it till later, when he and I were left alone over the fire in the smoking-room. He looked round to see that the door was shut behind the last bedgoer of my little party, and then turned to me.

"I've got to tell you something," he said. "It'll take half an hour, so to-morrow will do if you want to be off."

"But I don't," said I.

He pulled himself together from his sprawling sunkenness in his chair.

"Very well," he said. "What I want to tell you is the story of the breaking-off of my engagement with Sybil. I have often wanted to do so before, but while she was alive, as you will presently see, I could tell nobody. I shall ask you, when you know everything, whether you think I could have done otherwise. And please do not interrupt me till I have finished, unless there is something you don't understand, for it won't be very easy to get through with it. But I think I can make it intelligible."

He was silent a moment, and I saw his face working and twitching.

"I must tell somebody," he said, "and I choose you, unless you mind it awfully. But I simply can't bear it alone any more."

"Go on, then, old boy," I said. "I'm glad you chose me, do you know. And I won't interrupt."

Archie spoke.

"A week or two only before our marriage was to have taken place," he said, "I went down to Lincote for a couple of days. I had had the house done up and re-decorated, and now the work was finished and I wanted to see that all was in order. Nothing could be worthy of Sybil, but—well, you can guess, more or less, what my feelings were.

"For a week before there had been very heavy rains, and the lake—you know it—below the garden was very high, higher than I had ever seen it: the water poured over the road across the dam which leads to the village. Under the weight and press of it a great crack had appeared in the concrete with which it is faced, and there was danger of the dam being carried away. If that happened the whole lake would have been suddenly released and no end of damage might have been done. It was therefore necessary to draw off the water as fast as possible to relieve the pressure and repair the crack. This was done by means of big siphons. For two days we had them working, but the crack seemed to extend right to the foundations of the dam, and before it could be repaired all the water in the lake would have to be drawn off. I was just leaving for town, when the foreman came up to the house to tell me that they had found something there. In the ooze and mud at the base of the dam, twenty-five feet below water-level, they had come upon the body of a young girl."

92

He gripped the arms of his chair tight. Little did he know that I was horribly aware of what he was going to tell me next.

"About a month before my cousin Ernest's death," he said, "a mysterious affair happened in the village. A girl named Ellen Davenport had disappeared. She came up one afternoon to the house with a note, and was never seen again, dead or alive. Her disappearance was now explained. A chain of beads round the neck and various fragments of clothing established, beyond any doubt, the identity of what they had found at the bottom of the lake. I waited for the inquest, telegraphing to Sybil that business had detained me, and then returned to town, not intending to tell her what that business was, for our marriage was close at hand and it was not a topic one would choose. She was very superstitious, you know, and I thought that it would shock her. That she would feel it to be unlucky and ill-omened. So I said nothing to her.

"Sybil had extraordinary mediumistic powers. She did not often exercise them and she never would give a séance to any one she did not know extremely well, for she believed that people brought with them the spiritual influences with which they were surrounded, and that there was the possibility of very evil intelligences being set free. But she had sat several times with me, and I had witnessed some very remarkable manifestations. Her procedure was to put herself, by abstraction of her mind, into a state of trance, and spirits of the dead who were connected with the sitters could then communicate through her. On one occasion my mother, whom she had never seen, and who died many years ago, spoke through her and told me certain facts which Sybil could not have known, and which I did not know. But an old friend of my mother's, still alive, told me that they were correct. They were of an exceedingly private nature. Sybil also, so she told me, could produce materialisations, but up till now I had never seen any. A remarkable thing about her mediumship was that she would sometimes regain consciousness from her trance while still these communications were being made, and she knew what was going on. She could hear herself speak and be mentally aware of what she was saying. On the occasion, for instance, of which I have told you, when my mother spoke to me she was in this state. The same thing occurred at the sitting of which I shall now speak.

"That night, on my return to London, she and I dined alone. I felt a very strong desire, for which I could not account, that she should hold a sitting—just herself and me—and she consented. We sat in her room, with a shaded lamp, but there was sufficient illumination for me to see her quite distinctly, for her face was

93

towards the light. There was a small table in front of us covered with a dark cloth. She sat close to it, in a high chair, composed herself, and almost immediately went into trance. Her head fell forward and by her slow breathing and her absolute immobility I knew she was unconscious. For a long time we sat there in silence, and I began to think that we should get no manifestations at all, and that the sitting, as sometimes was the case, would be a failure; but then I saw that something was happening."

His hands, with which he gripped the arms of his chair, were trembling. Twice he tried to speak, but it was not till the third attempt that he mastered himself.

"There was forming a mist above the table," he said. "It was slightly luminous and it spread upwards, pillar-shaped, in height between two and three feet. Then I saw that below the outlying skeins of it something was materialising. It moulded itself into human shape, rising waist-high from the table, and presently shoulders and arms and neck and head were visible, and features began to outline themselves. For some time it remained vague and fluid, swaying backwards and forwards a little; then very quickly it solidified, and there, close in front of me, was the half-figure of a young girl. The eyes were still closed, but now they opened. Round her neck was a chain of beads just such as I had seen laid by the body that had been found in the lake. And then I spoke to her, asking her who she was, though I already knew.

"Her answer was no more than a whisper, but quite distinct.

"'Ellen Davenport,' she said.

"A disordered terror seized me. Yet perhaps this little white figure, with its wide-gazing eyes, was some hallucination, something that had no objective existence at all. All day the thought of the poor kiddie whose remains I had seen taken out of the ooze at the bottom of the lake had been vivid in my mind, and I tried to think that what I saw was no more than some strange projection of my thought. And yet I felt it was not so; it was independent of myself. And why was it made manifest, and on what errand had it come? I had pressed Sybil to give me this séance, and God knows what I would have given not to have done so! For one thing I was thankful, namely, that she was in unconscious trance. Perhaps the phantom would fade again before she came out of it.

"And then I heard a stir of movement from the chair where she sat, and, turning, I saw that she had raised her head. Her eyes were open and on her face such a mask of terror as I have never known human being could wear. Recognition was there, too; I saw that Sybil knew who the phantom was.

"The figure that palely gleamed above the table turned its head towards her, and once more the white lips opened.

"'Yes, I am Ellen Davenport,' she said.

"The whisper grew louder.

"'You might have saved me,' she said, 'or you might have tried to save me; but you watched me struggling till I sank.'

"And then the apparition vanished. It did not die away; it was there clear and distinct one moment, at the next it was gone. Sybil and I were sitting alone in her room with the low-burning lamp, and the silence sang in my ears.

"I got up and turned on the switch that kindled the electric lights, and knew that something within me had grown cold and that something had snapped. She still sat where she was, not looking at me at all, but blankly in front of her. She said no word of denial in answer to the terrible accusation that had been uttered. And I think I was glad of that, for there are times when it is not only futility to deny, but blasphemy. For my part, I could neither look at her nor speak to her. I remember holding out my hands to the empty grate, as if there had been a fire burning there. And standing there I heard her rise, and drearily wondered what she would say and knew how useless it would be. And then I heard the whisper of her dress on the carpet and the noise of the door opening and shutting, and when I turned I found that I was alone in the room. Presently I let myself out of the house."

There was a long pause, but I did not break it, for I felt he had not quite finished.

"I had loved her with my whole heart," he said, "and she knew it. Perhaps that was why I never attempted to see her again and why she did not attempt to see me. That little white figure would always have been with us, for she could not deny the reality of it and the truth of that which it had spoken. That's my story, then. You needn't even tell me if you think I could have done differently, for I knew I couldn't. And she couldn't."

He rose.

"I see there is to be an inquest," he said. "I hope they will find that she killed herself. It will mean, won't it, that her remorse was unbearable. And that's atonement."

He moved towards the door.

"Inscrutable decrees," he said.

# The Gardener

Two friends of mine, Hugh Grainger and his wife, had taken for a month of Christmas holiday the house in which we were to witness such strange manifestations, and when I received an invitation from them to spend a fortnight there I returned them an enthusiastic affirmative. Well already did I know that pleasant heathery country-side, and most intimate was my acquaintance with the subtle hazards of its most charming golf-links. Golf, I was given to understand, was to occupy the solid day for Hugh and me, so that Margaret should never be obliged to set her hand to the implements with which the game, so detestable to her, was conducted....

I arrived there while yet the daylight lingered, and as my hosts were out, I took a ramble round the place. The house and garden stood on a plateau facing south; below it were a couple of acres of pasture that sloped down to a vagrant stream crossed by a foot-bridge, by the side of which stood a thatched cottage with a vegetable patch surrounding it. A path ran close past this across the pasture from a wicket-gate in the garden, conducted you over the foot-bridge, and, so my remembered sense of geography told me, must constitute a short cut to the links that lay not half a mile beyond. The cottage itself was clearly on the land of the little estate, and I at once supposed it to be the gardener's house. What went against so obvious and simple a theory was that it appeared to be untenanted. No wreath of smoke, though the evening was chilly, curled from its chimneys, and, coming closer, I fancied it had that air of "waiting" about it which we so often conjure into unused habitations. There it stood, with no sign of life whatever about it, though ready, as its apparently perfect state of repair seemed to warrant, for fresh tenants to put the breath of life into it again. Its little garden, too, though the palings were neat and newly painted, told the same tale; the beds were untended and unweeded, and in the flower-border by the front door was a row of chrysanthemums, which had withered on their stems. But all this was but the impression of a moment, and I did not pause as I passed it, but crossed the foot-bridge and went on up the heathery slope that lay beyond. My geography was not at fault, for presently I saw the club-house just in front of me. Hugh no doubt would be just about coming in from his afternoon round, and so we would walk back together. On reaching the club-house, however, the steward told me that not five minutes before Mrs. Grainger had called in her car for

96

her husband, and I therefore retraced my steps by the path along which I had already come. But I made a detour, as a golfer will, to walk up the fairway of the seventeenth and eighteenth holes just for the pleasure of recognition, and looked respectfully at the yawning sandpit which so inexorably guards the eighteenth green, wondering in what circumstances I should visit it next, whether with a step complacent and superior, knowing that my ball reposed safely on the green beyond, or with the heavy footfall of one who knows that laborious delving lies before him.

The light of the winter evening had faded fast, and when I crossed the foot-bridge on my return the dusk had gathered. To my right, just beside the path, lay the cottage, the whitewashed walls of which gleamed whitely in the gloaming; and as I turned my glance back from it to the rather narrow plank which bridged the stream I thought I caught out of the tail of my eye some light from one of its windows, which thus disproved my theory that it was untenanted. But when I looked directly at it again I saw that I was mistaken: some reflection in the glass of the red lines of sunset in the west must have deceived me, for in the inclement twilight it looked more desolate than ever. Yet I lingered by the wicket gate in its low palings, for though all exterior evidence bore witness to its emptiness, some inexplicable feeling assured me, quite irrationally, that this was not so, and that there was somebody there. Certainly there was nobody visible, but, so this absurd idea informed me, he might be at the back of the cottage concealed from me by the intervening structure, and, still oddly, still unreasonably, it became a matter of importance to my mind to ascertain whether this was so or not, so clearly had my perceptions told me that the place was empty, and so firmly had some conviction assured me that it was tenanted. To cover my inquisitiveness, in case there was someone there, I could inquire whether this path was a short cut to the house at which I was staying, and, rather rebelling at what I was doing, I went through the small garden, and rapped at the door. There was no answer, and, after waiting for a response to a second summons, and having tried the door and found it locked, I made the circuit of the house. Of course there was no one there, and I told myself that I was just like a man who looks under his bed for a burglar and would be beyond measure astonished if he found one.

My hosts were at the house when I arrived, and we spent a cheerful two hours before dinner in such desultory and eager conversation as is proper between friends who have not met for some time. Between Hugh Grainger and his wife it is always impossible to light on a subject which does not vividly interest one or other of them, and golf, politics, the needs of Russia, cooking, ghosts, the possible victory over Mount Everest, and the income tax were among the topics which we passionately discussed. With all these plates spinning, it was easy to whip up any one of them, and the subject of spooks generally was lighted upon again and again.

"Margaret is on the high road to madness," remarked Hugh on one of these occasions, "for she has begun using planchette. If you use planchette for six months, I am told, most careful doctors will conscientiously certify you as insane. She's got five months more before she goes to Bedlam."

"Does it work?" I asked.

"Yes, it says most interesting things," said Margaret. "It says things that never entered my head. We'll try it to-night."

"Oh, not to-night," said Hugh. "Let's have an evening off."

Margaret disregarded this.

"It's no use asking planchette questions," she went on, "because there is in your mind some sort of answer to them. If I ask whether it will be fine to-morrow, for instance, it is probably I— though indeed I don't mean to push—who makes the pencil say 'yes.'"

"And then it usually rains," remarked Hugh.

"Not always: don't interrupt. The interesting thing is to let the pencil write what it chooses. Very often it only makes loops and curves—though they may mean something—and every now and then a word comes, of the significance of which I have no idea whatever, so I clearly couldn't have suggested it. Yesterday evening, for instance, it wrote 'gardener' over and over again. Now what did that mean? The gardener here is a Methodist with a chin-beard. Could it have meant him? Oh, it's time to dress. Please don't be late, my cook is so sensitive about soup."

We rose, and some connection of ideas about "gardener" linked itself up in my mind.

"By the way, what's that cottage in the field by the foot-bridge?" I asked. "Is that the gardener's cottage?"

"It used to be," said Hugh. "But the chin-beard doesn't live there: in fact nobody lives there. It's empty. If I was owner here, I should put the chin-beard into it, and take the rent off his wages. Some people have no idea of economy. Why did you ask?"

I saw Margaret was looking at me rather attentively.

"Curiosity," I said. "Idle curiosity."

"I don't believe it was," said she.

"But it was," I said. "It was idle curiosity to know whether the house was inhabited. As I passed it, going down to the club-house, I felt sure it was empty, but coming back I felt so sure that there was someone there that I rapped at the door, and indeed walked round it."

Hugh had preceded us upstairs, as she lingered a little.

"And there was no one there?" she asked. "It's odd: I had just the same feeling as you about it."

"That explains planchette writing 'gardener' over and over again," said I. "You had the gardener's cottage on your mind."

"How ingenious!" said Margaret. "Hurry up and dress."

A gleam of strong moonlight between my drawn curtains when I went up to bed that night led me to look out. My room faced the garden and the fields which I had traversed that afternoon, and all was vividly illuminated by the full moon. The thatched cottage with its white walls close by the stream was very distinct, and once more, I suppose, the reflection of the light on the glass of one of its windows made it appear that the room was lit within. It struck me as odd that twice that day this illusion should have been presented to me, but now a yet odder thing happened. Even as I looked the light was extinguished.

The morning did not at all bear out the fine promise of the clear night, for when I woke the wind was squealing, and sheets of rain from the south-west were dashed against my panes. Golf was wholly out of the question, and, though the violence of the storm abated a little in the afternoon, the rain dripped with a steady sullenness. But I wearied of indoors, and, since the two others entirely refused to set foot outside, I went forth mackintoshed to get a breath of air. By way of an object in my tramp, I took the road to the links in preference to the muddy short cut through the fields, with the intention of engaging a couple of caddies for Hugh and myself next morning, and lingered awhile over illustrated papers in the smoking-room. I must have read for longer than I knew, for a sudden beam of sunset light suddenly illuminated my page, and looking up, I saw that the rain had ceased, and that evening was fast coming on. So instead of taking the long detour by the road again, I set forth homewards by the path across the fields. That gleam of sunset was the last of the day, and once again, just as twenty-four hours ago, I crossed the foot-bridge in the gloaming. Till that moment, as far as I was aware, I had not thought at all about the cottage there, but now in a flash the light I had seen there last night, suddenly extinguished, recalled itself to my mind, and at the same moment I felt that invincible conviction that the cottage was tenanted. Simultaneously in these swift processes of thought I looked towards it, and saw standing by the door the figure of a man.

In the dusk I could distinguish nothing of his face, if indeed it was turned to me, and only got the impression of a tallish fellow, thickly built. He opened the door, from which there came a dim light as of a lamp, entered, and shut it after him.

So then my conviction was right. Yet I had been distinctly told that the cottage was empty: who, then, was he that entered as if returning home? Once more, this time with a certain qualm of fear, I rapped on the door, intending to put some trivial question; and rapped again, this time more drastically, so that there could be no question that my summons was unheard. But still I got no reply, and finally I tried the handle of the door. It was locked. Then, with difficulty mastering an increasing terror, I made the circuit of the cottage, peering into each unshuttered window. All was dark within, though but two minutes ago I had seen the gleam of light escape from the opened door.

Just because some chain of conjecture was beginning to form itself in my mind, I made no allusion to this odd adventure, and after dinner Margaret, amid protests from Hugh, got out the planchette which had persisted in writing "gardener." My surmise was, of course, utterly fantastic, but I wanted to convey no suggestion of any sort to Margaret.... For a long time the pencil skated over her paper making loops and curves and peaks like a temperature chart, and she had begun to yawn and weary over her experiment before any coherent word emerged. And then, in the oddest way, her head nodded forward and she seemed to have fallen asleep.

Hugh looked up from his book and spoke in a whisper to me.

"She fell asleep the other night over it," he said.

Margaret's eyes were closed, and she breathed the long, quiet breaths of slumber, and then her hand began to move with a curious firmness. Right across the big sheet of paper went a level line of writing, and at the end her hand stopped with a jerk, and she woke.

She looked at the paper.

"Hullo," she said. "Ah, one of you has been playing a trick on me!"

We assured her that this was not so, and she read what she had written.

"Gardener, gardener," it ran. "I am the gardener. I want to come in. I can't find her here."

"O Lord, that gardener again!" said Hugh.

Looking up from the paper, I saw Margaret's eyes fixed on mine, and even before she spoke I knew what her thought was.

"Did you come home by the empty cottage?" she asked.

"Yes: why?"

"Still empty?" she said in a low voice. "Or—or anything else?"

I did not want to tell her just what I had seen—or what, at any rate, I thought I had seen. If there was going to be anything odd, anything worth observation, it was far better that our respective impressions should not fortify each other.

"I tapped again, and there was no answer," I said.

Presently there was a move to bed: Margaret initiated it, and after she had gone upstairs Hugh and I went to the front door to interrogate the weather. Once more the moon shone in a clear sky, and we strolled out along the flagged path that fronted the house. Suddenly Hugh turned quickly and pointed to the angle of the house.

"Who on earth is that?" he said. "Look! There! He has gone round the corner."

I had but the glimpse of a tallish man of heavy build.

"Didn't you see him?" asked Hugh. "I'll just go round the house, and find him; I don't want anyone prowling round us at night. Wait here, will you, and if he comes round the other corner ask him what his business is."

Hugh had left me, in our stroll, close by the front door which was open, and there I waited until he should have made his circuit. He had hardly disappeared when I heard, quite distinctly, a rather quick but heavy footfall coming along the paved walk towards me from the opposite direction. But there was absolutely no one to be seen who made this sound of rapid walking. Closer and closer to me came the steps of the invisible one, and then with a shudder of horror I felt somebody unseen push by me as I stood on the threshold. That shudder was not merely of the spirit, for the touch of him was that of ice on my hand. I tried to seize this impalpable intruder, but he slipped from me, and next moment I heard his steps on the parquet of the floor inside. Some door within opened and shut, and I heard no more of him. Next moment Hugh came running round the corner of the house from which the sound of steps had approached.

"But where is he?" he asked. "He was not twenty yards in front of me—a big, tall fellow."

"I saw nobody," I said. "I heard his step along the walk, but there was nothing to be seen."

"And then?" asked Hugh.

"Whatever it was seemed to brush by me, and go into the house," said I.

There had certainly been no sound of steps on the bare oak

stairs, and we searched room after room through the ground floor of the house. The dining-room door and that of the smoking-room were locked, that into the drawing-room was open, and the only other door which could have furnished the impression of an opening and a shutting was that into the kitchen and servants' quarters. Here again our quest was fruitless; through pantry and scullery and boot-room and servants' hall we searched, but all was empty and quiet. Finally we came to the kitchen, which too was empty. But by the fire there was set a rocking-chair, and this was oscillating to and fro as if someone, lately sitting there, had just quitted it. There it stood gently rocking, and this seemed to convey the sense of a presence, invisible now, more than even the sight of him who surely had been sitting there could have done. I remember wanting to steady it and stop it, and yet my hand refused to go forth to it.

What we had seen, and in especial what we had not seen, would have been sufficient to furnish most people with a broken night, and assuredly I was not among the strong-minded exceptions. Long I lay wide-eyed and open-eared, and when at last I dozed I was plucked from the borderland of sleep by the sound, muffled but unmistakable, of someone moving about the house. It occurred to me that the steps might be those of Hugh conducting a lonely exploration, but even while I wondered a tap came at the door of communication between our rooms, and, in answer to my response, it appeared that he had come to see whether it was I thus uneasily wandering. Even as we spoke the step passed my door, and the stairs leading to the floor above creaked to its ascent. Next moment it sounded directly above our heads in some attics in the roof.

"Those are not the servants' bedrooms," said Hugh. "No one sleeps there. Let us look once more: it must be somebody."

With lit candles we made our stealthy way upstairs, and just when we were at the top of the flight, Hugh, a step ahead of me, uttered a sharp exclamation.

"But something is passing by me!" he said, and he clutched at the empty air. Even as he spoke, I experienced the same sensation, and the moment afterwards the stairs below us creaked again, as the unseen passed down.

All night long that sound of steps moved about the passages, as if someone was searching the house, and as I lay and listened that message which had come through the pencil of the planchette to Margaret's fingers occurred to me. "I want to come in. I cannot find her here."... Indeed someone had come in, and was sedulous in his

102

search. He was the gardener, it would seem. But what gardener was this invisible seeker, and for whom did he seek?

Even as when some bodily pain ceases it is difficult to recall with any vividness what the pain was like, so next morning, as I dressed, I found myself vainly trying to recapture the horror of the spirit which had accompanied these nocturnal adventures. I remembered that something within me had sickened as I watched the movements of the rocking-chair the night before and as I heard the steps along the paved way outside, and by that invisible pressure against me knew that someone had entered the house. But now in the sane and tranquil morning, and all day under the serene winter sun, I could not realise what it had been. The presence, like the bodily pain, had to be there for the realisation of it, and all day it was absent. Hugh felt the same; he was even disposed to be humorous on the subject.

"Well, he's had a good look," he said, "whoever he is, and whomever he was looking for. By the way, not a word to Margaret, please. She heard nothing of these perambulations, nor of the entry of—of whatever it was. Not gardener, anyhow: who ever heard of a gardener spending his time walking about the house? If there were steps all over the potato-patch, I might have been with you."

Margaret had arranged to drive over to have tea with some friends of hers that afternoon, and in consequence Hugh and I refreshed ourselves at the club-house after our game, and it was already dusk when for the third day in succession I passed homewards by the whitewashed cottage. But to-night I had no sense of it being subtly occupied; it stood mournfully desolate, as is the way of untenanted houses, and no light nor semblance of such gleamed from its windows. Hugh, to whom I had told the odd impressions I had received there, gave them a reception as flippant as that which he had accorded to the memories of the night, and he was still being humorous about them when we came to the door of the house.

"A psychic disturbance, old boy," he said. "Like a cold in the head. Hullo, the door's locked."

He rang and rapped, and from inside came the noise of a turned key and withdrawn bolts.

"What's the door locked for?" he asked his servant who opened it.

The man shifted from one foot to the other.

"The bell rang half an hour ago, sir," he said, "and when I came to answer it there was a man standing outside, and——"

"Well?" asked Hugh.

"I didn't like the looks of him, sir," he said, "and I asked him his business. He didn't say anything, and then he must have gone pretty smartly away, for I never saw him go."

"Where did he seem to go?" asked Hugh, glancing at me.

"I can't rightly say, sir. He didn't seem to go at all. Something seemed to brush by me."

"That'll do," said Hugh rather sharply.

Margaret had not come in from her visit, but when soon after the crunch of the motor wheels was heard Hugh reiterated his wish that nothing should be said to her about the impression which now, apparently, a third person shared with us. She came in with a flush of excitement on her face.

"Never laugh at my planchette again," she said. "I've heard the most extraordinary story from Maud Ashfield—horrible, but so frightfully interesting."

"Out with it," said Hugh.

"Well, there was a gardener here," she said. "He used to live at that little cottage by the foot-bridge, and when the family were up in London he and his wife used to be caretakers and live here."

Hugh's glance and mine met: then he turned away. I knew, as certainly as if I was in his mind, that his thoughts were identical with my own.

"He married a wife much younger than himself," continued Margaret, "and gradually he became frightfully jealous of her. And one day in a fit of passion he strangled her with his own hands. A little while after someone came to the cottage, and found him sobbing over her, trying to restore her. They went for the police, but before they came he had cut his own throat. Isn't it all horrible? But surely it's rather curious that the planchette said Gardener. 'I am the gardener. I want to come in. I can't find her here.' You see I knew nothing about it. I shall do planchette again to-night. Oh dear me, the post goes in half an hour, and I have a whole budget to send. But respect my planchette for the future, Hughie."

We talked the situation out when she had gone, but Hugh, unwillingly convinced and yet unwilling to admit that something more than coincidence lay behind that "planchette nonsense," still insisted that Margaret should be told nothing of what we had heard and seen in the house last night, and of the strange visitor who again this evening, so we must conclude, had made his entry.

"She'll be frightened," he said, "and she'll begin imagining things. As for the planchette, as likely as not it will do nothing but scribble and make loops. What's that? Yes: come in!"

There had come from somewhere in the room one sharp,

peremptory rap. I did not think it came from the door, but Hugh, when no response replied to his words of admittance, jumped up and opened it. He took a few steps into the hall outside, and returned.

"Didn't you hear it?" he asked.

"Certainly. No one there?"

"Not a soul."

Hugh came back to the fireplace and rather irritably threw a cigarette which he had just lit into the fender.

"That was rather a nasty jar," he observed; "and if you ask me whether I feel comfortable, I can tell you I never felt less comfortable in my life. I'm frightened, if you want to know, and I believe you are too."

I hadn't the smallest intention of denying this, and he went on.

"We've got to keep a hand on ourselves," he said. "There's nothing so infectious as fear, and Margaret mustn't catch it from us. But there's something more than our fear, you know. Something has got into the house and we're up against it. I never believed in such things before. Let's face it for a minute. What is it anyhow?"

"If you want to know what I think it is," said I, "I believe it to be the spirit of the man who strangled his wife and then cut his throat. But I don't see how it can hurt us. We're afraid of our own fear really."

"But we're up against it," said Hugh. "And what will it do? Good Lord, if I only knew what it would do I shouldn't mind. It's the not knowing.... Well, it's time to dress."

Margaret was in her highest spirits at dinner. Knowing nothing of the manifestations of that presence which had taken place in the last twenty-four hours, she thought it absorbingly interesting that her planchette should have "guessed" (so ran her phrase) about the gardener, and from that topic she flitted to an equally interesting form of patience for three which her friend had showed her, promising to initiate us into it after dinner. This she did, and, not knowing that we both above all things wanted to keep planchette at a distance, she was delighted with the success of her game. But suddenly she observed that the evening was burning rapidly away, and swept the cards together at the conclusion of a hand.

"Now just half an hour of planchette," she said.

"Oh, mayn't we play one more hand?" asked Hugh. "It's the best game I've seen for years. Planchette will be dismally slow after this."

"Darling, if the gardener will only communicate again, it won't be slow," said she.

"But it is such drivel," said Hugh.

"How rude you are! Read your book, then."

Margaret had already got out her machine and a sheet of paper, when Hugh rose.

"Please don't do it to-night, Margaret," he said.

"But why? You needn't attend."

"Well, I ask you not to, anyhow," said he.

Margaret looked at him closely.

"Hughie, you've got something on your mind," she said. "Out with it. I believe you're nervous. You think there is something queer about. What is it?"

I could see Hugh hesitating as to whether to tell her or not, and I gathered that he chose the chance of her planchette inanely scribbling.

"Go on, then," he said.

Margaret hesitated: she clearly did not want to vex Hugh, but his insistence must have seemed to her most unreasonable.

"Well, just ten minutes," she said, "and I promise not to think of gardeners."

She had hardly laid her hand on the board when her head fell forward, and the machine began moving. I was sitting close to her, and as it rolled steadily along the paper the writing became visible.

"I have come in," it ran, "but still I can't find her. Are you hiding her? I will search the room where you are."

What else was written but still concealed underneath the planchette I did not know, for at that moment a current of icy air swept round the room, and at the door, this time unmistakably, came a loud, peremptory knock. Hugh sprang to his feet.

"Margaret, wake up," he said, "something is coming!"

The door opened, and there moved in the figure of a man. He stood just within the door, his head bent forward, and he turned it from side to side, peering, it would seem, with eyes staring and infinitely sad, into every corner of the room.

"Margaret, Margaret," cried Hugh again.

But Margaret's eyes were open too; they were fixed on this dreadful visitor.

"Be quiet, Hughie," she said below her breath, rising as she spoke. The ghost was now looking directly at her. Once the lips above the thick, rust-coloured beard moved, but no sound came forth, the mouth only moved and slavered. He raised his head, and, horror upon horror, I saw that one side of his neck was laid open in a red, glistening gash....

For how long that pause continued, when we all three stood stiff and frozen in some deadly inhibition to move or speak, I have no idea: I suppose that at the utmost it was a dozen seconds. Then the spectre turned, and went out as it had come. We heard his steps pass along the parqueted floor; there was the sound of bolts withdrawn from the front door, and with a crash that shook the house it slammed to.

"It's all over," said Margaret. "God have mercy on him!"

Now the reader may put precisely what construction he pleases on this visitation from the dead. He need not, indeed, consider it to have been a visitation from the dead at all, but say that there had been impressed on the scene, where this murder and suicide happened, some sort of emotional record, which in certain circumstances could translate itself into images visible and invisible. Waves of ether, or what not, may conceivably retain the impress of such scenes; they may be held, so to speak, in solution, ready to be precipitated. Or he may hold that the spirit of the dead man indeed made itself manifest, revisiting in some sort of spiritual penance and remorse the place where his crime was committed. Naturally, no materialist will entertain such an explanation for an instant, but then there is no one so obstinately unreasonable as the materialist. Beyond doubt a dreadful deed was done there, and Margaret's last utterance is not inapplicable.

# Mr. Tilly's Séance

Mr. Tilly had only the briefest moment for reflection, when, as he slipped and fell on the greasy wood pavement at Hyde Park Corner, which he was crossing at a smart trot, he saw the huge traction-engine with its grooved ponderous wheels towering high above him.

"Oh, dear! oh, dear!" he said petulantly, "it will certainly crush me quite flat, and I shan't be able to be at Mrs. Cumberbatch's séance! Most provoking! A-ow!"

The words were hardly out of his mouth, when the first half of his horrid anticipations was thoroughly fulfilled. The heavy wheels passed over him from head to foot and flattened him completely out. Then the driver (too late) reversed his engine and passed over him again, and finally lost his head, whistled loudly and stopped. The policeman on duty at the corner turned quite faint at the sight of the catastrophe, but presently recovered sufficiently to hold up the traffic, and ran to see what on earth could be done. It was all so much "up" with Mr. Tilly that the only thing possible was to get the hysterical engine-driver to move clear. Then the ambulance from the hospital was sent for, and Mr. Tilly's remains, detached with great difficulty from the road (so firmly had they been pressed into it), were reverently carried away into the mortuary....

Mr. Tilly during this had experienced one moment's excruciating pain, resembling the severest neuralgia as his head was ground beneath the wheel, but almost before he realised it, the pain was past, and he found himself, still rather dazed, floating or standing (he did not know which) in the middle of the road. There had been no break in his consciousness; he perfectly recollected slipping, and wondered how he had managed to save himself. He saw the arrested traffic, the policeman with white wan face making suggestions to the gibbering engine-driver, and he received the very puzzling impression that the traction engine was all mixed up with him. He had a sensation of red-hot coals and boiling water and rivets all around him, but yet no feeling of scalding or burning or confinement. He was, on the contrary, extremely comfortable, and had the most pleasant consciousness of buoyancy and freedom. Then the engine puffed and the wheels went round, and immediately, to his immense surprise, he perceived his own crushed remains, flat as a biscuit, lying on the roadway. He identified them for certain by his clothes, which he had put on for the first time that morning, and one patent leather boot which had escaped demolition.

"But what on earth has happened?" he said. "Here am I, and yet that poor pressed flower of arms and legs is me—or rather I— also. And how terribly upset the driver looks. Why, I do believe that I've been run over! It did hurt for a moment, now I come to think of it.... My good man, where are you shoving to? Don't you see me?"

He addressed these two questions to the policeman, who appeared to walk right through him. But the man took no notice, and calmly came out on the other side: it was quite evident that he did not see him, or apprehend him in any way.

Mr. Tilly was still feeling rather at sea amid these unusual occurrences, and there began to steal into his mind a glimpse of the fact which was so obvious to the crowd which formed an interested but respectful ring round his body. Men stood with bared heads; women screamed and looked away and looked back again.

"I really believe I'm dead," said he. "That's the only hypothesis which will cover the facts. But I must feel more certain of it before I do anything. Ah! Here they come with the ambulance to look at me. I must be terribly hurt, and yet I don't feel hurt. I should feel hurt surely if I was hurt. I must be dead."

Certainly it seemed the only thing for him to be, but he was far from realising it yet. A lane had been made through the crowd for the stretcher-bearers, and he found himself wincing when they began to detach him from the road.

"Oh, do take care!" he said. "That's the sciatic nerve protruding there surely, isn't it? A-ow! No, it didn't hurt after all. My new clothes, too: I put them on to-day for the first time. What bad luck! Now you're holding my leg upside down. Of course all my money comes out of my trouser pocket. And there's my ticket for the séance; I must have that: I may use it after all."

He tweaked it out of the fingers of the man who had picked it up, and laughed to see the expression of amazement on his face as the card suddenly vanished. That gave him something fresh to think about, and he pondered for a moment over some touch of association set up by it.

"I have it," he thought. "It is clear that the moment I came into connection with that card, it became invisible. I'm invisible myself (of course to the grosser sense), and everything I hold becomes invisible. Most interesting! That accounts for the sudden appearances of small objects at a séance. The spirit has been holding them, and as long as he holds them they are invisible. Then he lets go, and there's the flower or the spirit-photograph on the

109

table. It accounts, too, for the sudden disappearances of such objects. The spirit has taken them, though the scoffers say that the medium has secreted them about his person. It is true that when searched he sometimes appears to have done so; but, after all, that may be a joke on the part of the spirit. Now, what am I to do with myself.... Let me see, there's the clock. It's just half-past ten. All this has happened in a few minutes, for it was a quarter past when I left my house. Half-past ten now: what does that mean exactly? I used to know what it meant, but now it seems nonsense. Ten what? Hours, is it? What's an hour?"

This was very puzzling. He felt that he used to know what an hour and a minute meant, but the perception of that, naturally enough, had ceased with his emergence from time and space into eternity. The conception of time was like some memory which, refusing to record itself on the consciousness, lies perdu in some dark corner of the brain, laughing at the efforts of the owner to ferret it out. While he still interrogated his mind over this lapsed perception, he found that space as well as time, had similarly grown obsolete for him, for he caught sight of his friend Miss Ida Soulsby, whom he knew was to be present at the séance for which he was bound, hurrying with bird-like steps down the pavement opposite. Forgetting for the moment that he was a disembodied spirit, he made the effort of will which in his past human existence would have set his legs in pursuit of her, and found that the effort of will alone was enough to place him at her side.

"My dear Miss Soulsby," he said, "I was on my way to Mrs. Cumberbatch's house when I was knocked down and killed. It was far from unpleasant, a moment's headache——"

So far his natural volubility had carried him before he recollected that he was invisible and inaudible to those still closed in by the muddy vesture of decay, and stopped short. But though it was clear that what he said was inaudible to Miss Soulsby's rather large intelligent-looking ears, it seemed that some consciousness of his presence was conveyed to her finer sense, for she looked suddenly startled, a flush rose to her face, and he heard her murmur, "Very odd. I wonder why I received so vivid an impression of dear Teddy."

That gave Mr. Tilly a pleasant shock. He had long admired the lady, and here she was alluding to him in her supposed privacy as "dear Teddy." That was followed by a momentary regret that he had been killed: he would have liked to have been possessed of this information before, and have pursued the primrose path of dalliance down which it seemed to lead. (His intentions, of course, would, as always, have been strictly honourable: the path of dalliance would have conducted them both, if she consented, to the altar, where the primroses would have been exchanged for orange blossom.) But his regret was quite short-lived; though the altar seemed inaccessible, the primrose path might still be open, for many of the spiritualistic circle in which he lived were on most affectionate terms with their spiritual guides and friends who, like himself, had passed over. From a human point of view these innocent and even elevating flirtations had always seemed to him rather bloodless; but now, looking on them from the far side, he saw how charming they were, for they gave him the sense of still having a place and an identity in the world he had just quitted. He pressed Miss Ida's hand (or rather put himself into the spiritual condition of so doing), and could vaguely feel that it had some hint of warmth and solidity about it. This was gratifying, for it showed that though he had passed out of the material plane, he could still be in touch with it. Still more gratifying was it to observe that a pleased and secret smile overspread Miss Ida's fine features as he gave this token of his presence: perhaps she only smiled at her own thoughts, but in any case it was he who had inspired them. Encouraged by this, he indulged in a slightly more intimate token of affection, and permitted himself a respectful salute, and saw that he had gone too far, for she said to herself, "Hush, hush!" and quickened her pace, as if to leave these amorous thoughts behind.

He felt that he was beginning to adjust himself to the new conditions in which he would now live, or, at any rate, was getting some sort of inkling as to what they were. Time existed no more for him, nor yet did space, since the wish to be at Miss Ida's side had instantly transported him there, and with a view to testing this further he wished himself back in his flat. As swiftly as the change of scene in a cinematograph show he found himself there, and perceived that the news of his death must have reached his servants, for his cook and parlour-maid with excited faces, were talking over the event.

"Poor little gentleman," said his cook. "It seems a shame it does. He never hurt a fly, and to think of one of those great engines laying him out flat. I hope they'll take him to the cemetery from the hospital: I never could bear a corpse in the house."

The great strapping parlour-maid tossed her head.

"Well, I'm not sure that it doesn't serve him right," she observed. "Always messing about with spirits he was, and the knockings and concertinas was awful sometimes when I've been laying out supper in the dining-room. Now perhaps he'll come himself and visit the rest of the loonies. But I'm sorry all the same. A less troublesome little gentleman never stepped. Always pleasant, too, and wages paid to the day."

These regretful comments and encomiums were something of a shock to Mr. Tilly. He had imagined that his excellent servants regarded him with a respectful affection, as befitted some sort of demigod, and the rôle of the poor little gentleman was not at all to his mind. This revelation of their true estimate of him, although what they thought of him could no longer have the smallest significance, irritated him profoundly.

"I never heard such impertinence," he said (so he thought) quite out loud, and still intensely earth-bound, was astonished to see that they had no perception whatever of his presence. He raised his voice, replete with extreme irony, and addressed his cook.

"You may reserve your criticism on my character for your saucepans," he said. "They will no doubt appreciate them. As regards the arrangements for my funeral, I have already provided for them in my will, and do not propose to consult your convenience. At present——"

"Lor'!" said Mrs. Inglis, "I declare I can almost hear his voice, poor little fellow. Husky it was, as if he would do better by clearing his throat. I suppose I'd best be making a black bow to my cap. His lawyers and what not will be here presently."

Mr. Tilly had no sympathy with this suggestion. He was immensely conscious of being quite alive, and the idea of his servants behaving as if he were dead, especially after the way in which they had spoken about him, was very vexing. He wanted to give them some striking evidence of his presence and his activity, and he banged his hand angrily on the dining-room table, from which the breakfast equipage had not yet been cleared. Three tremendous blows he gave it, and was rejoiced to see that his parlour-maid looked startled. Mrs. Inglis's face remained perfectly placid.

"Why, if I didn't hear a sort of rapping sound," said Miss Talton. "Where did it come from?"

"Nonsense! You've the jumps, dear," said Mrs. Inglis, picking up a remaining rasher of bacon on a fork, and putting it into her capacious mouth.

Mr. Tilly was delighted at making any impression at all on either of these impercipient females.

"Talton!" he called at the top of his voice.

"Why, what's that?" said Talton. "Almost hear his voice, do you say, Mrs. Inglis? I declare I did hear his voice then."

"A pack o' nonsense, dear," said Mrs. Inglis placidly. "That's a prime bit of bacon, and there's a good cut of it left. Why, you're all of a tremble! It's your imagination."

Suddenly it struck Mr. Tilly that he might be employing himself much better than, with such extreme exertion, managing to convey so slight a hint of his presence to his parlour-maid, and that the séance at the house of the medium, Mrs. Cumberbatch, would afford him much easier opportunities of getting through to the earth-plane again. He gave a couple more thumps to the table and, wishing himself at Mrs. Cumberbatch's, nearly a mile away, scarcely heard the faint scream of Talton at the sound of his blows before he found himself in West Norfolk Street.

He knew the house well, and went straight to the drawing-room, which was the scene of the séances he had so often and so eagerly attended. Mrs. Cumberbatch, who had a long spoon-shaped face, had already pulled down the blinds, leaving the room in total darkness except for the glimmer of the night-light which, under a shade of ruby-glass, stood on the chimney-piece in front of the coloured photograph of Cardinal Newman. Round the table were seated Miss Ida Soulsby, Mr. and Mrs. Meriott (who paid their guineas at least twice a week in order to consult their spiritual guide Abibel and received mysterious advice about their indigestion and investments), and Sir John Plaice, who was much interested in learning the details of his previous incarnation as a Chaldean priest, completed the circle. His guide, who revealed to him his sacerdotal career, was playfully called Mespot. Naturally many other spirits visited them, for Miss Soulsby had no less than three guides in her spiritual household, Sapphire, Semiramis, and Sweet William, while Napoleon and Plato were not infrequent guests. Cardinal Newman, too, was a great favourite, and they encouraged his presence by the singing in unison of "Lead, kindly Light": he could hardly ever resist that....

Mr. Tilly observed with pleasure that there was a vacant seat by the table which no doubt had been placed there for him. As he entered, Mrs. Cumberbatch peered at her watch.

"Eleven o'clock already," she said, "and Mr. Tilly is not here yet. I wonder what can have kept him. What shall we do, dear friends? Abibel gets very impatient sometimes if we keep him waiting."

Mr. and Mrs. Meriott were getting impatient too, for he terribly wanted to ask about Mexican oils, and she had a very vexing heartburn.

"And Mespot doesn't like waiting either," said Sir John,

jealous for the prestige of his protector, "not to mention Sweet William."

Miss Soulsby gave a little silvery laugh.

"Oh, but my Sweet William's so good and kind," she said; "besides, I have a feeling, quite a psychic feeling, Mrs. Cumberbatch, that Mr. Tilly is very close."

"So I am," said Mr. Tilly.

"Indeed, as I walked here," continued Miss Soulsby, "I felt that Mr. Tilly was somewhere quite close to me. Dear me, what's that?"

Mr. Tilly was so delighted at being sensed, that he could not resist giving a tremendous rap on the table, in a sort of pleased applause. Mrs. Cumberbatch heard it too.

"I'm sure that's Abibel come to tell us that he is ready," she said. "I know Abibel's knock. A little patience, Abibel. Let's give Mr. Tilly three minutes more and then begin. Perhaps, if we put up the blinds, Abibel will understand we haven't begun."

This was done, and Miss Soulsby glided to the window, in order to make known Mr. Tilly's approach, for he always came along the opposite pavement and crossed over by the little island in the river of traffic. There was evidently some lately published news, for the readers of early editions were busy, and she caught sight of one of the advertisement-boards bearing in large letters the announcement of a terrible accident at Hyde Park Corner. She drew in her breath with a hissing sound and turned away, unwilling to have her psychic tranquillity upset by the intrusion of painful incidents. But Mr. Tilly, who had followed her to the window and saw what she had seen, could hardly restrain a spiritual whoop of exultation.

"Why, it's all about me!" he said. "Such large letters, too. Very gratifying. Subsequent editions will no doubt contain my name."

He gave another loud rap to call attention to himself, and Mrs. Cumberbatch, sitting down in her antique chair which had once belonged to Madame Blavatsky, again heard.

"Well, if that isn't Abibel again," she said. "Be quiet, naughty. Perhaps we had better begin."

She recited the usual invocation to guides and angels, and leaned back in her chair. Presently she began to twitch and mutter, and shortly afterwards with several loud snorts, relapsed into cataleptic immobility. There she lay, stiff as a poker, a port of call, so to speak, for any voyaging intelligence. With pleased anticipation Mr. Tilly awaited their coming. How gratifying if Napoleon, with whom he had so often talked, recognised him and said, "Pleased to see you, Mr. Tilly. I perceive you have joined us...." The room was dark except for the ruby-shaded lamp in front of Cardinal Newman, but to Mr. Tilly's emancipated perceptions the withdrawal of mere material light made no difference, and he idly wondered why it was generally supposed that disembodied spirits like himself produced their most powerful effects in the dark. He could not imagine the reason for that, and, what puzzled him still more, there was not to his spiritual perception any sign of those colleagues of his (for so he might now call them) who usually attended Mrs. Cumberbatch's séances in such gratifying numbers. Though she had been moaning and muttering a long time now, Mr. Tilly was in no way conscious of the presence of Abibel and Sweet William and Sapphire and Napoleon. "They ought to be here by now," he said to himself.

But while he still wondered at their absence, he saw to his amazed disgust that the medium's hand, now covered with a black glove, and thus invisible to ordinary human vision in the darkness, was groping about the table and clearly searching for the megaphone-trumpet which lay there. He found that he could read her mind with the same ease, though far less satisfaction, as he had read Miss Ida's half an hour ago, and knew that she was intending to apply the trumpet to her own mouth and pretend to be Abibel or Semiramis or somebody, whereas she affirmed that she never touched the trumpet herself. Much shocked at this, he snatched up the trumpet himself, and observed that she was not in trance at all, for she opened her sharp black eyes, which always reminded him of buttons covered with American cloth, and gave a great gasp.

"Why, Mr. Tilly!" she said. "On the spiritual plane too!"

The rest of the circle was now singing "Lead, kindly Light" in order to encourage Cardinal Newman, and this conversation was conducted under cover of the hoarse crooning voices. But Mr. Tilly had the feeling that though Mrs. Cumberbatch saw and heard him as clearly as he saw her, he was quite imperceptible to the others.

"Yes, I've been killed," he said, "and I want to get into touch with the material world. That's why I came here. But I want to get into touch with other spirits too, and surely Abibel or Mespot ought to be here by this time."

He received no answer, and her eyes fell before his like those of a detected charlatan. A terrible suspicion invaded his mind.

"What? Are you a fraud, Mrs. Cumberbatch?" he asked. "Oh, for shame! Think of all the guineas I have paid you."

"You shall have them all back," said Mrs. Cumberbatch. "But don't tell of me."

She began to whimper, and he remembered that she often

115

made that sort of sniffling noise when Abibel was taking possession of her.

"That usually means that Abibel is coming," he said, with withering sarcasm. "Come along, Abibel: we're waiting."

"Give me the trumpet," whispered the miserable medium. "Oh, please give me the trumpet!"

"I shall do nothing of the kind," said Mr. Tilly indignantly. "I would sooner use it myself."

She gave a sob of relief.

"Oh do, Mr. Tilly!" she said. "What a wonderful idea! It will be most interesting to everybody to hear you talk just after you've been killed and before they know. It would be the making of me! And I'm not a fraud, at least not altogether. I do have spiritual perceptions sometimes; spirits do communicate through me. And when they won't come through it's a dreadful temptation to a poor woman to— to supplement them by human agency. And how could I be seeing and hearing you now, and be able to talk to you—so pleasantly, I'm sure—if I hadn't super-normal powers? You've been killed, so you assure me, and yet I can see and hear you quite plainly. Where did it happen, may I ask, if it's not a painful subject?"

"Hyde Park Corner, half an hour ago," said Mr. Tilly. "No, it only hurt for a moment, thanks. But about your other suggestion—"

While the third verse of "Lead, kindly Light" was going on, Mr. Tilly applied his mind to this difficult situation. It was quite true that if Mrs. Cumberbatch had no power of communication with the unseen she could not possibly have seen him. But she evidently had, and had heard him too, for their conversation had certainly been conducted on the spirit-plane, with perfect lucidity. Naturally, now that he was a genuine spirit, he did not want to be mixed up in fraudulent mediumship, for he felt that such a thing would seriously compromise him on the other side, where, probably, it was widely known that Mrs. Cumberbatch was a person to be avoided. But, on the other hand, having so soon found a medium through whom he could communicate with his friends, it was hard to take a high moral view, and say that he would have nothing whatever to do with her.

"I don't know if I trust you," he said. "I shouldn't have a moment's peace if I thought that you would be sending all sorts of bogus messages from me to the circle, which I wasn't responsible for at all. You've done it with Abibel and Mespot. How can I know that when I don't choose to communicate through you, you won't make up all sorts of piffle on your own account?"

She positively squirmed in her chair.

116

"Oh, I'll turn over a new leaf," she said. "I will leave all that sort of thing behind me. And I am a medium. Look at me! Aren't I more real to you than any of the others? Don't I belong to your plane in a way that none of the others do? I may be occasionally fraudulent, and I can no more get Napoleon here than I can fly, but I'm genuine as well. Oh, Mr. Tilly, be indulgent to us poor human creatures! It isn't so long since you were one of us yourself."

The mention of Napoleon, with the information that Mrs. Cumberbatch had never been controlled by that great creature, wounded Mr. Tilly again. Often in this darkened room he had held long colloquies with him, and Napoleon had given him most interesting details of his life on St. Helena, which, so Mr. Tilly had found, were often borne out by Lord Rosebery's pleasant volume The Last Phase. But now the whole thing wore a more sinister aspect, and suspicion as solid as certainty bumped against his mind.

"Confess!" he said. "Where did you get all that Napoleon talk from? You told us you had never read Lord Rosebery's book, and allowed us to look through your library to see that it wasn't there. Be honest for once, Mrs. Cumberbatch."

She suppressed a sob.

"I will," she said. "The book was there all the time. I put it into an old cover called 'Elegant Extracts....' But I'm not wholly a fraud. We're talking together, you a spirit and I a mortal female. They can't hear us talk. But only look at me, and you'll see.... You can talk to them through me, if you'll only be so kind. I don't often get in touch with a genuine spirit like yourself."

Mr. Tilly glanced at the other sitters and then back to the medium, who, to keep the others interested, was making weird gurgling noises like an undervitalised siphon. Certainly she was far clearer to him than were the others, and her argument that she was able to see and hear him had great weight. And then a new and curious perception came to him. Her mind seemed spread out before him like a pool of slightly muddy water, and he figured himself as standing on a header-board above it, perfectly able, if he chose, to immerse himself in it. The objection to so doing was its muddiness, its materiality; the reason for so doing was that he felt that then he would be able to be heard by the others, possibly to be seen by them, certainly to come into touch with them. As it was, the loudest bangs on the table were only faintly perceptible.

"I'm beginning to understand," he said.

"Oh, Mr. Tilly! Just jump in like a kind good spirit," she said. "Make your own test-conditions. Put your hand over my mouth to make sure that I'm not speaking, and keep hold of the trumpet."

"And you'll promise not to cheat any more?" he asked.

"Never!"

He made up his mind.

"All right then," he said, and, so to speak, dived into her mind.

He experienced the oddest sensation. It was like passing out of some fine, sunny air into the stuffiest of unventilated rooms. Space and time closed over him again: his head swam, his eyes were heavy. Then, with the trumpet in one hand, he laid the other firmly over her mouth. Looking round, he saw that the room seemed almost completely dark, but that the outline of the figures sitting round the table had vastly gained in solidity.

"Here I am!" he said briskly.

Miss Soulsby gave a startled exclamation.

"That's Mr. Tilly's voice!" she whispered.

"Why, of course it is," said Mr. Tilly. "I've just passed over at Hyde Park Corner under a traction engine...."

He felt the dead weight of the medium's mind, her conventional conceptions, her mild, unreal piety pressing in on him from all sides, stifling and confusing him. Whatever he said had to pass through muddy water....

"There's a wonderful feeling of joy and lightness," he said. "I can't tell you of the sunshine and happiness. We're all very busy and active, helping others. And it's such a pleasure, dear friends, to be able to get into touch with you all again. Death is not death: it is the gate of life...."

He broke off suddenly.

"Oh, I can't stand this," he said to the medium. "You make me talk such twaddle. Do get your stupid mind out of the way. Can't we do anything in which you won't interfere with me so much?"

"Can you give us some spirit lights round the room?" suggested Mrs. Cumberbatch in a sleepy voice. "You have come through beautifully, Mr. Tilly. It's too dear of you!"

"You're sure you haven't arranged some phosphorescent patches already?" asked Mr. Tilly suspiciously.

"Yes, there are one or two near the chimney-piece," said Mrs. Cumberbatch, "but none anywhere else. Dear Mr. Tilly, I swear there are not. Just give us a nice star with long rays on the ceiling!"

Mr. Tilly was the most good-natured of men, always willing to help an unattractive female in distress, and whispering to her, "I shall require the phosphorescent patches to be given into my hands after the séance," he proceeded, by the mere effort of his imagination, to light a beautiful big star with red and violet rays on the ceiling. Of course it was not nearly as brilliant as his own

118

conception of it, for its light had to pass through the opacity of the medium's mind, but it was still a most striking object, and elicited gasps of applause from the company. To enhance the effect of it he intoned a few very pretty lines about a star by Adelaide Anne Procter, whose poems had always seemed to him to emanate from the topmost peak of Parnassus.

"Oh, thank you, Mr. Tilly!" whispered the medium. "It was lovely! Would a photograph of it be permitted on some future occasion, if you would be so kind as to reproduce it again?"

"Oh, I don't know," said Mr. Tilly irritably. "I want to get out. I'm very hot and uncomfortable. And it's all so cheap."

"Cheap?" ejaculated Mrs. Cumberbatch. "Why, there's not a medium in London whose future wouldn't be made by a real genuine star like that, say, twice a week."

"But I wasn't run over in order that I might make the fortune of mediums," said Mr. Tilly. "I want to go: it's all rather degrading. And I want to see something of my new world. I don't know what it's like yet."

"Oh, but, Mr. Tilly," said she. "You told us lovely things about it, how busy and happy you were."

"No, I didn't. It was you who said that, at least it was you who put it into my head."

Even as he wished, he found himself emerging from the dull waters of Mrs. Cumberbatch's mind.

"There's the whole new world waiting for me," he said. "I must go and see it. I'll come back and tell you, for it must be full of marvellous revelations...."

Suddenly he felt the hopelessness of it. There was that thick fluid of materiality to pierce, and, as it dripped off him again, he began to see that nothing of that fine rare quality of life which he had just begun to experience, could penetrate these opacities. That was why, perhaps, all that thus came across from the spirit-world, was so stupid, so banal. They, of whom he now was one, could tap on furniture, could light stars, could abound with commonplace, could read as in a book the mind of medium or sitters, but nothing more. They had to pass into the region of gross perceptions, in order to be seen of blind eyes and be heard of deaf ears.

Mrs. Cumberbatch stirred.

"The power is failing," she said, in a deep voice, which Mr. Tilly felt was meant to imitate his own. "I must leave you now, dear friends——"

He felt much exasperated.

"The power isn't failing," he shouted. "It wasn't I who said that."

But he had emerged too far, and perceived that nobody except the medium heard him.

"Oh, don't be vexed, Mr. Tilly," she said. "That's only a formula. But you're leaving us very soon. Not time for just one materialisation? They are more convincing than anything to most inquirers."

"Not one," said he. "You don't understand how stifling it is even to speak through you and make stars. But I'll come back as soon as I find there's anything new that I can get through to you. What's the use of my repeating all that stale stuff about being busy and happy? They've been told that often enough already. Besides, I have got to see if it's true. Good-bye: don't cheat any more."

He dropped his card of admittance to the séance on the table and heard murmurs of excitement as he floated off.

The news of the wonderful star, and the presence of Mr. Tilly at the séance within half an hour of his death, which at the time was unknown to any of the sitters, spread swiftly through spiritualistic circles. The Psychical Research Society sent investigators to take independent evidence from all those present, but were inclined to attribute the occurrence to a subtle mixture of thought-transference and unconscious visual impression, when they heard that Miss Soulsby had, a few minutes previously, seen a news-board in the street outside recording the accident at Hyde Park Corner. This explanation was rather elaborate, for it postulated that Miss Soulsby, thinking of Mr. Tilly's non-arrival, had combined that with the accident at Hyde Park Corner, and had probably (though unconsciously) seen the name of the victim on another news-board and had transferred the whole by telepathy to the mind of the medium. As for the star on the ceiling, though they could not account for it, they certainly found remains of phosphorescent paint on the panels of the wall above the chimney-piece, and came to the conclusion that the star had been produced by some similar contrivance. So they rejected the whole thing, which was a pity, since, for once, the phenomena were absolutely genuine.

Miss Soulsby continued to be a constant attendant at Mrs. Cumberbatch's séance, but never experienced the presence of Mr. Tilly again. On that the reader may put any interpretation he pleases. It looks to me somewhat as if he had found something else to do.

# Mrs. Amworth

The village of Maxley, where, last summer and autumn, these strange events took place, lies on a heathery and pine-clad upland of Sussex. In all England you could not find a sweeter and saner situation. Should the wind blow from the south, it comes laden with the spices of the sea; to the east high downs protect it from the inclemencies of March; and from the west and north the breezes which reach it travel over miles of aromatic forest and heather. The village itself is insignificant enough in point of population, but rich in amenities and beauty. Half-way down the single street, with its broad road and spacious areas of grass on each side, stands the little Norman Church and the antique graveyard long disused: for the rest there are a dozen small, sedate Georgian houses, red-bricked and long-windowed, each with a square of flower-garden in front, and an ampler strip behind; a score of shops, and a couple of score of thatched cottages belonging to labourers on neighbouring estates, complete the entire cluster of its peaceful habitations. The general peace, however, is sadly broken on Saturdays and Sundays, for we lie on one of the main roads between London and Brighton and our quiet street becomes a race-course for flying motor-cars and bicycles. A notice just outside the village begging them to go slowly only seems to encourage them to accelerate their speed, for the road lies open and straight, and there is really no reason why they should do otherwise. By way of protest, therefore, the ladies of Maxley cover their noses and mouths with their handkerchiefs as they see a motor-car approaching, though, as the street is asphalted, they need not really take these precautions against dust. But late on Sunday night the horde of scorchers has passed, and we settle down again to five days of cheerful and leisurely seclusion. Railway strikes which agitate the country so much leave us undisturbed because most of the inhabitants of Maxley never leave it at all.

I am the fortunate possessor of one of these small Georgian houses, and consider myself no less fortunate in having so interesting and stimulating a neighbour as Francis Urcombe, who, the most confirmed of Maxleyites, has not slept away from his house, which stands just opposite to mine in the village street, for nearly two years, at which date, though still in middle life, he resigned his Physiological Professorship at Cambridge University and devoted himself to the study of those occult and curious phenomena which seem equally to concern the physical and the psychical sides of human nature. Indeed his retirement was not unconnected with his passion for the strange uncharted places that lie on the confines and borders of science, the existence of which is so stoutly denied by the more materialistic minds, for he advocated that all medical students should be obliged to pass some sort of examination in mesmerism, and that one of the tripos papers should be designed to test their knowledge in such subjects as appearances at time of death, haunted houses, vampirism, automatic writing, and possession.

"Of course they wouldn't listen to me," ran his account of the matter, "for there is nothing that these seats of learning are so frightened of as knowledge, and the road to knowledge lies in the study of things like these. The functions of the human frame are, broadly speaking, known. They are a country, anyhow, that has been charted and mapped out. But outside that lie huge tracts of undiscovered country, which certainly exist, and the real pioneers of knowledge are those who, at the cost of being derided as credulous and superstitious, want to push on into those misty and probably perilous places. I felt that I could be of more use by setting out without compass or knapsack into the mists than by sitting in a cage like a canary and chirping about what was known. Besides, teaching is very bad for a man who knows himself only to be a learner: you only need to be a self-conceited ass to teach."

Here, then, in Francis Urcombe, was a delightful neighbour to one who, like myself, has an uneasy and burning curiosity about what he called the "misty and perilous places"; and this last spring we had a further and most welcome addition to our pleasant little community, in the person of Mrs. Amworth, widow of an Indian civil servant. Her husband had been a judge in the North-West Provinces, and after his death at Peshawar she came back to England, and after a year in London found herself starving for the ampler air and sunshine of the country to take the place of the fogs and griminess of town. She had, too, a special reason for settling in Maxley, since her ancestors up till a hundred years ago had long been native to the place, and in the old church-yard, now disused, are many grave-stones bearing her maiden name of Chaston. Big and energetic, her vigorous and genial personality speedily woke Maxley up to a higher degree of sociality than it had ever known. Most of us were bachelors or spinsters or elderly folk not much inclined to exert ourselves in the expense and effort of hospitality, and hitherto the gaiety of a small tea-party, with bridge afterwards and goloshes (when it was wet) to trip home in again for a solitary dinner, was about the climax of our festivities. But Mrs. Amworth

122

showed us a more gregarious way, and set an example of luncheon-parties and little dinners, which we began to follow. On other nights when no such hospitality was on foot, a lone man like myself found it pleasant to know that a call on the telephone to Mrs. Amworth's house not a hundred yards off, and an inquiry as to whether I might come over after dinner for a game of piquet before bed-time, would probably evoke a response of welcome. There she would be, with a comrade-like eagerness for companionship, and there was a glass of port and a cup of coffee and a cigarette and a game of piquet. She played the piano, too, in a free and exuberant manner, and had a charming voice and sang to her own accompaniment; and as the days grew long and the light lingered late, we played our game in her garden, which in the course of a few months she had turned from being a nursery for slugs and snails into a glowing patch of luxuriant blossoming. She was always cheery and jolly; she was interested in everything, and in music, in gardening, in games of all sorts was a competent performer. Everybody (with one exception) liked her, everybody felt her to bring with her the tonic of a sunny day. That one exception was Francis Urcombe; he, though he confessed he did not like her, acknowledged that he was vastly interested in her. This always seemed strange to me, for pleasant and jovial as she was, I could see nothing in her that could call forth conjecture or intrigued surmise, so healthy and unmysterious a figure did she present. But of the genuineness of Urcombe's interest there could be no doubt; one could see him watching and scrutinising her. In matter of age, she frankly volunteered the information that she was forty-five; but her briskness, her activity, her unravaged skin, her coal-black hair, made it difficult to believe that she was not adopting an unusual device, and adding ten years on to her age instead of subtracting them.

Often, also, as our quite unsentimental friendship ripened, Mrs. Amworth would ring me up and propose her advent. If I was busy writing, I was to give her, so we definitely bargained, a frank negative, and in answer I could hear her jolly laugh and her wishes for a successful evening of work. Sometimes, before her proposal arrived, Urcombe would already have stepped across from his house opposite for a smoke and a chat, and he, hearing who my intending visitor was, always urged me to beg her to come. She and I should play our piquet, said he, and he would look on, if we did not object, and learn something of the game. But I doubt whether he paid much attention to it, for nothing could be clearer than that, under that penthouse of forehead and thick eyebrows, his attention was fixed not on the cards, but on one of the players. But he seemed to enjoy an hour spent thus, and often, until one particular evening in July, he would watch her with the air of a man who has some deep problem in front of him. She, enthusiastically keen about our game, seemed not to notice his scrutiny. Then came that evening, when, as I see in the light of subsequent events, began the first twitching of the veil that hid the secret horror from my eyes. I did not know it then, though I noticed that thereafter, if she rang up to propose coming round, she always asked not only if I was at leisure, but whether Mr. Urcombe was with me. If so, she said, she would not spoil the chat of two old bachelors, and laughingly wished me good night.

Urcombe, on this occasion, had been with me for some half-hour before Mrs. Amworth's appearance, and had been talking to me about the mediæval beliefs concerning vampirism, one of those borderland subjects which he declared had not been sufficiently studied before it had been consigned by the medical profession to the dust-heap of exploded superstitions. There he sat, grim and eager, tracing, with that pellucid clearness which had made him in his Cambridge days so admirable a lecturer, the history of those mysterious visitations. In them all there were the same general features: one of those ghoulish spirits took up its abode in a living man or woman, conferring supernatural powers of bat-like flight and glutting itself with nocturnal blood-feasts. When its host died it continued to dwell in the corpse, which remained undecayed. By day it rested, by night it left the grave and went on its awful errands. No European country in the Middle Ages seemed to have escaped them; earlier yet, parallels were to be found, in Roman and Greek and in Jewish history.

"It's a large order to set all that evidence aside as being moonshine," he said. "Hundreds of totally independent witnesses in many ages have testified to the occurrence of these phenomena, and there's no explanation known to me which covers all the facts. And if you feel inclined to say 'Why, then, if these are facts, do we not come across them now?' there are two answers I can make you. One is that there were diseases known in the Middle Ages, such as the black death, which were certainly existent then and which have become extinct since, but for that reason we do not assert that such diseases never existed. Just as the black death visited England and decimated the population of Norfolk, so here in this very district about three hundred years ago there was certainly an outbreak of vampirism, and Maxley was the centre of it. My second answer is even more convincing, for I tell you that vampirism is by no means extinct now. An outbreak of it certainly occurred in India a year or two ago."

At that moment I heard my knocker plied in the cheerful and peremptory manner in which Mrs. Amworth is accustomed to announce her arrival, and I went to the door to open it.

"Come in at once," I said, "and save me from having my blood curdled. Mr. Urcombe has been trying to alarm me."

Instantly her vital, voluminous presence seemed to fill the room.

"Ah, but how lovely!" she said. "I delight in having my blood curdled. Go on with your ghost-story, Mr. Urcombe. I adore ghost-stories."

I saw that, as his habit was, he was intently observing her.

"It wasn't a ghost-story exactly," said he. "I was only telling our host how vampirism was not extinct yet. I was saying that there was an outbreak of it in India only a few years ago."

There was a more than perceptible pause, and I saw that, if Urcombe was observing her, she on her side was observing him with fixed eye and parted mouth. Then her jolly laugh invaded that rather tense silence.

"Oh, what a shame!" she said. "You're not going to curdle my blood at all. Where did you pick up such a tale, Mr. Urcombe? I have lived for years in India and never heard a rumour of such a thing. Some story-teller in the bazaars must have invented it: they are famous at that."

I could see that Urcombe was on the point of saying something further, but checked himself.

"Ah! very likely that was it," he said.

But something had disturbed our usual peaceful sociability that night, and something had damped Mrs. Amworth's usual high spirits. She had no gusto for her piquet, and left after a couple of games. Urcombe had been silent too, indeed he hardly spoke again till she departed.

"That was unfortunate," he said, "for the outbreak of—of a very mysterious disease, let us call it, took place at Peshawar, where she and her husband were. And——"

"Well?" I asked.

"He was one of the victims of it," said he. "Naturally I had quite forgotten that when I spoke."

The summer was unreasonably hot and rainless, and Maxley suffered much from drought, and also from a plague of big black night-flying gnats, the bite of which was very irritating and virulent. They came sailing in of an evening, settling on one's skin so quietly that one perceived nothing till the sharp stab announced that one had been bitten. They did not bite the hands or face, but chose always the neck and throat for their feeding-ground, and most of us, as the poison spread, assumed a temporary goitre. Then about the middle of August appeared the first of those mysterious cases of illness which our local doctor attributed to the long-continued heat coupled with the bite of these venomous insects. The patient was a boy of sixteen or seventeen, the son of Mrs. Amworth's gardener, and the symptoms were an anæmic pallor and a languid prostration, accompanied by great drowsiness and an abnormal appetite. He had, too, on his throat two small punctures where, so Dr. Ross conjectured, one of these great gnats had bitten him. But the odd thing was that there was no swelling or inflammation round the place where he had been bitten. The heat at this time had begun to abate, but the cooler weather failed to restore him, and the boy, in spite of the quantity of good food which he so ravenously swallowed, wasted away to a skin-clad skeleton.

I met Dr. Ross in the street one afternoon about this time, and in answer to my inquiries about his patient he said that he was afraid the boy was dying. The case, he confessed, completely puzzled him: some obscure form of pernicious anæmia was all he could suggest. But he wondered whether Mr. Urcombe would consent to see the boy, on the chance of his being able to throw some new light on the case, and since Urcombe was dining with me that night, I proposed to Dr. Ross to join us. He could not do this, but said he would look in later. When he came, Urcombe at once consented to put his skill at the other's disposal, and together they went off at once. Being thus shorn of my sociable evening, I telephoned to Mrs. Amworth to know if I might inflict myself on her for an hour. Her answer was a welcoming affirmative, and between piquet and music the hour lengthened itself into two. She spoke of the boy who was lying so desperately and mysteriously ill, and told me that she had often been to see him, taking him nourishing and delicate food. But to-day—and her kind eyes moistened as she spoke—she was afraid she had paid her last visit. Knowing the antipathy between her and Urcombe, I did not tell her that he had been called into consultation; and when I returned home she accompanied me to my door, for the sake of a breath of night air, and in order to borrow a magazine which contained an article on gardening which she wished to read.

"Ah, this delicious night air," she said, luxuriously sniffing in the coolness. "Night air and gardening are the great tonics. There is nothing so stimulating as bare contact with rich mother earth. You are never so fresh as when you have been grubbing in the soil—

black hands, black nails, and boots covered with mud." She gave her great jovial laugh.

"I'm a glutton for air and earth," she said. "Positively I look forward to death, for then I shall be buried and have the kind earth all round me. No leaden caskets for me—I have given explicit directions. But what shall I do about air? Well, I suppose one can't have everything. The magazine? A thousand thanks, I will faithfully return it. Good night: garden and keep your windows open, and you won't have anæmia."

"I always sleep with my windows open," said I.

I went straight up to my bedroom, of which one of the windows looks out over the street, and as I undressed I thought I heard voices talking outside not far away. But I paid no particular attention, put out my lights, and falling asleep plunged into the depths of a most horrible dream, distortedly suggested no doubt, by my last words with Mrs. Amworth. I dreamed that I woke, and found that both my bedroom windows were shut. Half-suffocating I dreamed that I sprang out of bed, and went across to open them. The blind over the first was drawn down, and pulling it up I saw, with the indescribable horror of incipient nightmare, Mrs. Amworth's face suspended close to the pane in the darkness outside, nodding and smiling at me. Pulling down the blind again to keep that terror out, I rushed to the second window on the other side of the room, and there again was Mrs. Amworth's face. Then the panic came upon me in full blast; here was I suffocating in the airless room, and whichever window I opened Mrs. Amworth's face would float in, like those noiseless black gnats that bit before one was aware. The nightmare rose to screaming point, and with strangled yells I awoke to find my room cool and quiet with both windows open and blinds up and a half-moon high in its course, casting an oblong of tranquil light on the floor. But even when I was awake the horror persisted, and I lay tossing and turning. I must have slept long before the nightmare seized me, for now it was nearly day, and soon in the east the drowsy eyelids of morning began to lift.

I was scarcely downstairs next morning—for after the dawn I slept late—when Urcombe rang up to know if he might see me immediately. He came in, grim and preoccupied, and I noticed that he was pulling on a pipe that was not even filled.

"I want your help," he said, "and so I must tell you first of all what happened last night. I went round with the little doctor to see his patient, and found him just alive, but scarcely more. I instantly

127

diagnosed in my own mind what this anæmia, unaccountable by any other explanation, meant. The boy is the prey of a vampire."

He put his empty pipe on the breakfast-table, by which I had just sat down, and folded his arms, looking at me steadily from under his overhanging brows.

"Now about last night," he said. "I insisted that he should be moved from his father's cottage into my house. As we were carrying him on a stretcher, whom should we meet but Mrs. Amworth? She expressed shocked surprise that we were moving him. Now why do you think she did that?"

With a start of horror, as I remembered my dream that night before, I felt an idea come into my mind so preposterous and unthinkable that I instantly turned it out again.

"I haven't the smallest idea," I said.

"Then listen, while I tell you about what happened later. I put out all light in the room where the boy lay, and watched. One window was a little open, for I had forgotten to close it, and about midnight I heard something outside, trying apparently to push it farther open. I guessed who it was—yes, it was full twenty feet from the ground—and I peeped round the corner of the blind. Just outside was the face of Mrs. Amworth and her hand was on the frame of the window. Very softly I crept close, and then banged the window down, and I think I just caught the tip of one of her fingers."

"But it's impossible," I cried. "How could she be floating in the air like that? And what had she come for? Don't tell me such——"

Once more, with closer grip, the remembrance of my nightmare seized me.

"I am telling you what I saw," said he. "And all night long, until it was nearly day, she was fluttering outside, like some terrible bat, trying to gain admittance. Now put together various things I have told you."

He began checking them off on his fingers.

"Number one," he said: "there was an outbreak of disease similar to that which this boy is suffering from at Peshawar, and her husband died of it. Number two: Mrs. Amworth protested against my moving the boy to my house. Number three: she, or the demon that inhabits her body, a creature powerful and deadly, tries to gain admittance. And add this, too: in mediæval times there was an epidemic of vampirism here at Maxley. The vampire, so the accounts run, was found to be Elizabeth Chaston ... I see you remember Mrs. Amworth's maiden name. Finally, the boy is

128

stronger this morning. He would certainly not have been alive if he had been visited again. And what do you make of it?"

There was a long silence, during which I found this incredible horror assuming the hues of reality.

"I have something to add," I said, "which may or may not bear on it. You say that the—the spectre went away shortly before dawn."

"Yes."

I told him of my dream, and he smiled grimly.

"Yes, you did well to awake," he said. "That warning came from your subconscious self, which never wholly slumbers, and cried out to you of deadly danger. For two reasons, then, you must help me: one to save others, the second to save yourself."

"What do you want me to do?" I asked.

"I want you first of all to help me in watching this boy, and ensuring that she does not come near him. Eventually I want you to help me in tracking the thing down, in exposing and destroying it. It is not human: it is an incarnate fiend. What steps we shall have to take I don't yet know."

It was now eleven of the forenoon, and presently I went across to his house for a twelve-hour vigil while he slept, to come on duty again that night, so that for the next twenty-four hours either Urcombe or myself was always in the room where the boy, now getting stronger every hour, was lying. The day following was Saturday and a morning of brilliant, pellucid weather, and already when I went across to his house to resume my duty the stream of motors down to Brighton had begun. Simultaneously I saw Urcombe with a cheerful face, which boded good news of his patient, coming out of his house, and Mrs. Amworth, with a gesture of salutation to me and a basket in her hand, walking up the broad strip of grass which bordered the road. There we all three met. I noticed (and saw that Urcombe noticed it too) that one finger of her left hand was bandaged.

"Good morning to you both," said she. "And I hear your patient is doing well, Mr. Urcombe. I have come to bring him a bowl of jelly, and to sit with him for an hour. He and I are great friends. I am overjoyed at his recovery."

Urcombe paused a moment, as if making up his mind, and then shot out a pointing finger at her.

"I forbid that," he said. "You shall not sit with him or see him. And you know the reason as well as I do."

I have never seen so horrible a change pass over a human face as that which now blanched hers to the colour of a grey mist. She put up her hand as if to shield herself from that pointing finger, which drew the sign of the cross in the air, and shrank back cowering on to the road. There was a wild hoot from a horn, a grinding of brakes, a shout—too late—from a passing car, and one long scream suddenly cut short. Her body rebounded from the roadway after the first wheel had gone over it, and the second followed. It lay there, quivering and twitching, and was still.

She was buried three days afterwards in the cemetery outside Maxley, in accordance with the wishes she had told me that she had devised about her interment, and the shock which her sudden and awful death had caused to the little community began by degrees to pass off. To two people only, Urcombe and myself, the horror of it was mitigated from the first by the nature of the relief that her death brought; but, naturally enough, we kept our own counsel, and no hint of what greater horror had been thus averted was ever let slip. But, oddly enough, so it seemed to me, he was still not satisfied about something in connection with her, and would give no answer to my questions on the subject. Then as the days of a tranquil mellow September and the October that followed began to drop away like the leaves of the yellowing trees, his uneasiness relaxed. But before the entry of November the seeming tranquillity broke into hurricane.

I had been dining one night at the far end of the village, and about eleven o'clock was walking home again. The moon was of an unusual brilliance, rendering all that it shone on as distinct as in some etching. I had just come opposite the house which Mrs. Amworth had occupied, where there was a board up telling that it was to let, when I heard the click of her front gate, and next moment I saw, with a sudden chill and quaking of my very spirit, that she stood there. Her profile, vividly illuminated, was turned to me, and I could not be mistaken in my identification of her. She appeared not to see me (indeed the shadow of the yew hedge in front of her garden enveloped me in its blackness) and she went swiftly across the road, and entered the gate of the house directly opposite. There I lost sight of her completely.

My breath was coming in short pants as if I had been running—and now indeed I ran, with fearful backward glances, along the hundred yards that separated me from my house and Urcombe's. It was to his that my flying steps took me, and next minute I was within.

"What have you come to tell me?" he asked. "Or shall I guess?"

"You can't guess," said I.

"No; it's no guess. She has come back and you have seen her. Tell me about it."

I gave him my story.

"That's Major Pearsall's house," he said. "Come back with me there at once."

"But what can we do?" I asked.

"I've no idea. That's what we have got to find out."

A minute later, we were opposite the house. When I had passed it before, it was all dark; now lights gleamed from a couple of windows upstairs. Even as we faced it, the front door opened, and next moment Major Pearsall emerged from the gate. He saw us and stopped.

"I'm on my way to Dr. Ross," he said quickly. "My wife has been taken suddenly ill. She had been in bed an hour when I came upstairs, and I found her white as a ghost and utterly exhausted. She had been to sleep, it seemed—— but you will excuse me."

"One moment, Major," said Urcombe. "Was there any mark on her throat?"

"How did you guess that?" said he. "There was: one of those beastly gnats must have bitten her twice there. She was streaming with blood."

"And there's someone with her?" asked Urcombe.

"Yes, I roused her maid."

He went off, and Urcombe turned to me. "I know now what we have to do," he said. "Change your clothes, and I'll join you at your house."

"What is it?" I asked.

"I'll tell you on our way. We're going to the cemetery."

He carried a pick, a shovel, and a screwdriver when he rejoined me, and wore round his shoulders a long coil of rope. As we walked, he gave me the outlines of the ghastly hour that lay before us.

"What I have to tell you," he said, "will seem to you now too fantastic for credence, but before dawn we shall see whether it outstrips reality. By a most fortunate happening, you saw the spectre, the astral body, whatever you choose to call it, of Mrs. Amworth, going on its grisly business, and therefore, beyond doubt, the vampire spirit which abode in her during life animates her again in death. That is not exceptional—indeed, all these weeks since her death I have been expecting it. If I am right, we shall find her body undecayed and untouched by corruption."

"But she has been dead nearly two months," said I.

"If she had been dead two years it would still be so, if the vampire has possession of her. So remember: whatever you see done, it will be done not to her, who in the natural course would now be feeding the grasses above her grave, but to a spirit of untold evil and malignancy, which gives a phantom life to her body."

"But what shall I see done?" said I.

"I will tell you. We know that now, at this moment, the vampire clad in her mortal semblance is out; dining out. But it must get back before dawn, and it will pass into the material form that lies in her grave. We must wait for that, and then with your help I shall dig up her body. If I am right, you will look on her as she was in life, with the full vigour of the dreadful nutriment she has received pulsing in her veins. And then, when dawn has come, and the vampire cannot leave the lair of her body, I shall strike her with this"—and he pointed to his pick—"through the heart, and she, who comes to life again only with the animation the fiend gives her, she and her hellish partner will be dead indeed. Then we must bury her again, delivered at last."

We had come to the cemetery, and in the brightness of the moonshine there was no difficulty in identifying her grave. It lay some twenty yards from the small chapel, in the porch of which, obscured by shadow, we concealed ourselves. From there we had a clear and open sight of the grave, and now we must wait till its infernal visitor returned home. The night was warm and windless, yet even if a freezing wind had been raging I think I should have felt nothing of it, so intense was my preoccupation as to what the night and dawn would bring. There was a bell in the turret of the chapel, that struck the quarters of the hour, and it amazed me to find how swiftly the chimes succeeded one another.

The moon had long set, but a twilight of stars shone in a clear sky, when five o'clock of the morning sounded from the turret. A few minutes more passed, and then I felt Urcombe's hand softly nudging me; and looking out in the direction of his pointing finger, I saw that the form of a woman, tall and large in build, was approaching from the right. Noiselessly, with a motion more of gliding and floating than walking, she moved across the cemetery to the grave which was the centre of our observation. She moved round it as if to be certain of its identity, and for a moment stood directly facing us. In the greyness to which now my eyes had grown accustomed, I could easily see her face, and recognise its features.

She drew her hand across her mouth as if wiping it, and broke into a chuckle of such laughter as made my hair stir on my head. Then she leaped on to the grave, holding her hands high above her head, and inch by inch disappeared into the earth. Urcombe's hand was laid on my arm, in an injunction to keep still, but now he removed it.

"Come," he said.

With pick and shovel and rope we went to the grave. The earth was light and sandy, and soon after six struck we had delved down to the coffin lid. With his pick he loosened the earth round it, and, adjusting the rope through the handles by which it had been lowered, we tried to raise it. This was a long and laborious business, and the light had begun to herald day in the east before we had it out, and lying by the side of the grave. With his screwdriver he loosed the fastenings of the lid, and slid it aside, and standing there we looked on the face of Mrs. Amworth. The eyes, once closed in death, were open, the cheeks were flushed with colour, the red, full-lipped mouth seemed to smile.

"One blow and it is all over," he said. "You need not look."

Even as he spoke he took up the pick again, and, laying the point of it on her left breast, measured his distance. And though I knew what was coming I could not look away....

He grasped the pick in both hands, raised it an inch or two for the taking of his aim, and then with full force brought it down on her breast. A fountain of blood, though she had been dead so long, spouted high in the air, falling with the thud of a heavy splash over the shroud, and simultaneously from those red lips came one long, appalling cry, swelling up like some hooting siren, and dying away again. With that, instantaneous as a lightning flash, came the touch of corruption on her face, the colour of it faded to ash, the plump cheeks fell in, the mouth dropped.

"Thank God, that's over," said he, and without pause slipped the coffin lid back into its place.

Day was coming fast now, and, working like men possessed, we lowered the coffin into its place again, and shovelled the earth over it.... The birds were busy with their earliest pipings as we went back to Maxley.

# In the Tube

"It's a convention," said Anthony Carling cheerfully, "and not a very convincing one. Time, indeed! There's no such thing as Time really; it has no actual existence. Time is nothing more than an infinitesimal point in eternity, just as space is an infinitesimal point in infinity. At the most, Time is a sort of tunnel through which we are accustomed to believe that we are travelling. There's a roar in our ears and a darkness in our eyes which makes it seem real to us. But before we came into the tunnel we existed for ever in an infinite sunlight, and after we have got through it we shall exist in an infinite sunlight again. So why should we bother ourselves about the confusion and noise and darkness which only encompass us for a moment?"

For a firm-rooted believer in such immeasurable ideas as these, which he punctuated with brisk application of the poker to the brave sparkle and glow of the fire, Anthony has a very pleasant appreciation of the measurable and the finite, and nobody with whom I have acquaintance has so keen a zest for life and its enjoyments as he. He had given us this evening an admirable dinner, had passed round a port beyond praise, and had illuminated the jolly hours with the light of his infectious optimism. Now the small company had melted away, and I was left with him over the fire in his study. Outside the tattoo of wind-driven sleet was audible on the window-panes, over-scoring now and again the flap of the flames on the open hearth, and the thought of the chilly blasts and the snow-covered pavement in Brompton Square, across which, to skidding taxicabs, the last of his other guests had scurried, made my position, resident here till to-morrow morning, the more delicately delightful. Above all there was this stimulating and suggestive companion, who, whether he talked of the great abstractions which were so intensely real and practical to him, or of the very remarkable experiences which he had encountered among these conventions of time and space, was equally fascinating to the listener.

"I adore life," he said. "I find it the most entrancing plaything. It's a delightful game, and, as you know very well, the only conceivable way to play a game is to treat it extremely seriously. If you say to yourself, 'It's only a game,' you cease to take the slightest interest in it. You have to know that it's only a game, and behave as if it was the one object of existence. I should like it to go on for

134

many years yet. But all the time one has to be living on the true plane as well, which is eternity and infinity. If you come to think of it, the one thing which the human mind cannot grasp is the finite, not the infinite, the temporary, not the eternal."

"That sounds rather paradoxical," said I.

"Only because you've made a habit of thinking about things that seem bounded and limited. Look it in the face for a minute. Try to imagine finite Time and Space, and you find you can't. Go back a million years, and multiply that million of years by another million, and you find that you can't conceive of a beginning. What happened before that beginning? Another beginning and another beginning? And before that? Look at it like that, and you find that the only solution comprehensible to you is the existence of an eternity, something that never began and will never end. It's the same about space. Project yourself to the farthest star, and what comes beyond that? Emptiness? Go on through the emptiness, and you can't imagine it being finite and having an end. It must needs go on for ever: that's the only thing you can understand. There's no such thing as before or after, or beginning or end, and what a comfort that is! I should fidget myself to death if there wasn't the huge soft cushion of eternity to lean one's head against. Some people say—I believe I've heard you say it yourself—that the idea of eternity is so tiring; you feel that you want to stop. But that's because you are thinking of eternity in terms of Time, and mumbling in your brain, 'And after that, and after that?' Don't you grasp the idea that in eternity there isn't any 'after,' any more than there is any 'before'? It's all one. Eternity isn't a quantity: it's a quality."

Sometimes, when Anthony talks in this manner, I seem to get a glimpse of that which to his mind is so transparently clear and solidly real, at other times (not having a brain that readily envisages abstractions) I feel as though he was pushing me over a precipice, and my intellectual faculties grasp wildly at anything tangible or comprehensible. This was the case now, and I hastily interrupted.

"But there is a 'before' and 'after,'" I said. "A few hours ago you gave us an admirable dinner, and after that—yes, after—we played bridge. And now you are going to explain things a little more clearly to me, and after that I shall go to bed——"

He laughed.

"You shall do exactly as you like," he said, "and you shan't be a slave to Time either to-night or to-morrow morning. We won't even mention an hour for breakfast, but you shall have it in eternity whenever you awake. And as I see it is not midnight yet, we'll slip the bonds of Time, and talk quite infinitely. I will stop the clock, if

135

that will assist you in getting rid of your illusion, and then I'll tell you a story, which to my mind, shows how unreal so-called realities are; or, at any rate, how fallacious are our senses as judges of what is real and what is not."

"Something occult, something spookish?" I asked, pricking up my ears, for Anthony has the strangest clairvoyances and visions of things unseen by the normal eye.

"I suppose you might call some of it occult," he said, "though there's a certain amount of rather grim reality mixed up in it."

"Go on; excellent mixture," said I.

He threw a fresh log on the fire.

"It's a longish story," he said. "You may stop me as soon as you've had enough. But there will come a point for which I claim your consideration. You, who cling to your 'before' and 'after,' has it ever occurred to you how difficult it is to say when an incident takes place? Say that a man commits some crime of violence, can we not, with a good deal of truth, say that he really commits that crime when he definitely plans and determines upon it, dwelling on it with gusto? The actual commission of it, I think we can reasonably argue, is the mere material sequel of his resolve: he is guilty of it when he makes that determination. When, therefore, in the term of 'before' and 'after,' does the crime truly take place? There is also in my story a further point for your consideration. For it seems certain that the spirit of a man, after the death of his body, is obliged to re-enact such a crime, with a view, I suppose we may guess, to his remorse and his eventual redemption. Those who have second sight have seen such re-enactments. Perhaps he may have done his deed blindly in this life; but then his spirit re-commits it with its spiritual eyes open, and able to comprehend its enormity. So, shall we view the man's original determination and the material commission of his crime only as preludes to the real commission of it, when with eyes unsealed he does it and repents of it?... That all sounds very obscure when I speak in the abstract, but I think you will see what I mean, if you follow my tale. Comfortable? Got everything you want? Here goes, then."

He leaned back in his chair, concentrating his mind, and then spoke:

"The story that I am about to tell you," he said, "had its beginning a month ago, when you were away in Switzerland. It reached its conclusion, so I imagine, last night. I do not, at any rate, expect to experience any more of it. Well, a month ago I was returning late on a very wet night from dining out. There was not a taxi to be had, and I hurried through the pouring rain to the tube-station at Piccadilly Circus, and thought myself very lucky to catch the last train in this direction. The carriage into which I stepped was quite empty except for one other passenger, who sat next the door immediately opposite to me. I had never, to my knowledge, seen him before, but I found my attention vividly fixed on him, as if he somehow concerned me. He was a man of middle age, in dress-clothes, and his face wore an expression of intense thought, as if in his mind he was pondering some very significant matter, and his hand which was resting on his knee clenched and unclenched itself. Suddenly he looked up and stared me in the face, and I saw there suspicion and fear, as if I had surprised him in some secret deed.

"At that moment we stopped at Dover Street, and the conductor threw open the doors, announced the station and added, 'Change here for Hyde Park Corner and Gloucester Road.' That was all right for me since it meant that the train would stop at Brompton Road, which was my destination. It was all right apparently, too, for my companion, for he certainly did not get out, and after a moment's stop, during which no one else got in, we went on. I saw him, I must insist, after the doors were closed and the train had started. But when I looked again, as we rattled on, I saw that there was no one there. I was quite alone in the carriage.

"Now you may think that I had had one of those swift momentary dreams which flash in and out of the mind in the space of a second, but I did not believe it was so myself, for I felt that I had experienced some sort of premonition or clairvoyant vision. A man, the semblance of whom, astral body or whatever you may choose to call it, I had just seen, would sometime sit in that seat opposite to me, pondering and planning."

"But why?" I asked. "Why should it have been the astral body of a living man which you thought you had seen? Why not the ghost of a dead one?"

"Because of my own sensations. The sight of the spirit of someone dead, which has occurred to me two or three times in my life, has always been accompanied by a physical shrinking and fear, and by the sensation of cold and of loneliness. I believed, at any rate, that I had seen a phantom of the living, and that impression was confirmed, I might say proved, the next day. For I met the man himself. And the next night, as you shall hear, I met the phantom again. We will take them in order.

"I was lunching, then, the next day with my neighbour Mrs. Stanley: there was a small party, and when I arrived we waited but for the final guest. He entered while I was talking to some friend, and presently at my elbow I heard Mrs. Stanley's voice—

137

"'Let me introduce you to Sir Henry Payle,' she said.

"I turned and saw my vis-à-vis of the night before. It was quite unmistakably he, and as we shook hands he looked at me I thought with vague and puzzled recognition.

"'Haven't we met before, Mr. Carling?' he said. 'I seem to recollect——'

"For the moment I forgot the strange manner of his disappearance from the carriage, and thought that it had been the man himself whom I had seen last night.

"'Surely, and not so long ago,' I said. 'For we sat opposite each other in the last tube-train from Piccadilly Circus yesterday night.'

"He still looked at me, frowning, puzzled, and shook his head.

"'That can hardly be,' he said. 'I only came up from the country this morning.'

"Now this interested me profoundly, for the astral body, we are told, abides in some half-conscious region of the mind or spirit, and has recollections of what has happened to it, which it can convey only very vaguely and dimly to the conscious mind. All lunch-time I could see his eyes again and again directed to me with the same puzzled and perplexed air, and as I was taking my departure he came up to me.

"'I shall recollect some day,' he said, 'where we met before, and I hope we may meet again. Was it not——?'—and he stopped. 'No: it has gone from me,' he added."

The log that Anthony had thrown on the fire was burning bravely now, and its high-flickering flame lit up his face.

"Now, I don't know whether you believe in coincidences as chance things," he said, "but if you do, get rid of the notion. Or if you can't at once, call it a coincidence that that very night I again caught the last train on the tube going westwards. This time, so far from my being a solitary passenger, there was a considerable crowd waiting at Dover Street, where I entered, and just as the noise of the approaching train began to reverberate in the tunnel I caught sight of Sir Henry Payle standing near the opening from which the train would presently emerge, apart from the rest of the crowd. And I thought to myself how odd it was that I should have seen the phantom of him at this very hour last night and the man himself now, and I began walking towards him with the idea of saying, 'Anyhow, it is in the tube that we meet to-night.'... And then a terrible and awful thing happened. Just as the train emerged from the tunnel he jumped down on to the line in front of it, and the train swept along over him up the platform.

"For a moment I was stricken with horror at the sight, and I remember covering my eyes against the dreadful tragedy. But then I perceived that, though it had taken place in full sight of those who were waiting, no one seemed to have seen it except myself. The driver, looking out from his window, had not applied his brakes, there was no jolt from the advancing train, no scream, no cry, and the rest of the passengers began boarding the train with perfect nonchalance. I must have staggered, for I felt sick and faint with what I had seen, and some kindly soul put his arm round me and supported me into the train. He was a doctor, he told me, and asked if I was in pain, or what ailed me. I told him what I thought I had seen, and he assured me that no such accident had taken place.

"It was clear then to my own mind that I had seen the second act, so to speak, in this psychical drama, and I pondered next morning over the problem as to what I should do. Already I had glanced at the morning paper, which, as I knew would be the case, contained no mention whatever of what I had seen. The thing had certainly not happened, but I knew in myself that it would happen. The flimsy veil of Time had been withdrawn from my eyes, and I had seen into what you would call the future. In terms of Time of course it was the future, but from my point of view the thing was just as much in the past as it was in the future. It existed, and waited only for its material fulfilment. The more I thought about it, the more I saw that I could do nothing."

I interrupted his narrative.

"You did nothing?" I exclaimed. "Surely you might have taken some step in order to try to avert the tragedy."

He shook his head.

"What step precisely?" he said. "Was I to go to Sir Henry and tell him that once more I had seen him in the tube in the act of committing suicide? Look at it like this. Either what I had seen was pure illusion, pure imagination, in which case it had no existence or significance at all, or it was actual and real, and essentially it had happened. Or take it, though not very logically, somewhere between the two. Say that the idea of suicide, for some cause of which I knew nothing, had occurred to him or would occur. Should I not, if that was the case, be doing a very dangerous thing, by making such a suggestion to him? Might not the fact of my telling him what I had seen put the idea into his mind, or, if it was already there, confirm it and strengthen it? 'It's a ticklish matter to play with souls,' as Browning says."

"But it seems so inhuman not to interfere in any way," said I, "not to make any attempt."

"What interference?" asked he. "What attempt?"

139

The human instinct in me still seemed to cry aloud at the thought of doing nothing to avert such a tragedy, but it seemed to be beating itself against something austere and inexorable. And cudgel my brain as I would, I could not combat the sense of what he had said. I had no answer for him, and he went on.

"You must recollect, too," he said, "that I believed then and believe now that the thing had happened. The cause of it, whatever that was, had begun to work, and the effect, in this material sphere, was inevitable. That is what I alluded to when, at the beginning of my story, I asked you to consider how difficult it was to say when an action took place. You still hold that this particular action, this suicide of Sir Henry, had not yet taken place, because he had not yet thrown himself under the advancing train. To me that seems a materialistic view. I hold that in all but the endorsement of it, so to speak, it had taken place. I fancy that Sir Henry, for instance, now free from the material dusks, knows that himself."

Exactly as he spoke there swept through the warm lit room a current of ice-cold air, ruffling my hair as it passed me, and making the wood flames on the hearth to dwindle and flare. I looked round to see if the door at my back had opened, but nothing stirred there, and over the closed window the curtains were fully drawn. As it reached Anthony, he sat up quickly in his chair and directed his glance this way and that about the room.

"Did you feel that?" he asked.

"Yes: a sudden draught," I said. "Ice-cold."

"Anything else?" he asked. "Any other sensation?"

I paused before I answered, for at the moment there occurred to me Anthony's differentiation of the effects produced on the beholder by a phantasm of the living and the apparition of the dead. It was the latter which accurately described my sensations now, a certain physical shrinking, a fear, a feeling of desolation. But yet I had seen nothing. "I felt rather creepy," I said.

As I spoke I drew my chair rather closer to the fire, and sent a swift and, I confess, a somewhat apprehensive scrutiny round the walls of the brightly lit room. I noticed at the same time that Anthony was peering across to the chimney-piece, on which, just below a sconce holding two electric lights, stood the clock which at the beginning of our talk he had offered to stop. The hands I noticed pointed to twenty-five minutes to one.

"But you saw nothing?" he asked.

"Nothing whatever," I said. "Why should I? What was there to see? Or did you——"

"I don't think so," he said.

140

Somehow this answer got on my nerves, for the queer feeling which had accompanied that cold current of air had not left me. If anything it had become more acute.

"But surely you know whether you saw anything or not?" I said.

"One can't always be certain," said he. "I say that I don't think I saw anything. But I'm not sure, either, whether the story I am telling you was quite concluded last night. I think there may be a further incident. If you prefer it, I will leave the rest of it, as far as I know it, unfinished till to-morrow morning, and you can go off to bed now."

His complete calmness and tranquillity reassured me.

"But why should I do that?" I asked.

Again he looked round on the bright walls.

"Well, I think something entered the room just now," he said, "and it may develop. If you don't like the notion, you had better go. Of course there's nothing to be alarmed at; whatever it is, it can't hurt us. But it is close on the hour when on two successive nights I saw what I have already told you, and an apparition usually occurs at the same time. Why that is so, I cannot say, but certainly it looks as if a spirit that is earth-bound is still subject to certain conventions, the conventions of time for instance. I think that personally I shall see something before long, but most likely you won't. You're not such a sufferer as I from these—these delusions—"

I was frightened and knew it, but I was also intensely interested, and some perverse pride wriggled within me at his last words. Why, so I asked myself, shouldn't I see whatever was to be seen?...

"I don't want to go in the least," I said. "I want to hear the rest of your story."

"Where was I, then? Ah, yes: you were wondering why I didn't do something after I saw the train move up to the platform, and I said that there was nothing to be done. If you think it over, I fancy you will agree with me.... A couple of days passed, and on the third morning I saw in the paper that there had come fulfilment to my vision. Sir Henry Payle, who had been waiting on the platform of Dover Street Station for the last train to South Kensington, had thrown himself in front of it as it came into the station. The train had been pulled up in a couple of yards, but a wheel had passed over his chest, crushing it in and instantly killing him.

"An inquest was held, and there emerged at it one of those dark stories which, on occasions like these, sometimes fall like a midnight shadow across a life that the world perhaps had thought prosperous. He had long been on bad terms with his wife, from whom he had lived apart, and it appeared that not long before this he had fallen desperately in love with another woman. The night before his suicide he had appeared very late at his wife's house, and had a long and angry scene with her in which he entreated her to divorce him, threatening otherwise to make her life a hell to her. She refused, and in an ungovernable fit of passion he attempted to strangle her. There was a struggle, and the noise of it caused her manservant to come up, who succeeded in over-mastering him. Lady Payle threatened to proceed against him for assault with the intention to murder her. With this hanging over his head, the next night, as I have already told you, he committed suicide."

He glanced at the clock again, and I saw that the hands now pointed to ten minutes to one. The fire was beginning to burn low and the room surely was growing strangely cold.

"That's not quite all," said Anthony, again looking round. "Are you sure you wouldn't prefer to hear it to-morrow?"

The mixture of shame and pride and curiosity again prevailed.

"No: tell me the rest of it at once," I said.

Before speaking, he peered suddenly at some point behind my chair, shading his eyes. I followed his glance, and knew what he meant by saying that sometimes one could not be sure whether one saw something or not. But was that an outlined shadow that intervened between me and the wall? It was difficult to focus; I did not know whether it was near the wall or near my chair. It seemed to clear away, anyhow, as I looked more closely at it.

"You see nothing?" asked Anthony.

"No: I don't think so," said I. "And you?"

"I think I do," he said, and his eyes followed something which was invisible to mine. They came to rest between him and the chimney-piece. Looking steadily there, he spoke again.

"All this happened some weeks ago," he said, "when you were out in Switzerland, and since then, up till last night, I saw nothing further. But all the time I was expecting something further. I felt that, as far as I was concerned, it was not all over yet, and last night, with the intention of assisting any communication to come through to me from—from beyond, I went into the Dover Street tube-station at a few minutes before one o'clock, the hour at which both the assault and the suicide had taken place. The platform when I arrived on it was absolutely empty, or appeared to be so, but presently, just as I began to hear the roar of the approaching train, I saw there was the figure of a man standing some twenty yards from me, looking into the tunnel. He had not come down with me in the lift, and the

142

moment before he had not been there. He began moving towards me, and then I saw who it was, and I felt a stir of wind icy-cold coming towards me as he approached. It was not the draught that heralds the approach of a train, for it came from the opposite direction. He came close up to me, and I saw there was recognition in his eyes. He raised his face towards me and I saw his lips move, but, perhaps in the increasing noise from the tunnel, I heard nothing come from them. He put out his hand, as if entreating me to do something, and with a cowardice from which I cannot forgive myself, I shrank from him, for I knew, by the sign that I have told you, that this was one from the dead, and my flesh quaked before him, drowning for the moment all pity and all desire to help him, if that was possible. Certainly he had something which he wanted of me, but I recoiled from him. And by now the train was emerging from the tunnel, and next moment, with a dreadful gesture of despair, he threw himself in front of it."

As he finished speaking he got up quickly from his chair, still looking fixedly in front of him. I saw his pupils dilate, and his mouth worked.

"It is coming," he said. "I am to be given a chance of atoning for my cowardice. There is nothing to be afraid of: I must remember that myself...."

As he spoke there came from the panelling above the chimney-piece one loud shattering crack, and the cold wind again circled about my head. I found myself shrinking back in my chair with my hands held in front of me as instinctively I screened myself against something which I knew was there but which I could not see. Every sense told me that there was a presence in the room other than mine and Anthony's, and the horror of it was that I could not see it. Any vision, however terrible, would, I felt, be more tolerable than this clear certain knowledge that close to me was this invisible thing. And yet what horror might not be disclosed of the face of the dead and the crushed chest.... But all I could see, as I shuddered in this cold wind, was the familiar walls of the room, and Anthony standing in front of me stiff and firm, making, as I knew, a call on his courage. His eyes were focused on something quite close to him, and some semblance of a smile quivered on his mouth. And then he spoke again.

"Yes, I know you," he said. "And you want something of me. Tell me, then, what it is."

There was absolute silence, but what was silence to my ears could not have been so to his, for once or twice he nodded, and once he said, "Yes: I see. I will do it." And with the knowledge that, even

143

as there was someone here whom I could not see, so there was speech going on which I could not hear, this terror of the dead and of the unknown rose in me with the sense of powerlessness to move that accompanies nightmare. I could not stir, I could not speak. I could only strain my ears for the inaudible and my eyes for the unseen, while the cold wind from the very valley of the shadow of death streamed over me. It was not that the presence of death itself was terrible; it was that from its tranquillity and serene keeping there had been driven some unquiet soul unable to rest in peace for whatever ultimate awakening rouses the countless generations of those who have passed away, driven, no less, from whatever activities are theirs, back into the material world from which it should have been delivered. Never, until the gulf between the living and the dead was thus bridged, had it seemed so immense and so unnatural. It is possible that the dead may have communication with the living, and it was not that exactly that so terrified me, for such communication, as we know it, comes voluntarily from them. But here was something icy-cold and crime-laden, that was chased back from the peace that would not pacify it.

And then, most horrible of all, there came a change in these unseen conditions. Anthony was silent now, and from looking straight and fixedly in front of him, he began to glance sideways to where I sat and back again, and with that I felt that the unseen presence had turned its attention from him to me. And now, too, gradually and by awful degrees I began to see....

There came an outline of shadow across the chimney-piece and the panels above it. It took shape: it fashioned itself into the outline of a man. Within the shape of the shadow details began to form themselves, and I saw wavering in the air, like something concealed by haze, the semblance of a face, stricken and tragic, and burdened with such a weight of woe as no human face had ever worn. Next, the shoulders outlined themselves, and a stain livid and red spread out below them, and suddenly the vision leaped into clearness. There he stood, the chest crushed in and drowned in the red stain, from which broken ribs, like the bones of a wrecked ship, protruded. The mournful, terrible eyes were fixed on me, and it was from them, so I knew, that the bitter wind proceeded....

Then, quick as the switching off of a lamp, the spectre vanished, and the bitter wind was still, and opposite to me stood Anthony, in a quiet, bright-lit room. There was no sense of an unseen presence any more; he and I were then alone, with an interrupted conversation still dangling between us in the warm air. I came round to that, as one comes round after an anæsthetic. It all

144

swam into sight again, unreal at first, and gradually assuming the texture of actuality.

"You were talking to somebody, not to me," I said. "Who was it? What was it?"

He passed the back of his hand over his forehead, which glistened in the light.

"A soul in hell," he said.

Now it is hard ever to recall mere physical sensations, when they have passed. If you have been cold and are warmed, it is difficult to remember what cold was like: if you have been hot and have got cool, it is difficult to realise what the oppression of heat really meant. Just so, with the passing of that presence, I found myself unable to recapture the sense of the terror with which, a few moments ago only, it had invaded and inspired me.

"A soul in hell?" I said. "What are you talking about?"

He moved about the room for a minute or so, and then came and sat on the arm of my chair.

"I don't know what you saw," he said, "or what you felt, but there has never in all my life happened to me anything more real than what these last few minutes have brought. I have talked to a soul in the hell of remorse, which is the only possible hell. He knew, from what happened last night, that he could perhaps establish communication through me with the world he had quitted, and he sought me and found me. I am charged with a mission to a woman I have never seen, a message from the contrite.... You can guess who it is...."

He got up with a sudden briskness.

"Let's verify it anyhow," he said. "He gave me the street and the number. Ah, there's the telephone book! Would it be a coincidence merely if I found that at No. 20 in Chasemore Street, South Kensington, there lived a Lady Payle?"

He turned over the leaves of the bulky volume.

"Yes, that's right," he said.

# Roderick's Story

My powers of persuasion at first seemed quite ineffectual; I could not induce my friend Roderick Cardew to strike his melancholy tent in Chelsea, and (leaving it struck) steal away like the Arabs and spend this month of spring with me at my newly acquired house at Tilling to observe the spell of April's wand making magic in the country. I seemed to have brought out all the arguments of which I was master; he had been very ill, and his doctor recommended a clearer air with as mild a climate as he could conveniently attain; he loved the great stretches of drained marsh-land which lay spread like a pool of verdure round the little town; he had not seen my new home which made a breach in the functions of hospitality, and he really could not be expected to object to his host, who, after all, was one of his oldest friends. Besides (to leave no stone unturned) as he regained his strength he could begin to play golf again, and it entailed, as he well remembered, a very mild exertion for him to keep me in my proper position in such a pursuit.

At last there was some sign of yielding.

"Yes. I should like to see the marsh and the big sky once more," he said.

A rather sinister interpretation of his words "once more," made a sudden flashed signal of alarm in my mind. It was utterly fanciful, no doubt, but that had better be extinguished first.

"Once more?" I asked. "What does that mean?"

"I always say 'once more,'" he said. "It's greedy to ask for too much."

The very fact that he fenced so ingeniously deepened my suspicion.

"That won't do," I said. "Tell me, Roddie."

He was silent a moment.

"I didn't intend to," he said, "for there can be no use in it. But if you insist, as apparently you mean to do, I may as well give in. It's what you think; 'once more' will very likely be the most. But you mustn't fuss about it; I'm not going to. No proper person fusses about death; that's a train which we are all sure to catch. It always waits for you."

I have noticed that when one learns tidings of that sort, one feels, almost immediately, that one has known them a long time. I felt so now.

"Go on," I said.

"Well, that's about all there is. I've had sentence of death passed upon me, and it will probably be carried out, I'm delighted to say, in the French fashion. In France, you know, they don't tell you when you are to be executed till a few minutes before. It is likely that I shall have even less than that, so my doctor informs me. A second or two will be all I shall get. Congratulate me, please."

I thought it over for a moment.

"Yes, heartily," I said. "I want to know a little more though."

"Well, my heart's all wrong, quite unmendably so. Heart-disease! Doesn't it sound romantic? In mid-Victorian romance, heroes and heroines alone die of heart-disease. But that's by the way. The fact is that I may die at any time without a moment's warning. I shall give a couple of gasps, so he told me when I insisted on knowing details, and that'll be all. Now, perhaps, you understand why I was unwilling to come and stay with you. I don't want to die in your house; I think it's dreadfully bad manners to die in other people's houses. I long to see Tilling again, but I think I shall go to an hotel. Hotels are fair game, for the management over-charges those who live there to compensate themselves for those who die there. But it would be rude of me to die in your house; it might entail a lot of bother for you, and I couldn't apologize——"

"But I don't mind your dying in my house," I said. "At least you see what I mean——"

He laughed.

"I do, indeed," he said. "And you couldn't give a warmer assurance of friendship. But I couldn't come and stay with you in my present plight without telling you what it was, and yet I didn't mean to tell you. But there we are now. Think again; reconsider your decision."

"I don't," I said. "Come and die in my house by all means, if you've got to. I would much sooner you lived there: your dying will, in any case, annoy me immensely. But it would annoy me even more to know that you had done it in some beastly hotel among plush and looking-glasses. You shall have any bedroom you like. And I want you dreadfully to see my house, which is adorable.... O Roddie, what a bore it all is!"

It was impossible to speak or to think differently. I knew well how trivial a matter death was to my friend, and I was not sure that at heart I did not agree with him. We were quite at one, too, in that we had so often gossiped about death with cheerful conjecture and interested surmise based on the steady assurance that something of new and delightful import was to follow, since neither of us happened to be of that melancholy cast of mind that can envisage annihilation. I had promised, in case I was the first to embark on the great adventure, to do my best to "get through," and give him some irrefutable proof of the continuance of my existence, just by way of endorsement of our belief, and he had given a similar pledge, for it appeared to us both, that, whatever the conditions of the future might turn out to be, it would be impossible when lately translated there, not to be still greatly concerned with what the present world still held for us in ties of love and affection. I laughed now to remember how he had once imagined himself begging to be excused for a few minutes, directly after death, and saying to St. Peter: "May I keep your Holiness waiting for a minute before you finally lock me into Heaven or Hell with those beautiful keys? I won't be a minute, but I do want so much to be a ghost, and appear to a friend of mine who is on the look-out for such a visit. If I find I can't make myself visible I will come back at once.... Oh, thank you, your Holiness."

So we agreed that I should run the risk of his dying in my house, and promised not to make any reproaches posthumously (as far as he was concerned) in case he did so. He on his side promised not to die if he could possibly help it, and next week or so he would come down to me in the heart of the country that he loved, and see April at work.

"And I haven't told you anything about my house yet," I said. "It's right at the top of the hill, square and Georgian and red-bricked. A panelled hall, dining-room and panelled sitting-room downstairs, and more panelled rooms upstairs. And there's a garden with a lawn, and a high brick wall round it, and there is a big garden room, full of books, with a bow-window looking down the cobbled street. Which bedroom will you have? Do you like looking on to the garden or on to the street? You may even have my room if you like."

He looked at me a moment with eager attention. "I'll have the square panelled bedroom that looks out on to the garden, please," he said. "It's the second door on the right when you stand at the top of the stairs."

"But how do you know?" I asked.

"Because I've been in the house before, once only, three years ago," he said. "Margaret Alton took it furnished and lived there for a year or so. She died there, and I was with her. And if I had known that this was your house, I should never have dreamed of hesitating whether I should accept your invitation. I should have thrown my good manners about not dying in other people's houses to the winds. But the moment you began to describe the garden and garden-room I knew what house it was. I have always longed to go

148

there again. When may I come, please? Next week is too far ahead. You're off there this afternoon, aren't you?"

I rose: the clock warned me that it was time for me to go to the station.

"Yes. Come this afternoon," I suggested. "Come with me."

"I wish I could, but I take that to mean that it will suit you if I come to-morrow. For I certainly will. Good Lord! To think of your having got just that house! It ought to be a wonderfully happy one, for I saw—— But I'll tell you about that perhaps when I'm there. But don't ask me to: I'll tell you if and when I can, as the lawyers say. Are you really off?"

I was really off, for I had no time to spare, but before I got to the door he spoke again.

"Of course, the room I have chosen was the room," he said, and there was no need for me to ask what he meant by the room.

I knew no more than the barest and most public outline of that affair, distant now by the space of many years, but, so I conceived, ever green in Roderick's heart, and, as my train threaded its way through the gleams of this translucent spring evening, I retraced this outline as far as I knew it. It was the one thing of which Roderick never spoke (even now he was not sure that he could manage to tell me the end of it), and I had to rummage in my memory for the reconstruction of the half-obliterated lines.

Margaret—her maiden-name would not be conjured back into memory—had been an extremely beautiful girl when Roderick first met her, and, not without encouragement, he had fallen head over ears in love with her. All seemed to be going well with his wooing, he had the air of a happy lover, when there appeared on the scene that handsome and outrageous fellow, Richard Alton. He was the heir to his uncle's barony and his really vast estates, and the girl, when he proceeded to lay siege, very soon capitulated. She may have fallen in love with him, for he was an attractive scamp, but the verdict at the time was that it was her ambition, not her heart, that she indulged. In any case, there was the end of Roderick's wooing, and before the year was out she had married the other.

I remembered seeing her once or twice in London about this time, splendid and brilliant, of a beauty that dazzled, with the world very much at her feet. She bore him two sons; she succeeded to a great position; and then with the granting of her heart's desire, the leanness withal followed. Her husband's infidelities were numerous and notorious; he treated her with a subtle cruelty that just kept on the right side of the law, and, finally, seeking his freedom, he deserted her, and openly lived with another woman. Whether it was pride that kept her from divorcing him, or whether she still loved him (if she had ever done so) and was ready to take him back, or whether it was out of revenge that she refused to have done with him legally, was an affair of which I knew nothing. Calamity followed on calamity; first one and then the other of her sons was killed in the European War, and I remembered having heard that she was the victim of some malignant and disfiguring disease, which caused her to lead a hermit life, seeing nobody. It was now three years or so since she had died.

Such, with the addition that she had died in my house, and that Roderick had been with her, was the sum of my meagre knowledge, which might or might not, so he had intimated, be supplemented by him. He arrived next day, having motored down from London for the avoidance of fatigue, and certainly as we sat after dinner that night in the garden-room, he had avoided it very successfully, for never had I seen him more animated.

"Oh, I have been so right to come here," he said, "for I feel steeped in tranquillity and content. There's such a tremendous sense of Margaret's presence here, and I never knew how much I wanted it. Perhaps that is purely subjective, but what does that matter so long as I feel it? How a scene soaks into the place where it has been enacted; my room, which you know was her room, is alive with her. I want nothing better than to be here, prowling and purring over the memory of the last time, which was the only one, that I was here. Yes, just that; and I know how odd you must think it. But it's true, it was here that I saw her die, and instead of shunning the place, I bathe myself in it. For it was one of the happiest hours of my life."

"Because——" I began.

"No; not because it gave her release, if that's in your mind," he said. "It's because I saw——"

He broke off, and remembering his stipulation that I should ask him nothing, but that he would tell me "if and when" he could, I put no question to him. His eyes were dancing with the sparkle of fire that burned on the hearth, for though April was here, the evenings were still chilly, and it was not the fire that gave them their light, but a joyousness that was as bright as glee, and as deep as happiness.

"No, I'm not going on with that now," he said, "though I expect I shall before my days are out. At present I shall leave you wondering why a place that should hold such mournful memories for me, is such a well-spring. And as I am not for telling you about me, let me enquire about you. Bring yourself up to date; what have

150

you been doing, and much more important, what have you been thinking about?"

"My doings have chiefly been confined to settling into this house," I said. "I've been pulling and pushing furniture into places where it wouldn't go, and cursing it."

He looked round the room.

"It doesn't seem to bear you any grudge," he said. "It looks contented. And what else?"

"In the intervals, when I couldn't push and curse any more," I said, "I've been writing a few spook stories. All about the borderland, which I love as much as you do."

He laughed outright.

"Do you, indeed?" he said. "Then it's no use my saying that it is quite impossible. But I should like to know your views on the borderland."

I pointed to a sheaf of typewritten stuff that littered my table.

"Them's my sentiments," I said, "and quite at your service."

"Good; then I'll take them to bed with me when I go, if you'll allow me. I've always thought that you had a pretty notion of the creepy, but the mistake that you make is to imagine that creepiness is characteristic of the borderland. No doubt there are creepy things there, but so there are everywhere, and a thunder-storm is far more terrifying than an apparition. And when you get really close to the borderland, you see how enchanting it is, and how vastly more enchanting the other side must be. I got right on to the borderland once, here in this house, as I shall probably tell you, and I never saw so happy and kindly a place. And without doubt I shall soon be careering across it in my own person. That'll be, as we've often determined, wildly interesting, and it will have the solemnity of a first night at a new play about it. There'll be the curtain close in front of you, and presently it will be raised, and you will see something you never saw before. How well, on the whole, the secret has been kept, though from time to time little bits of information, little scraps of dialogue, little descriptions of scenery have leaked out. Enthrallingly interesting; one wonders how they will come into the great new drama."

"You don't mean the sort of thing that mediums tell us?" I asked.

"Of course I don't. I hate the sloshy—really there's no other word for it, and why should there be, since that word fits so admirably—the sloshy utterances of the ordinary high-class, beyond-suspicion medium at half a guinea a sitting, who asks if there's anybody present who once knew a Charles, or if not Charles,

Thomas or William. Naturally somebody has known a Charles, Thomas or William who has passed over, and is the son, brother, father or cousin of a lady in black. So when she claims Thomas, he tells her that he is very busy and happy, helping people.... O Lord, what rot! I went to one such séance a month ago, just before I was taken ill, and the medium said that Margaret wanted to get into touch with somebody. Two of us claimed Margaret, but Margaret chose me and said she was the spirit of my wife. Wife, you know! You must allow that this was a very unfortunate shot. When I said that I was unmarried, Margaret said that she was my mother, whose name was Charlotte. Oh dear, oh dear! Well, I shall go to bed with joy, bringing your spooks with me...."

"Sheaves," said I.

"Yes, but aren't they the sheaves? Isn't one's gleaning of sheaves in this world what they call spooks? That is, the knowledge of what one takes across?"

"I don't understand one word," said I.

"But you must understand. All the knowledge—worth anything—which you or I have collected here, is the beginning of the other life. We toil and moil, and make our gleanings and our harvestings, and all our decent efforts help us to realize what the real harvest is. Surely we shall take with us exactly that which we have reaped...."

After he had gone up to bed I sat trying to correct the errors of a typist, but still between me and the pages there dwelt that haunting sense of all that we did here being only the grist for what was to come. Our achievements were rewarded, so he seemed to say, by a glimpse. And those glimpses—so I tried to follow him—were the hints that had leaked out of the drama for which the curtain was twitching. Was that it?

Roderick came down to breakfast next morning, superlatively frank and happy.

"I didn't read a single line of your stories," he said. "When I got into my bedroom I was so immeasurably content that I couldn't risk getting interested in anything else. I lay awake a long time, pinching myself in order to prolong my sheer happiness, but the flesh was weak, and at last, from sheer happiness, I slept and probably snored. Did you hear me? I hope not. And then sheer happiness dictated my dreams, though I don't know what they were, and the moment I was called I got up, because ... because I didn't want to miss anything. Now, to be practical again, what are you doing this morning?"

"I was intending to play golf," I said, "unless——"

152

"There isn't an 'unless,' if you mean Me. My plan made itself for me, and I intend—this is my plan—to drive out with you, and sit in the hollow by the fourth tee, and read your stories there. There's a great south-westerly wind, like a celestial housemaid, scouring the skies, and I shall be completely sheltered there, and in the intervals of my reading, I shall pleasantly observe the unsuccessful efforts of the golfers to carry the big bunker. I can't personally play golf any more, but I shall enjoy seeing other people attempting to do it."

"And no prowling or purring?" I asked.

"Not this morning. That's all right: it's there. It's so much all right that I want to be active in other directions. Sitting in a windless hollow is about the range of my activities. I say that for fear that you should."

I found a match when we arrived at the club-house, and Roderick strolled away to the goal of his observations. Half an hour afterwards I found him watching with criminally ecstatic joy the soaring drives that, in the teeth of the great wind, were arrested and blown back into the unholiest bunker in all the world or the low clever balls that never rose to the height of the shored-up cliff of sand. The couple in front of my partner and me were sarcastic dogs, and bade us wait only till they had delved themselves over the ridge, and then we might follow as soon as we chose. After violent deeds in the bunker they climbed over the big dune, thirty yards beyond which lay the green on which they would now be putting.

As soon as they had disappeared, Roderick snatched my driver from my hand.

"I can't bear it," he said. "I must hit a ball again. Tee it low, caddie.... No, no tee at all."

He hit a superb shot, just high enough to carry the ridge, and not so high that it caught the opposing wind and was stopped towards the end of its flight. He gave a loud croak of laughter.

"That'll teach them not to insult my friend," he said. "It must have been pitched right among their careful puttings. And now I shall read his ghost-stories."

I have recorded this athletic incident because better than any analysis of his attitude towards life and death it conveys just what that attitude was. He knew perfectly well that any swift exertion might be fatal to him, but he wanted to hit a golf ball again as sweetly and as hard as it could be hit. He had done it: he had scored off death. And as I went on my way I felt perfectly confident that if, with that brisk free effort, he had fallen dead on the tee, he would have thought it well worth while, provided only that he had made that irreproachable shot. While alive, he proposed to partake in the

153

pleasures of life, amongst which he had always reckoned that of hitting golf balls, not caring, though he liked to be alive, whether the immediate consequence was death, just because he did not in the least object to being dead. The choice was of such little consequence.... The history of that I was to know that evening.

The stories which Roderick had taken to read were designed to be of an uncomfortable type: one concerned a vampire, one an elemental, the third the reincarnation of a certain execrable personage, and as we sat in the garden-room after tea, he with these pages on his knees, I had the pleasure of seeing him give hasty glances round, as he read, as if to assure himself that there was nothing unusual in the dimmer corners of the room.... I liked that; he was doing as I intended that a reader should.

Before long he came to the last page.

"And are you intending to make a book of them?" he asked. "What are the other stories like?"

"Worse," said I, with the complacency of the horror-monger.

"Then—did you ask for criticism? I shall give it in any case—you will make a book that not only is inartistic, all shadows and no light, but a false book. Fiction can be false, you know, inherently false. You play godfather to your stories, you see: you tell them in the first person, those at least that I have read, and that, though it need not be supposed that those experiences were actually yours, yet gives a sort of guarantee that you believe the borderland of which you write to be entirely terrible. But it isn't: there are probably terrors there—I think for instance that I believe in elemental spirits, of some ghastly kind—but I am sure that I believe that the borderland, for the most part, is almost inconceivably delightful. I've got the best of reasons for believing that."

"I'm willing to be convinced," said I.

Again, as he looked at the fire, his eye sparkled, not with the reflected flame, but with the brightness of some interior vision.

"Well, there's an hour yet before dinner," he said, "and my story won't take half of that. It's about my previous experience of this house; what I saw, in fact, in the room which I now occupy. It was because of that, naturally, that I wanted the same room again. Here goes, then.

"For the twenty years of Margaret's married life," he said, "I never saw her except quite accidentally and casually. Casually, like that, I had seen her at theatres and what not with her two boys whom thus I knew by sight. But I had never spoken to either of them, nor, after her marriage, to their mother. I knew, as all the world knew, that she had a terrible life, but circumstances being

154

what they were, I could not bring myself to her notice, the more so because she made no sign or gesture of wanting me. But I am sure that no day passed on which I did not long to be able to show her that my love and sympathy were hers. Only, so I thought, I had to know that she wanted them.

"I heard, of course, of the death of her sons. They were both killed in France within a few days of each other; one was eighteen, the other nineteen. I wrote to her then formally, so long had we been strangers, and she answered formally. After that, she took this house, where she lived alone. A year later, I was told that she had now for some months been suffering from a malignant and disfiguring disease.

"I was in London, strolling down Piccadilly when my companion mentioned it, and I at once became aware that I must go to see her, not to-morrow or soon, but now. It is difficult to describe the quality of that conviction, or tell you how instinctive and over-mastering it was. There are some things which you can't help doing, not exactly because you desire to do them, but because they must be done. If, for instance, you are in the middle of the road, and see a motor coming towards you at top-speed, you have to step to the side of the road, unless you deliberately choose to commit suicide. It was just like that; unless I intended to commit a sort of spiritual suicide there was no choice.

"A few hours later I was at your door here, asked to see her, and was told that she was desperately ill and could see nobody. But I got her maid to take the message that I was here, and presently her nurse came down to tell me that she would see me. I should find Margaret, she said, wearing a veil so as to conceal from me the dreadful ravages which the disease had inflicted on her face, and the scars of the two operations which she had undergone. Very likely she would not speak to me, for she had great difficulty in speaking at all, and in any case I was not to stay for more than a few minutes. Probably she could not live many hours: I had only just come in time. And at that moment I wished I had done anything rather than come here, for though instinct had driven me here, yet instinct now recoiled with unspeakable horror. The flesh wars against the spirit, you know, and under its stress I now suggested that it was better perhaps that I should not see her.... But the nurse merely said again that Margaret wished to see me, and guessing perhaps the cause of my unwillingness, 'Her face will be quite invisible,' she added. 'There will be nothing to shock you.'

"I went in alone: Margaret was propped up in bed with pillows, so that she sat nearly upright, and over her head was a dark veil through which I could see nothing whatever. Her right hand lay on the coverlet, and as I seated myself by her bedside, where the nurse had put a chair for me, Margaret advanced her hand towards me, shyly, hesitatingly, as if not sure that I would take it. But it was a sign, a gesture."

He paused, his face beaming and radiant with the light of that memory.

"I am speaking of things unspeakable," he said. "I can no more convey to you all that meant than by a mere enumeration of colours can I steep your soul in the feeling of a sunset.... So there I sat, with her hand covered and clasped in mine. I had been told that very likely she would not speak, and for myself there was no word in the world which would not be dross in the gold of that silence.

"And then from behind her veil there came a whisper.

"'I couldn't die without seeing you,' she said. 'I was sure you would come. I've one thing to say to you. I loved you, and I tried to choke my love. And for years, my dear, I have been reaping the harvest of what I did. I tried to kill love, but it was so much stronger than I. And now the harvest is gathered. I have suffered cruelly, you know, but I bless every pang of it. I needed it all....'

"Only a few minutes before, I had quaked at the thought of seeing her. But now I could not suffer that the veil should cover her face.

"'Put up your veil, darling,' I said. 'I must see you.'

"'No, no,' she whispered. 'I should horrify you. I am terrible.'

"'You can't be terrible to me,' I said. 'I am going to lift it.'

"I raised her veil. And what did I see? I might have known, I think: I might have guessed that at this moment, supreme and perfect, I should see with vision.

"There was no scar or ravage of disease or disfigurement there. She was far lovelier than she had ever been, and on her face there shone the dawn of the everlasting day. She had shed all that was perishable and subject to decay, and her immortal spirit was manifested to me, purged and punished if you will, but humble and holy. There was granted to my frail mortal sight the power of seeing truly; it was permitted to me to be with her beyond the bounds of mortality....

"And then, even as I was lost in an amazement of love and wonder, I saw we were not alone in the room. Two boys, whom I recognized, were standing at the other side of the bed, looking at her. It seemed utterly natural that they should be there.

"'We've been allowed to come for you, mother darling,' said one. 'Get up.'

"She turned her face to them.

"'Ah, my dears,' she said. 'How lovely of you. But just one moment.'

"She bent over towards me and kissed me.

"'Thank you for coming, Roderick,' she said. 'Good-bye, just for a little while.'

"At that my power of sight—my power of true sight—failed. Her head fell back on the pillows and turned over on one side. For one second, before I let the veil drop over it again, I had a glimpse of her face, marred and cruelly mutilated. I saw that, I say, but never then nor afterwards could I remember it. It was like a terrible dream, which utterly fades on the awaking. Then her hand, which had been clasping mine, in that moment of her farewell slackened its hold, and dropped on to the bed. She had just moved away, somewhere out of sight, with her two boys to look after her."

He paused.

"That's all," he said. "And do you wonder that I chose that room? How I hope that she will come for me."

My room was next to Roderick's, the head of his bed being just opposite the head of mine on the other side of the wall. That night I had undressed, lain down, and had just put out my light, when I heard a sharp tap just above me. I thought it was some fortuitous noise, as of a picture swinging in a draught, but the moment after it was repeated, and it struck me that it was perhaps a summons from Roderick who wanted something. Still quite unalarmed, I got out of bed, and, candle in hand, went to his door. I knocked, but receiving no answer, opened it an inch or two.

"Did you want anything?" I asked, and, again receiving no answer, I went in.

His lights were burning, and he was sitting up in bed. He did not appear to see me or be conscious of my presence, and his eyes were fixed on some point a few feet away in front of him. His mouth smiled, and in his eyes was just such a joy as I had seen there when he told me his story. Then, leaning on his arm, he moved as if to rise.

"Oh, Margaret, my dear...." he cried.

He drew a couple of short breaths, and fell back.